LUMP

LUMP

A COLLECTION OF SHORT STORIES

CLAIRE L. FISHBACK

Copyright © 2019 Claire L. Fishback.

ISBN: 978-1-970121-04-9 (eBook)
ISBN: 978-1-970121-05-6 (eBook)
ISBN: 978-1-970121-06-3 (Paperback)
ISBN: 978-1-970121-08-7 (Paperback)

Library of Congress Control Number: 2019902515

This is a work of fiction. Any references to historical events, real people, or real places are used fictitiously. Names, characters, and places are products of the author's imagination.

Cover Art by Brian Sakti
Cover Design by Steven Novak

Printed in the United States of America.

First edition. March 22, 2019.

Dark Doorways Press, LLC
PO Box 620514
Littleon, CO 80162

DarkDoorwaysPress.com

For Tim
Who read all of these stories and married me anyway

And for my dad, my other favorite person of the male
persuasion

CONTENTS

PART III
GOITERS

"Short stories are tiny windows into other worlds and other minds and other dreams. They are journeys you can make to the far side of the universe and still be back in time for dinner."
– Neil Gaiman

I don't know about you, but when we sit down to watch TV in the evening after a busy day, we choose what to watch depending on how much time we have before our self-inflicted bedtime. Sometimes we have time for two long shows, sometimes a long show and a short show.

I set this book up with the binge-watching craze in mind. Choose the length of story you want to read, depending on the time you have.

Got a few minutes before a meeting? Stuck in the exam room while you wait for the doctor to check out the strange bite mark on your shoulder? Scratch some Bug Bites. These stories are all under 500 words and include my very first story featuring the title character, Lump. He shows up a lot throughout the book, sometimes despicable, other times piteous. In all instances, he is someone's pawn, doing mindless, senseless, and horrific work.

Maybe you're at the DMV or waiting in the security line at the airport with suspicious contents in your carry on. Squeeze in a Furuncle or two. They range from 501-1,000 words. There's something for everyone here, as long as everyone has a twisty mind.

Are you on the train? A plane? In the trunk of someone's car? Goiters are enlarged tales over 1,001 words. The feature is Lump's expanded story, "Lump's Dream," in which we learn his true motivation. A few of these stories have been published, and one of my personal favorites, which was short-listed for a "binge-reading" anthology, is "Old O." Grab some tissues. This one's a tear jerker.

Enjoy!

Claire L. Fishback
Morrison, Colorado
2019

PART I

BUG BITES

LUMP WANTS NEW SKIN

His skin was covered in lumpy scars, deep and uncared for wounds from his past. He ran the blade along the whetting stone slowly. He looked to his right, through eyes mostly hidden by flaps of swollen tissue, at the girl. He exposed his gums and the three crooked and oversized teeth embedded within them.

"Lump want . . . new skin." His lips contorted in anguish. He stood up, his thick fist clenched around the filet knife. The girl screamed as he gripped her wrist and dug the knife in. He pulled down, peeling a strip of skin away from her arm.

THE BEETLE

SLIME COVERED HER FACE AS FAT NIGHT CRAWLERS squirmed through the dirt, exploring this new cavity placed in the ground. It was snug and cool. An underground burrow with few entries.

She woke to an insect feeling its way over her lips, pausing at her nostril. When it slipped inside she tried to sit up but was stopped short when she hit her head. Dust crumbled into her eyes. Her scream was cut short as the bug explored her sinuses and made its way into her throat. She was faintly aware of muffled laughter above, as she choked and suffocated on the beetle.

THE HARVESTER

A MOLAR RESTS ON THE HARDWOOD FLOOR, CLOTTED blood dangling from the roots. A woman's scream pierces the air. Another tooth lands next to the first.

"I'll have them all," a hoarse voice croaks. He wipes his lumpy brow with a bloodstained cloth.

The woman screams again as another tooth is ripped mercilessly from her mouth. When he is finished, he collects them into a jar, and places them on a shelf next to the eyeballs. He pulls a spoon from his belt and approaches her again.

He cackles, "The better to see you with!"

The woman's piercing scream can be heard from outside the cabin, but at the edge of the forest there is not a sound.

THE WAX COLLECTION

THE CANDLES DRIPPED WAX INTO HOT VATS. STEVE struggled against his bindings, stiff ropes that dug into his wrists and ankles. Dainty footsteps followed by heavy thudding entered the stone chamber.

The seductress leaned over him, her face soft and gentle. She motioned to a lumpy man with deep scars. He lifted a vat over his head and poured it over Steve's body. Steve cried out in burning anguish.

"You'll make a nice addition to my collection," she breathed. She motioned to a wall of men, standing, wrists bound, mouths gagged, all waxy and still. She looked at the thug who lifted another vat over his head. He smiled with three crooked teeth and poured the wax on Steve's face.

THE BIG TOE

THE TOENAIL ON HIS RIGHT BIG TOE WAS YELLOW, ingrown, and bulging. He always wore sandals, and he always touched that toe. He was obsessed with it, like he had to know it was still there. He rarely washed his hands.

One day, he reached out after molesting his toe, sock fuzz from long ago sticking to his fingers, and fondled several tea cakes on a tray on the table. He finally decided on one and popped it into his mouth. The fuzz was gone from his hand.

I took the knife from the table and swung it hard. All his toes scattered onto the floor like dice in a game of Yahtzee.

BOX ON THE DOORSTEP

THE BOX LEANED, SLOPING TO ONE SIDE. THE TAPE was worn and weak, threatening to allow the flaps to pop open, spoiling the surprise. The right side was dented in. The left side had a puncture wound, too small to see inside. A bottom corner had an oily, reddish stain.

It sat on the doorstep, waiting for someone to open it. A strange scent of old garbage and rotting meat hovered around.

Inside the box, his face was frozen in terror. His hair matted with blood. His eyes were missing, as were a few of his teeth. The neck, a gaping wound, oozed blood. He would never cheat again, and his lover would know it.

ALICE'S INK

THE RED INK SLITHERED ACROSS THE PAGE, THE PEN left unattended. Gliding and oozing it spelled out words on its own, ink glistening in the candle light. When the writer returned, he stared at the page.

You will die, the words said.

He dropped his tea cup, suddenly unable to breathe. The cup broke against the hardwood floor. The writer dropped to his knees, clawing at his throat. He stared at the words, a pleading look in his eyes. He looked past the page at the young, blond girl staring from the chair. She twitched, causing the tubes, extending from her veins and into a jar, to tremble.

"Alice, please . . . " the writer managed to get out.

She only stared.

SHADOW GHOSTS

Dedicated to Angela Alsaleem. I hope you no longer see them.

SHADOWS CREPT ACROSS THE WALL. THE SAME shadows I've seen every night since we moved into this old dump of a house. I haven't slept for a week.

In the beginning, I tried to convince myself they were nothing. A trick of the eyes in the silent blackness filling my room. I closed my eyes, and knew better, for I no longer saw the shadows slipping along the wall and disappearing into the dark corners of the room. Instead, I saw the shadow's faces.

The female frightens me the most. She has a round, purple face. It's as if she's held her breath far too long and her skin craves the oxygen she denies herself. Her hair is a mess of greasy tangles. Her eyes are bloodshot. I can smell her, too. That hot, oily smell a terminally ill person exudes. Sweat and inner decay.

The male has an orange moustache. The way he looks at me forces my eyes to stay open.

I watch their shadows drift across the wall and I wonder if I'll ever get some sleep. I close my eyes. The female holds a knife above me.

The male licks his lips.

THE BOY ON THE BRIDGE

They called him Henry. He lost his left hand in an accident in the woods before they moved to the city by the water. They said it was an accident, anyway.

They said Henry was born on Friday the thirteenth. He was cursed with bad luck, they said. They said a lot of things like that. Blaming these accidents on his bad luck. I call it bad parenting, but who am I to judge? We share the same parents, after all.

Before the hand, he usually only suffered minor scrapes and bruises. A black eye. A bloody nose was the least of his worries. Sometimes there were burns. Once or twice he broke a finger or two.

I often wondered when Child Protective Services would come take us away from our neglectful parents. Parents who disregarded our tattered clothes and dirty faces. Parents who hardly gave us a pat on the head, let alone a hug. Parents who didn't even notice the blood-soaked bandage on Henry's stump.

We were on the bridge now. Henry kicked a ball in the street.

The car coming up the lane swerved too late.

Now will they come? Now will they save us?

OCTOPUS SOUP

THE FIRST THING YOU NOTICE IS THE SMELL. IT IS
onions, garlic, and basil. You think you might be having
pizza, but when you open your eyes, you're sitting in a
pan with potatoes, carrots, and mushrooms, inside a giant
oven. The temperature is slowly rising.

You don't remember quite how you got into this
predicament, but you do recall meeting some very strange
characters the night before who asked a lot of personal
questions about your health. How much did you weigh,
what did you eat in the last week, what kind of exercise
did you do, things of that nature.

You struggle against bindings that hold you in the
pan, they aren't thick, but they bite into your bare skin.
You suddenly remember more.

Earlier that day, before meeting the odd individuals,
you ate half a gallon of ice cream. You didn't mention that
to them during their questioning. Who would admit to
such a feat? It was gluttonous and disgusting, and you
remember feeling that way about yourself after the last

bite went down. Before that you were at the gym. Before that you were at a friend's house trying to teach her child how to tie his shoes.

The oven opens and light spills inside. Bright, luminous light, much different than the red glow cast from the elements in the top and bottom of the oven. Something is stuck into the pan and you feel a hot liquid wash over your legs. You cry out in pain. Then comes another sensation. Something has been stabbed into your thigh. You struggle to look and see a meat thermometer sticking from your leg. You watch as the temperature rises. The needle stops on a line that reads, "Martian." Above that is Venusian, Jupiterite, and Earthling.

You gasp, trying to breathe the hot air inside the oven. Your lungs burn. Your eyes feel like they may burst.

Suddenly, when a tentacle, complete with suction cups, reaches into the oven, you remember what may have spawned the idea of eating you in the individual's heads.

Last night, when you met them, you were eating the octopus soup.

FROG TRAP

IF I DREW A SCHEMATIC OF WHAT I WANTED, BOYD could make it. His shop was called "I Made It," featuring any number of homemade items: lamps, toasters, microwaves. You name it, Boyd made it.

He put on his glasses and examined the drawing. "Frog trap?" he asked.

"I need it Friday," I said.

The device was simple: frog swims in, can't swim out. The frog was *not* an ordinary frog. It was smart. It *reasoned*. It was . . . *different*.

Boyd delivered. I eagerly took the trap to the pond and placed it in the shallow water. After a while, the alarm sounded, and inside the trap was the frog. I cackled maniacally and pulled it out. I stared into its face.

There was a splat, and I looked down into the watery eyes of hundreds of frogs. I was surrounded. I looked at the frog in my hand. His tongue lashed out, striking my eye. I dropped him and grabbed my face. When I pulled my hand away, it was covered in blood.

The others flicked their tongues. I stumbled backward and fell. One jumped onto my chest, and inched closer before shooting his tongue and snagging my other eye.

Tiny, slimy hands touched my lips and a cold mass entered my mouth. It struggled down my throat blocking my windpipe. I clawed at my throat. I gasped hard as the frog passed down into my gut.

Frogs around me croaked in anticipation. Suddenly, pain in my abdomen forced a scream from my lips. I felt a lump in my stomach with blind fingers. The resulting surges of agony split through the air with the tearing of skin and fabric. The frog climbed out.

The last thing I felt were hundreds of frogs jumping into the open wound and burrowing inside my body.

THE WINE OF LIFE

Death by Food sat between Huxley's Tux Shoppe and Write Your Life Down Biography Services on Main Street in what was called the Death District, mainly for the skyrocketing death rates–suicides, murders, accidents. Whatever they were called, the majority of crimes that took place involved someone's life expiring. Death by Food was a ritzy place with high-priced meals, sultry mood, and the only place that catered to the macabre individuals that resided in the Death District: People who claimed to be vampires, witches, and artists with no souls, having sold them to the Devil in the name of their craft. The restaurant was also a cover. They had ways to dispose of . . . carcasses.

The man in black sat down at the table with a woman in a golden dress with red curls. She did not greet him; barely looked at him. He didn't mind. It was all part of the price he paid to sit with her. He ordered The Wine of Life that was advertised as the table's special.

The crystal decanter came accompanied by two small glasses. It sloshed, coating the sides with each step the server took. She approached the table with a wide smile and delicately placed the glasses on the white tablecloth. She set the tray aside and uncorked the decanter, her smile never wavering.

After each glass was full of thick, red liquid, she left.

"The wine of life, my sweet." the man in black said to the lady across from him.

Her pale skin shined in the candle light. He lifted a glass to his lips and sipped. A tremor ran through his body, a quiet moan escaped his lips. He looked at his date. Her glassy eyes stared at nothing, her plastic skin tight across her facial structure. She slumped a little further to the left as the man in black sipped again from his glass.

"Do you mind if I drink yours, my dear?" He asked of his dead companion. "Of course you don't."

He looked around the room at the patrons of the restaurant, wondering what their lives were like. Their dates were very obviously alive, talking, laughing, chatting, intoxicated with life, love, or alcohol. He looked at his date with disgust.

"You never talk to me anymore," he said with a false pout. He sat in silence, staring at her frozen features. He started to laugh—a low, rhythmic noise in his throat. Building, it reached his lips and spilled out, loud, grating. He wiped a tear from his eye and beckoned to the server.

"Take care of her, will you?" he asked. The server bowed slightly, gripped the woman under the armpits and dragged her away. "Her blood is delicious," he said to himself, sipping from the tiny glass once more. "But she isn't very good company."

OATMEAL

Dedicated to my Belle, who always gets the last bite.

Sunshine comes in through the window and presses a warm hand to her cheek. She shifts in the bed, lowers her feet to the floor, and rises. She pads across the floor, quiet, careful. She doesn't want to wake him. In the kitchen, the shelves are spare. Their food is almost gone. A cylindrical canister sits on the shelf by the fridge. She opens it. Only one scoop of oats remains in the bottom of the can. Not even enough for one serving. She shakes it out into a bowl and prepares it the usual way, making sure to add just a pinch of salt—that's all she has left— and stirring occasionally for ten minutes.

She pours the oatmeal into a bowl and places it on the table. It isn't much. She hears him rise upstairs above her. The flap of his long ears. The ticking of his claws on the bare floor, slow. Steady. His padded feet on the stairs, thumping down each step.

"My dear," she says, "your breakfast."

She helps him up onto the chair, just a hand to support his hop. He gazes at her from a face speckled with white. She nods and he laps the oatmeal into his mouth. When he is finished, he looks up at her, licking his lips, and she knows she is a good girl, and she knows that he knows he is a good dog.

Her stomach growls. He cocks his head at the sound. She pets his head, his ears, and pulls him against her belly. He rubs his face against her apron.

They are short of food, but they will never be short of love.

PART II

FURUNCLES

THE DOOR CLOSED BEHIND HER WITH A SOFT CLICK. Marissa looked down the hall, her left hand gripping the shaft of the IV tree. She wheeled it next to her as she snuck down the hallway, her bare feet slapping on the cold tiles. She had to get out of there. Something wasn't right with the hospital, and definitely not with the attending doctor.

She wasn't sure what floor she was on, and the hallways were long and blank, void of any landmarks that would suggest she had been there before. As far as she knew she was wandering through a circular hallway. A door opened. She pressed herself into a shallow alcove in the wall.

A stout nurse with chunky white heels backed out, wheeling a gurney through the doors. As the double doors swung shut against the sides of the gurney, the nurse cursed. Marissa's need to leave the hospital suddenly became more urgent as a severed arm fell from beneath the stained sheet, splattering blood onto the floor.

The nurse picked it up and shoved it back beneath the sheet with a quick look around the hallway, then wheeled the gurney down the hall. She disappeared around a corner.

Marissa moved slowly and paused at the door the nurse had come through. It had caught on a red stained cloth, leaving a few inches of viewing space. Inside she saw a doctor, Dr. Cadaver, her attending physician, preparing a needle. On the table in front of him was a squirming woman. He shoved the needle deep into her chest until she stopped moving. Marissa watched as he caressed her all over, cooing and talking in low tones that she couldn't hear. Finally, with a laugh, he turned and took out a surgical saw.

Marissa ripped the needle out of her arm and ran. She turned the corner just as the nurse disappeared at the end of the hall through a set of doors labeled KITCHEN. Marissa peered through a circular window and watched the nurse sort the body parts into bins. Each bin had a different label. Meatloaf, Lasagna, Beef Stroganoff. Marissa choked on bile and spit on the floor when the nurse tossed a head into a dumpster.

The nurse looked up. Her eyes locked on Marissa's through the window.

"What are you doing out of your bed?" she asked with a twisted smile. Her red lipstick had bled into her face powder.

Marissa turned to run but was stopped by a thick hand around her neck. Dr. Cadaver smiled at her, the surgical saw, dripping with blood and flecks of flesh, was propped on his shoulder.

"Let's get started," he said in a low voice, eyeing the front of her gown.

Marissa screamed, but it was no use. She was the only one left.

MOUNTAIN VIEW HOSPITAL

THEY PUT ME IN MOUNTAIN VIEW SIX YEARS AGO. They said I was crazy. But I could see things no one else could. I sat in a padded room with dingy gray walls. I acquired one black crayon that I used to draw symbols on the walls. Protection symbols. But after six years, the black of the crayon has grown dull. In some places, it blends away into the wall and disappears.

Every night for six months the same thing happened. I heard it lurking. A low purring sound, like a large cat, came from outside my door. It stopped by my door and smelled the crack at the bottom with long, sucking sniffs. The sound of it made my stomach turn. I pushed myself into the corner. My toes curled involuntarily. I trembled. I heard a faint scratching that sent my flesh tingling and my heart pounding.

The doors to the rooms along the hallway all have a barred window near the top, almost too high up to see through. A dark shadow appeared in the window. Red eyes glared at me. A twisted mouth with sharp teeth and long fangs opened and a low, long rattle issued from within.

I turned my head away and wrapped my arms around my body. I prayed for it to go away. I squeezed my eyes shut tight and tried to melt into the wall.

The doorknob jiggled, and I jerked my head to look.

"No!" I cried. I jumped to my feet and grabbed the doorknob, keeping it in place. The doors were supposed to be locked. They were supposed to keep us safe in here. It twisted beneath my hand, and I squeezed harder. It dug into my flesh. The beast outside looked suddenly to the right and fled.

I swallowed hard, my hand gripping the doorknob. I pulled it away and flexed my stiff fingers. I took a deep breath and tried the knob. It was unlocked. I backed away a few steps. It was supposed to be locked. I was supposed to be safe here. Tears burned in my eyes and nose. My breathing quickened. I felt panicked. My knees shook, threatening to buckle. I had to get out. This place was no longer safe for me. I ran to the door and tried to look out the window. On my tiptoes, I could just see over the bottom edge.

The black form appeared suddenly in the window, knocking me on my back. I scooted into the corner as the doorknob slowly turned and the door creaked open. I gasped for air. My face felt hot, blackness threatened my vision. The dark shape loomed closer, rattling and sniffing. The red eyes glowed. The fangs dripped saliva that singed the floor.

I screamed for help, knowing no one would come. No one else could see them. Only I could see them. My scream was mingled with the cries of the other patients as the beast ripped into my flesh.

DEATH IS NOT AN EXCUSE

ONE WOULD THINK THAT DEATH WOULD BE AN excuse for missing a deadline, however, at Spinkman's & Snott's that was not the case.

It was the day before my project was due. I was nowhere near completing it. There was a knock at the door. I was half relieved and half annoyed that I was pulled away from my project.

When I got to the door, I was shocked to see a young woman in a low-cut, knee-length red dress, heaving bosom and all, standing on my porch. She pushed her way inside and slammed the door.

"You've got to help me," she said. "Do you have any boards?"

"Boards?" I asked. I was still shocked that this beautiful woman was in my house.

"Yes, boards!" she screeched. "Two by fours, eight by tens, boards! You know? Wood?"

"No," I said with a raised eyebrow. I lived in a town house, it wasn't like I kept lumber lying around.

She made an exasperated noise and brushed her hair out of her face. I saw she had some blood on her forehead.

"What's going on?" I asked. "Are you in some sort of trouble?"

At this she laughs. "Am I in trouble?" She asks in a mocking tone. "The whole town's in trouble! Haven't you seen the news?"

She looked around and grabbed the television remote off the coffee table and turned it to Channel 4. A frazzled set of newscasters shouted to get inside, bar the doors and windows if you could, do anything to stay safe and indoors. This is not a test.

"What's going on?" I asked.

Before she could answer, there was a bang at the door. I turned to answer it, but she grabbed my wrist.

"Listen to me," she said her eyes wide. "Don't open that door. If you value your life, do not open it!"

"What? What's wrong with you?" I stepped backward toward the door.

"Please," she begged. "There's, oh you idiot! You'll never believe me!" She fell to her knees by the couch and hugged the arm, waiting for me to open the door.

When I reached the door, I listened. Outside there were sounds of movement and moaning. Perhaps someone outside was injured?

"Please," the girl whimpered. "Just stay inside," she was crying.

I grabbed the door knob, jerked the door open and gasped at the spectacle before me.

There on my lawn, milling around like cattle, were about fifty people, only they weren't normal people.

Their skin was grayish. Some of them looked the worse for wear with tattered clothes. Their eyes were what caught my attention the most. All of them had light blue eyes, almost as if they were blind. They were all moving around each other, unaware, moaning.

"Zombies!" I screamed. I slammed the door, but it was too late. They knew we were inside. They started to bang on the door. I heard a window in the kitchen break and their terrible moans increased. The kitchen door was closed. I ran to it and locked it as quick as I could.

"Boards!" the girl cried. "You don't have any boards!"

"We're as good as dead," I said. I crumbled to the floor beside her and held her. A perfect stranger.

We waited. Listening to them scrape at the kitchen door. The squeak of their fingers and faces against the glass of the windows by the door.

Finally, they broke through the barriers of door and window and they were upon us. Biting and gnashing.

I woke up with an immense hunger for brains, but I'm a vegetarian. I've never eaten meat, so I dismissed my craving and went back to work on my project. My brain felt foggy, like a bad hangover, and the words on the screen and on my documents didn't make any sense.

I tried to say something, but it came out a low, wheezing moan.

"Wha?"

I ran to the bathroom and looked in the mirror.

Gray skin. Tattered clothes. Disheveled hair. Blue eyes.

The phone rang.

I answered it. There was a series of moans and groans that, oddly, I understood.

"You're late! Where is your project?"

It was my boss, Mr. Spinkman, and indeed, I was late. I missed my deadline.

GOODBYE LIVER

HUGH MCGUMPFREY WAS DRUNK AFTER SIX RUM and cokes, a shot of Jaegermeister, and a snort of lime juice–the latter taken on a dare.

"Elvis are you out there somewhere?" He sang. "Lookin' like a happy man?" He turned to the woman beside him. "I wrote that song," he said. She gave him a disgusted look and left.

In all actuality, his ex-friend Brian wrote that song. Hugh merely played the keyboard for that number, and that was as a favor for Hugh's brother Murphy.

"McGump," the bartender, Josephine, said. "You better get out of here before you cause a disturbance." She always warned her customers before having them removed from her bar.

"Josie, lady, I ain't causin' no trouble," Hugh said. He sipped some water from a random glass of melting ice.

"I know," she winked at him. "But you've had your fill and you ought to get home."

Hugh considered the two of her for a moment,

wobbled dangerously on his stool, and decided that he should honor her wishes. He gathered his coat and left the bar.

He stumbled and grabbed onto the first thing he touched, which happened to be an enormous pink elephant.

The elephant took his hat from his hand with her trunk and put it on his head, then helped him stumble home.

The next morning, Hugh woke up with a massive headache.

"Jager," he scowled. "I should know better by now." He spit into the sink and waited for the nausea to subside.

In the mirror, something caught his attention and he turned around.

An attractive woman in a towel stood behind him. She smiled and flung herself into his arms and planted a sloppy kiss on his lips.

"Who are you?" Hugh asked.

She removed the towel—Hugh surprised himself by turning around abruptly—and started to dry her long pink hair with it. Hugh just then realized that her hair was in fact pink.

"I'm Pinky," she said with an upside-down grin. "I'm your liver." She straightened up, planted a kiss on his lips and left the bathroom. Hugh followed her. She had a big red bag, packed full, that she gripped in a tiny hand.

"You need help?" Hugh asked.

"No," Pinky said. She giggled. "Maybe a long time ago." With that she left his apartment.

Hugh suddenly felt very tired and worn down. He went to the couch and dropped onto it, no sooner had he done this, he jumped back up and ran to the bathroom to throw up. After rinsing his mouth, he looked in the mirror and saw his skin held a yellow tinge.

I'm dying, was his first though, and in fact, he was. He fell to the floor just as his liver burst.

Hugh sat up straight in bed with a gasp. He had an empty bottle of Jack in his hand.

"Holy shit," he said. "That was some dream." He started to rub his eyes just as a woman with pink hair dragged a big red bag across the room.

JUDGMENT

Modern World, 2099. A war has broken out among the folk of Modern World and of Old World. Beliefs and technologies have clashed for decades. Finally, in an attempt to bring peace or destroy Old World, a trio was formed and sent deep into the center.

AFTER TRAVELING THROUGH WINDING OUTER AND inner caves and tunnels, traversing steep inclines, scaling vertical walls, and swimming across dangerous underground lakes, the trio stood before the tall wood and metal door. The entrance to Old World.

"This is it," Bruce said. He was the fighter. The modern-day warrior, equipped with both knowledge and strength. He had the cunning manipulation of the best salesman, the business savvy of a Wall Street trader, and the strength of ten men. He could take on the world, or a simple, financial negotiation.

"Yeah," Tiera replied. She was the thief. Stealthy by day and by night. She had the double-edged personality of a pure Gemini, she could be sweet and innocent and pick your pocket at the same time. She was dangerously alert, artfully silent. She could step in and out, take your most precious belongings, without you knowing she even existed.

"Let's go." Coo gripped his staff. He was the healer. The doctor who cared for sick children, ailing seniors, and everyone in between. He could take a temperature, probe an abdomen, write a prescription and raise stamina all at the same time. A real magician of herbs and chemistry. He was equipped to handle a severed arm as well as a tummy ache.

Through the door was Ginocka, the largest of the four titans to rule over Old World. He sat in his throne, a mixture of sloppy mud and hard granite. He moved with the sound of grating stone and ordered his minions to do his bidding.

He was in the middle of sending out a scout when the trio came through the doors.

"Ginocka," Bruce said, catching his attention. "Today you shall die."

Ginocka laughed a deep, resonating laugh.

Bruce laughed back, a hearty chuckle. He stopped suddenly and unsheathed his sword. "No, I'm serious."

"Let's talk," Ginocka said. "All this fighting and no one ever talks anymore. You're skilled in verbal communication, let's talk."

"There will be time for talking later," Tiera said. She loosed an arrow at a low-flying bat-bird. It hit its mark with clear accuracy and pinned the beast to the wall above Ginocka's head.

"Now Tiera," Bruce said, turning to her. "You're supposed to wait for my mark,"

"There's no time for waiting, Bruce," she said through clenched teeth, her eyes unmoving from the face of Ginocka. "We must destroy him,"

"Listen to me," Bruce said. He placed a hand on her arm, forcing her to lower her arrow.

Tiera turned to him, removing her eyes from their enemy. "What is it now?"

Bruce and Tiera argued.

Coo wondered why he ever joined a husband/wife team, then remembered he was assigned to them as well as this mission. He cleared his throat a couple of times, his eyes locked on Ginocka. Ginocka's mud hand moved toward a lever. A small gate opened to his left.

"Guys," Coo said. "Guys I think something's happening," he watched as a black form emerged slowly, like smoke seeping under a door during a house fire. "Bruce," Coo said. "Tiera, something's happening."

Ginocka laughed again. "This is Judgment," he said, gesturing to the form. "I'm sure you have all heard of him."

Bruce and Tiera stopped arguing and looked to where Ginocka pointed. There sat the black mass. Oh, yes, they had heard of Judgment. Everyone had been exposed to some diluted form of him for centuries, millennia even.

Judgment was unforgiving and cruel. He was the best at the worst punishments and torture techniques. He was a backstabber and a friend all at one time. He hated everyone before he even met them. He turned friends on each other, ripped apart families, and destroyed everything in his path. He was the Old World's oldest weapon and at that very moment, he oozed across the floor toward them.

Bruce looked from Tiera to Coo.

"Run," he said in a harsh whisper.

They turned and fled through the massive front doors. They ran back through the caves, scaled the vertical wall, swam across the lake. When Bruce stopped, Tiera and Coo ran into him.

"What's going on?" Tiera said, panicked. She looked over her shoulder. There was no sign of Judgment.

"I think we lost him," Bruce said. He fumbled around in various pouches on his belt.

A scrape like a blade on a whetstone pulled Bruce from his search.

"Run," he said again. They reached the outer caves and tore toward the opening.

"This way!" Tiera yelled, catching a glimpse of white light.

Bruce's BMW was parked just outside in a clearing. Tiera stopped at the passenger door, Coo at a back door. Bruce ran around to the driver's side, patting his vest, his pants. He scrambled to look through all his pouches again.

Finally, he looked across the car at Tiera, and then at Coo. He looked past them at the dark form emerging from the cave and seeping into the forest clearing.

He panted, breathless after their run.

"What are you waiting for?" Tiera yelled at him.

"Unlock the doors, Bruce!" Coo said, after a panicked look over his shoulder. He jerked on the door handle.

"I can't," Bruce said. He took a couple of breaths and swallowed hard. He looked at his friends for the last time. "I've lost my keys!"

MARCI LOVES MY BOOTS

I HATED MARCI ROGERS, BUT NOT AS MUCH AS I hated her friends, Georgia and Vicky. When it was only Marci, she was at least civil. When Georgia and Vicky were around, I was a slime ball, and they made sure I knew that.

I made the mistake, years ago, of telling Georgia how I felt about Marci. She told Marci in front of me. I think I saw a hint of a smile, but her expression turned to disgust.

"Him? He likes me?" She flipped her golden hair. "Gross." The three girls walked off, but Marci looked over her shoulder with a soft expression.

It wasn't until Marci started dating Brett Jones that my hatred began. She flaunted her relationship through the halls at school and out on the grounds, and at the mall, and at the movies, and everywhere they went. She showed up wearing his letterman jacket and his class ring on a chain. Georgia and Vicky laughed and hugged her. They saw me watching and they pulled Marci away, giving me dirty looks.

Brett Jones was tall, handsome, chiseled. I would never look like him no matter how hard I tried. In fact, I was the exact opposite of him. I heard him talking to some buddies in the hall about getting into Marci's pants and how easy it was. I felt my face flush, my fists clenched at my sides, but I kept walking. I followed him after school. He lived close enough to walk home. When he entered the wooded trail that led to his neighborhood, I pulled out the hunting knife my dad gave me before he left us. It was old and rusted, but it was sharp.

In an upward motion, I plunged the knife into his rib cage. He gasped, turned toward me, his mouth opened and closed like a fish. He reached out and I kicked him in the chest, knocking him back onto the knife.

I dragged his body home. I lived close by, too. In the basement of my house I skinned him. It was almost an erotic experience, slicing the flesh from his muscle. I looked up at the walls where I had various other skins stretched and tanned. A cat, the neighbor's yapping dog, my little sister who was 'kidnapped.' My mom will never know the truth. I locked the basement every time I left so she couldn't get in. She thought I was an anguished teen, full of angst and other teen feelings. Really? I was doing Marci a service. He talked about her like she was nothing to him. He fucked her and told his friends.

I made Brett Jones into a pair of boots and wore them to school. Marci told me she liked them. By the end of the day, her face was filled with worry. I saw her on her cell phone, leaving Brett a message at least a dozen times. I chuckled silently, knowing his cell phone was in my basement, ringing away.

NORTH BY NORTHWEST

"North by Northwest," the old man said. He pointed.

"That's south," I said. "North's that way." I thrust a thumb over my shoulder.

"North by northwest." Again, he pointed to the south. "You wanna take that road.

Don't stop there, you'll be sorry you ever did."

I climbed into the taxi.

"North by northwest?" He nodded in the rearview mirror. "Don't go there much no more," he said. "Hafta charge you extra for that one."

I didn't answer. From the rear window I watched the old man and the small town disappear on the horizon.

I fell asleep on the way. When the taxi jolted from the smooth highway onto a bumpy road I woke up and rubbed my eyes.

"Where are we?" I asked, groggy.

"North by northwest," the taxi driver answered. The taxi stopped.

"Is there a hotel?" I rubbed jagged sleep from my eyes.

The driver pointed to a building just outside the window.

"Thanks," I said. I grabbed my bag, paid him, and stepped out into a cool and starless night. He drove off no sooner had I shut the door, leaving me in a cloud of dust.

The building before me listed to one side as if something large and invisible were lounging against it. The wood siding was missing in some places, shutters hung at precarious angles. The windows were all dark. A breeze sent tumbleweed rolling in front of me and a swirl of dust blew by.

I knocked on the door. It opened a crack and an eye on a wrinkled face peered out.

"Can I help you?" A grainy voice asked.

"I need a room please," I said.

The eye seemed to peer around outside. The voice whispered, "Where are the birds?"

I looked over my shoulder. I looked up at the sky. I took a step back and looked at the roof.

"I don't see any birds," I said.

The door jerked open. The eye belonged to an elderly woman in a pink bathrobe and curlers.

"I'm sorry if I woke you," I said.

"Quite alright," she answered. She looked out the door one more time before closing it and latching several locks. "Not many visitors come through these parts anymore," she said, eyeing me oddly. "I have one room left," she said.

"Are there other visitors?" I asked.

"No, I've just got the one room." She handed me a key. "Upstairs, second door on the left. Don't go snooping around late at night. You'll disturb them."

She shuffled off through a doorway before I could ask any questions.

I climbed the creaking stairs. When I reached the second door on the left I shuddered. It was room thirteen.

"I thought there was only one room," I muttered to myself. It was apparent that there were at least thirteen rooms on this floor. I shrugged and let myself in.

The room was sparse and unfeeling, furnished with a single bed and a dresser. The bathroom light cast a cold beam down on the sink, leaving the shower and toilet in shadow. I chanced a glance in the mirror. The light made my face look gaunt and pale. I washed up and got into bed. The springs in the worn mattress jabbed my back and the frame groaned with every movement. I finally fell asleep.

A bang against the wall and muffled yelling brought me from slumber. Two voices. A couple fighting? Did they just arrive? I heard sobbing, and I went into the hallway. I tentatively knocked on the door.

The voices inside stopped. I heard footsteps and the door opened. A man with a mustache peered out.

"Isn't it late to be knocking on doors?" he asked.

"I'm sorry," I said. "I could hear you yelling through the wall, I woke up. Is everything alright?"

His expression changed from annoyance to worry. "Did you hear the birds?" He asked.

"Birds?" I said. "No, I didn't hear birds, I heard yelling."

"Quick, come inside," he grabbed my arm with an icy grip.

A woman wept on the bed. She wore a Victorian dress complete with bustle, and a velvet hat with a feather sticking out of it. The man, I noticed, wore a three-piece, brown, pinstriped suit, also characteristic from the Victorian era.

"Did they wake you?" she asked.

"No," I said. "I heard yelling,"

"What kind of yelling?" the man asked, his face intent on mine.

"Yelling, like arguing," I said. "It wasn't you?"

"We don't argue anymore," the woman said. "Not since . . . the birds."

"It wasn't since the birds, it was after the man who knew too much came," the man said.

The woman gasped and covered her face.

"Who is the man who knew too much?"

They both looked at me. I could hear the faint call of crows.

The woman began to cry.

"North by Northwest was once a bustling town," he said. "A trade town. One day, a furious and violent windstorm swept through. The only thing that could be heard over the wind was the call of crows. When the storm was over, people were surprised to see a man all in black standing out in the street. He grinned at them and left as another storm smote the town."

"The birds are constantly calling, warning," the woman sobbed. "The man, he takes it all away."

"What does he take?" I asked.

They looked at each other, then slowly back at me.

"He takes the souls."

I woke up the next morning and went to check out, but no one was around. I decided to leave $100 on the counter and stepped outside. When my eyes adjusted to the bright sunlight, I took a step back. All around, covering the ground, on rooftops, stationed on fence posts were crows. They were silent, staring at me. The only sound was the crunch of gravel as a man all in black stepped from the shadow of a building and grinned at me.

PARTS 'R' US

THE BOOTS WERE FASHIONED OUT OF FEET AND nailed into the ground outside in the grass. I wasn't quite sure what the nails were for until I approached the feet. They wriggled, toes flexing and un-flexing. I backed away in disgust.

"If I didn't keep 'em nailed down," the proprietor said. "They would hop right out of here!" He stood in the doorway smoking a pipe. He was a tall man with thin gangly legs and arms, a large belly. His bearded head sat upon his shoulders with no transition between. He smiled, exposing a row of long, crooked yellow teeth and black gums. Periodontitis came to mind and I grimaced. "Oh, don't mind them, they harmless." He laughed a wheezing laugh that ended in a spasm of coughing.

"What can I do for you, sir?" he asked, sobering quickly when I didn't join his laughter. The feet-boots continued to wriggle and squirm beneath the nails.

"Just wanted to look around," I said. The man motioned inside with a sweeping arm, and I went in. It was frigid as I started looking around at the shelves of strange items. There were face parts, each in different labeled boxes. Ears, noses, lips, eyes. The eyes made me shudder. A couple of them were turned up and they followed me as I walked by, or at least that's how it seemed. Another shelf held limbs. Legs and arms were tossed onto this shelf. One of the arms was draped over the edge. When I walked by, it grabbed my shirt. I screamed.

The man laughed. When he sobered again, he took a long drag from the pipe.

"Is there anything in particular you're looking for?" he asked.

"No," I said. I looked in a bin of hands. "Well, maybe." I stood up and went to the counter. "I'm looking for a hand," I said.

"Male or female?" he asked, sucking on the end of the pipe.

"Female," I answered. "There was a ring."

"So, it's a left hand, eh?" the proprietor said. He walked in long strides to a corner in the store where he unlocked a glass case. "Is this the hand you are looking for?" He held the hand as if he were shaking it and laughed his raucous laugh again.

"Not exactly," I said. "That's not the right ring." I peered over his shoulder at the other hands in the case, each had at least one ring on it. The hand I was looking for had a two-carat diamond ring attached to it. "I think it might be that one," I said. I could have kicked myself for not knowing my own fiancés hand. We'd been together for years, and in all the times we held hands in the park, laughing and enjoying the sun, I never thought to examine it. Of course, back then, I never thought I'd be picking through a parts shop for it.

"Ah, yes," the proprietor said. "This one was found down by the lake." He held the hand gently, and I was grateful for his care.

"The lake," I said, taking the hand carefully. It was definitely hers and I was relieved that I remembered something about it. There was a mole on the first joint of the thumb. "She loved the lake." I sniffled.

"You can have it," the man said, patting my shoulder. I looked at him, tears in my eyes. "For three thousand dollars," he finished.

"Three thousand dollars?" I exclaimed. "The ring is only worth fifteen hundred!"

He stared hard at me. "Two thousand," he negotiated.

"Fine," I said. I paid him, and he wrapped my purchase in a silk scarf and placed it into a wooden box with a glass door.

I left the store, the package under my arm. As I walked past the boots I noticed there were wires leading from each nail. I followed the wires to a young man in the bushes. He was pulling on them, making the boots dance and squirm. I scowled at him and kept walking.

The days of the past were over. The days where the dead were properly buried, ceremonies given to honor them, wakes to give friends and family a last chance to say good bye. The dead were no longer honored, they were mutilated. Parts chopped off and sold to stores like this one, scavenged, salvaged. Murder was at an all-time high. With the selling price for rare parts, like hands with jewelry, arms with tattoos, ears with piercings, one could make a profit, a living even. People always searched, looking for pieces of their loved ones. Last remnants to bury and pray for, to keep as a memory. My fiancé was killed in the park we used to enjoy so much together. The only thing I ever found was her left hand.

ROOM BY AGE

Dr. Delaware approached me with his hands behind his back. An air of arrogance enveloped him everywhere he went.

"The five-year-olds are screaming again," he informed me.

I sighed and went to the five-year-old storage. I peeked through the window. Sure enough, all of them were screaming.

I turned to Dr. Delaware. "What did you do?" I asked him.

He smiled, displaying a row of yellow teeth. "I only tapped on the glass," he said.

I pulled him away from the door by his upper arm. He looked at me, shocked at my action.

"They have very sensitive hearing," I whispered. "Tapping on the glass for them is like firing a shotgun to us."

"Well, I had no idea," Dr. Delaware said. His wicked smile told me differently, however.

There were twelve of them. All five years old, all transferred from the four-year-old storage room just days ago. I didn't like that their rooms were referred to as storage. They were living creatures, not surplus objects to get out of sight.

It was about thirteen years ago when the first of them arrived. They came down with the annual rain showers as seeds. Vines grew from the seeds at rapid paces. Flowers appeared on the vines, similar to melons. The flowers grew into pods that looked like a cross between a cantaloupe and a watermelon. The color and texture of the first, the size of the latter.

When the pods split open, tiny babies squirmed inside. They looked like human babies, but instead of having the pinky peach flesh tones, they had cool flesh tones; greens, blues, purples. Occasionally one showed up with yellow skin, but it died hours after hatching.

We opened a research lab to keep the infants under control and out of the cruel eyes of the media and anyone who might object to our research. Since they only landed in one location, we built the lab close to that spot and began harvesting them annually.

As they aged, we built different rooms according to the years since they hatched. It was easier to keep them organized this way as we found, over the years, as they aged, they required different attention, environment, food, etc.

We only have one in the thirteen-year-old room and have found that ages seven and eight are the most difficult. They begin to change. It is rapid, and they require constant monitoring. At age seven, they can no longer walk as their legs fuse together. At age eight, they cannot breathe air. They are placed into a tank of water and monitored closer still. As the eight-year-olds develop into nine-year-olds, they are back to normal. Their legs un-fuse, they can breathe air again, and they are moved into the nine-year-old room for further observation.

We believe that these changes are hereditary and evolutionary. Perhaps on their home planet, before they began to rain down upon us, these changes are necessary for their survival. They only "talk" from ages one to six, and it comes out in the form of shrill screams. After age six they become mute. We are hoping that at some point they will begin to speak so we may learn more about them.

I donned my earplugs and went into the five-year-old room and looked around at the purple, green, and blue children inside. All of them had their heads thrown back, faces white with anger or some other emotion, all screaming. I touched each of them on the head. I found this technique worked only long enough to get to the last one, then the first one would start to scream. As I reached baby number twelve I started to hum. I didn't have to hum anything particular, just the humming sound was enough to soothe them. Sometimes they would hum, too, either mimicking, as children often do, or to join in.

When they all fell asleep, I crept from the storage room and back into the hall. I closed the door and peered through the window at the slumbering children.

Dr. Delaware was behind me looking over my shoulder at them.

"Disgusting creatures," he hissed. "Why are we even continuing this stupid research?"

I turned around and looked him in the eye. "They are not disgusting." I said through gritted teeth. "And we are doing this research because this is the first good bit of evidence we have that there is life somewhere else in this universe."

Dr. Delaware leaned closer, leered at me and said, "Who cares?" He backed away abruptly. "Who cares if there is life elsewhere? We obviously cannot communicate with them!" He threw something against the five-year-old's door, and they all began to scream again.

"Go check on the thirteen-year-old," I said.

Dʀ. Dᴇʟᴀᴡᴀʀᴇ ʟᴀᴜɢʜᴇᴅ as the assistant disappeared into the five-year-old room. He sauntered down the hall toward the room with the thirteen-year-old. It was obviously a female specimen. She had long dark-blue hair that she enjoyed brushing as she sat in her storage room.

Dr. Delaware entered her room and looked at her. He rubbed his hands together and gave her a wicked grin. The thirteen-year-old turned toward him and her mouth twitched. Dr. Delaware took a step forward.

"Useless creatures, can't even talk," he said out loud. The thirteen-year-old smiled at him. As he neared her, she opened her mouth. "What are you doing?" Dr. Delaware asked her.

Her mouth opened further, as if she was going to answer him, but instead, a serpent shot out, grabbed Dr.

Delaware around the middle, bent him in two, swallowed him whole and disappeared back into her mouth. All the while, she combed her long hair. She began to hum.

WHEN I ENTERED the thirteen-year-old's room, she was humming and combing her hair.

"Did you have a good lunch?" I asked her. She looked at me and nodded emphatically.

A CALL FROM GODZILLA

"This is not my phone," Bill said, his brow furrowed. "Someone stole my phone and switched it with this one, look," he handed his phone to his girlfriend, the busty and blonde Lucille.

"Who the hell is Francine?" She asked, her lips turning down into a pout.

"I don't know. This isn't my phone."

Lucille handed the phone back to Bill and he continued to scroll through the numbers.

Suddenly, it rang. The assigned ring tone for a caller called "Godzilla" was the theme from *Friends*.

Bill pressed the answer button. "Hello?" he asked, brow still furrowed.

Lucille pulled a nail file from her purse and started vigorously filing her middle finger.

The voice on the phone was deep and mechanical.

"Go to the Eight of Clubs. There you will meet a man called Leibniz, he has the secret. You will receive a phone call from Restricted Number. Give them the secret and you will live. Deny them the secret, and you and your busty little girlfriend will die."

"Eight of Clubs the bar or the pawn shop?" Bill asked. The phone went dead. "Hello? Hello?"

"Who was that?" Lucille asked.

"Godzilla," Bill said. "We have to go."

Bill hoped on his Harley, Lucille in the sidecar, and drove first to the pawn shop, though something told him this Leibniz guy would be at the bar. He went inside, instructing Lucille to stay by the bike, and asked for Leibniz.

The pawn shop owner shrugged. "Ain't no Leibniz here," he said. "Try the bar."

Bill entered the bar and looked around. A haze of smoke drifted above eye level, fighting the fans that spun lackadaisically on the yellowed ceiling. An obese gentleman at the bar in a tight-fitting brown, pinstripe suit sucked on a cigar. He flipped a couple bills out of his money clip and put them on the counter.

"Thanks, Leibniz!" he called, waving across the bar. Bill looked to where he was waving but didn't see anyone. He approached the bar.

"Where can I find Leibniz?" he asked.

"Who wants to know?" The bartender asked, uninterested while he wiped the counter. He was a bulky man with rippling biceps in a black muscle shirt.

"I do," Bill said. "Bill Billsly," he said.

"Oh, hey!" The bartender said, eyes brightening. He stopped wiping the bar. "Bill Billsly is here!" He yelled over Bill's head. Bill turned to look. When he turned back around, the bartender had his arms crossed. "Who the hell cares who Bill Billsly is?" He said. "Get outta my bar."

Lucille leaned on the counter and popped her gum. "Hi," she said with a bright, toothy smile.

Bartender leaned on the counter on one elbow. "Heyhowareya," he said, like it was one word.

"Fine," she said with a sassy flip of her hair. "Where's Leibniz," she asked. Bartender's eye balls would have fallen into her cleavage if they hadn't been lodged securely in their sockets.

"In the back corner," he said, visibly drooling.

Bill rolled his eyes, grabbed Lucille's wrist and dragged her to the back corner.

On the table was a name card that read, *Leibniz.*

"Sit down." A man, who was obscured completely by a newspaper, said. "You want the secret?"

"Yes." Bill slid into the booth. Leibniz lowered the newspaper.

"Here it is, listen and listen closely." He could have been related to Woody Allen. He was old, with gray hair and a large nose with big, dark-rimmed glasses perched on top. His accent was from New York. "One cup of sugar, two teaspoons of lemon juice, a shot of Crown, and a drop, just a drop you hear, of pure vanilla extract. It has to be pure or else it won't work." He raised the paper back in front of him.

"Wait, can you say it again? I need to write this down," Bill said. He grabbed a napkin.

"Nope, that's all you get," Leibniz said.

Lucille shrugged. "I remember it," she said. She pulled a little pink notebook from her little pink purse and wrote the secret in pink ink with a little pink pen.

"Thank you, Leibniz." Bill said.

When they left the bar, the cell phone rang with the familiar TV show theme. It was Godzilla.

"Did you get the secret?"

"Yes," Bill answered.

"Good," Godzilla replied. "Restricted Number will be calling you shortly."

No sooner had Bill hung up with Godzilla, the phone rang again with Restricted Number's theme—Jaws.

"Give me the secret," Restricted Number said before Bill had the chance to say Hello. His voice was deep and gruff, as if he just woke up with a sore throat.

He looked at Lucille who handed him the paper she had written the secret on. He relayed the message.

"What?" Restricted Number said.

Bill repeated the secret.

"That can't be right," Restricted Number said. "That's not a combination, that's a recipe!"

Before Bill and Lucille could do anything, they were surrounded by a group of teenagers in white shirts. Each held a different type of weapon. Bill wondered if they got to choose their weapons when they joined up with whatever agency it was that they belonged to.

A girl with a backwards ball cap on swung a chain around in a circle. "Let's get 'em boys."

Back at the Eight of Clubs, Leibniz stood up and

looked at his name card. "Oh darn, they spelled my name wrong, again!" He crossed out the z and added a *ck* to the end. "No wonder those kids thanked me by the wrong name, sheesh!" He tucked the paper under his arm and left the bar.

MYCELIA

MYCELIANS LOVE PRUNES AND LIVE UNDER BEDS, that's what the book *Mycelian Facts and Falsehoods* claimed. I placed a plate of prunes on the floor and waited. I was old—eighty-eight—to believe in monsters under the bed, and that's probably the reason my family put me in here. 'Here' is the claustrophobic room in Mountain View, a hospital for the elderly.

The reason I wanted to catch a Mycelian was because they could transport me to a better place. The book said that, too.

I heard three coins drop into the vending machine outside, and a can clatter into the bin. I scrambled to my window to see what they got. As the person passed, I strained to look, but I couldn't see.

"What did you get?" I yelled. "What did you get, let me see!"

A middle-aged man turned, held up a can of cola, and kept walking.

"Cola . . ." I said. I flipped through the book, full of

brightly-colored pictures of the Mycelian and Mycelia, to see if they liked cola. It didn't say whether they did or not.

When I looked at the plate, the prunes were gone.

Dr. Carthian finished applying her red lipstick, placed the tube back in her purse and pulled the zipper shut. She looked up at me.

"Mycelians?" She said. "What are Mycelians?"

I didn't like her. She showed no compassion, no understanding. I sat in a hard, plastic chair. This was my weekly therapy session.

"They live under my bed," I said quietly, looking at my hands in a lap that had become frail over the past months.

"Where did you hear about them?" She jotted notes on a yellow pad.

"In a book," I said.

"What book?" She asked.

I met her eyes, a piercing, icy blue. I told her the title of my beloved book.

"The children's book?" She said with a scowl. She rolled her eyes and continued writing.

When we were finished, I heard her say to someone, "remove the books from room 19."

When I got back to my room, the book was gone. I sat on my bed and cried.

A moment later, there was a tug on my sleeve. I looked down into the eye of a female Mycelian! I knew she was female because of her three long eyelashes on her one large, blue, saucer-like eye. She still held my sleeve in her long fingers. Her little pink lips formed a smile as she handed me the book. She gripped my hand and pulled at it. I got up from the bed.

The Mycelian stood to my knee and wore a mushroom-shaped hat over her long, golden hair that trailed down her back, nearly to the floor. Her cat-like tail lashed as she pointed underneath the bed.

"Am I to go under there?" I asked.

She nodded, fluttering her dragonfly wings. She swept a hand over her eye, indicating that I was to close my own.

I lay on my back and slid under the bed, eyes closed. When I opened them, I was in a mystical land, full of color, like the pictures of the book. Rolling green hills dappled with colorful flowers, sparkling ponds full of rainbow-colored fish, a blue sky with white, cotton candy clouds. Mycelians danced and ran around giggling. I saw people I hadn't seen in years, thought to be dead; friends from my past.

We joined hands and danced in a circle, reveling in the greatness of Mycelia!

THE NURSE PAUSED in the doorway. She turned and rushed down the hall to Dr. Carthian's office.

"The tenant of room 19 is dead," she told him.

THE AUCTION

THE AUCTION HOUSE WAS A TALL STRUCTURE WITH missing shingles, drooping shutters, and an all-around creepy visage. It was in dire need of paint and was in a sad state of disrepair. It was here where the Private Auction was held by invitation only.

The Auctioneer was a tall man with sallow skin and deep-set eyes. He had long fingers that he waved around when he spoke in his low voice.

"Lot number 327," he said, gesturing to the table. A canvas tarp covered the table. The Auctioneer's assistant, a squat fellow with a toad-like face, whipped the tarp off the table with a flourish. "The left arm of Isabella Rothberger,"

The arm lay among a beautiful display of flowers. It was dressed in a lacy white sleeve and had a beautiful two-carat diamond ring on the ring finger.

"Bidding will start at one-hundred dollars," The Auctioneer said.

After Isabella Rothberger's arm was sold to a lady in a yellow hat for $25,000, the next lot was brought out.

"Lot number 328," The Auctioneer said.

When the assistant pulled the canvas tarp off lot 328, there was a quiet gasp in the audience.

"Mr. Hinkelheim's head."

A woman in the front row fainted. Her husband caught her and fanned her face with his wooden paddle.

"Five hundred dollars to the man fanning the lady," The Auctioneer said.

The man looked up, eyes wide. "No, sir, you see I'm merely fanning her, I'm not bidding! Can't you see she's passed out?" The man shouted.

"Sir you already bid, no need to bid again," The Auctioneer said.

"Five hundred, do I see five fifty?" The Auctioneer said. "Five hundred going once, going twice," The Auctioneer looked around the room one more time before bringing his mallet down on the podium. "Sold to the man fanning the lady for $500."

The man stopped fanning his wife and looked up at The Auctioneer and then at the table where Mr. Hinkelheim's head sat. The eyes were closed, and the face looked serene.

"I don't want that silly head," the man said. "Certainly not for five hundred dollars!"

"Sir, you bid, you won, you pay," The Auctioneer said with a sneer. He looked up at the audience. "Moving right along to lot number 329," the tarp was pulled from the table. "Mr. Hinkelheim's mistress, Lady Florington,"

Lady Florington lay on the table on her back in a

lovely rose-colored dress. There was a knife jutting from her abdomen, and a circle of red around the knife.

"The bidding will start at $10,000," The Auctioneer said.

Lady Florington was sold for $30,000.

There were several macabre lots to follow. Finally, lot number 342 was brought out; Isabella Rothberger, intact with the exception of her left arm.

"Lot number 342, Isabella Rothberger," The Auctioneer said. Isabella Rothberger looked altogether peaceful in her white dress with lacy sleeves. She was wearing a veil that whoever set up the lots had placed gently over her face.

As it goes, according to the article published in the newspaper if one had read the paper a few days before the auction, Isabella Rothberger was engaged to Mr. Hinkelheim. On the day of their wedding, she was unfortunate enough to open the door to Lady Florington, Mr. Hinkelheim's mistress. Florington cut off Rothberger's left arm in order to get the ring that she believed belonged to her. Rothberger, in retaliation, stabbed Florington in the stomach with the knife in the dressing room. She then hunted down Mr. Hinkelheim. The only part of Mr. Hinckelheim that was found was his head. Rothberger bled to death.

"The next auction will be held next Saturday," The Auctioneer said. "After the man fanning the lady kills myself and my assistant. Does anyone wish to be an auctioneer?"

THE DOOR

I WISH I'D NEVER GONE THROUGH THAT DOOR. IT WAS frightening to look at. The long stairway ended with the door, and over the years the wood around the door had turned gray and old. It had aged much faster than it should have, given that it was never exposed to the outside elements. The gray spread partway down the staircase. The stairs became warped.

Sometimes it sounded like there were a dozen people up there stomping around. Other times it sounded like a being with clawed feet was running back and forth. Scratching sounds, moaning, crying, shrieking. No one knew what was behind that door because if anyone came back, they were shells of their former selves.

It was an old house set in the center of a swamp surrounded by willow trees that swayed and moaned in a breeze that always flowed through. I always felt trapped there, like I would suffocate.

One night, I found myself halfway up the stairs before I woke from a trance. I had my right foot poised on the first of the warped gray steps. Some force drew me forward.

When I stood on the landing in front of the door, I reached out a hand and pressed it against the rough, grayed wood. It was warm. I touched the knob gently at first, in case it was hot. It was quite cool. I gripped it and turned slowly.

All light was enveloped by the darkness within. I stepped inside, slightly aware of the door closing gently behind me. There wasn't a shred of light, not even from under the door. I saw lights flashing before my eyes, and I felt hope, until I realized it was because I couldn't breathe. I closed my eyes and was dully aware of striking my head on the floor.

When I woke up, I was in a land full of writhing creatures that were mostly mist-like beings. There was a great winding pathway down a hill. At the bottom was a throne and on the throne was a gargoyle, or perhaps a demon. She was chained to the throne by a large shackle around her neck. Her giant wings formed the ceiling of this cavern. When she moved, bits of stone fell from where her wings scraped the walls.

She moaned, and I was filled with sadness. Who was this demon who had such a commanding presence, yet full of such sorrow?

I wandered down the winding path and stood before her. Her figure, and the throne she was imprisoned on, stood at least fifty feet above me. She looked at me with cat eyes that were the same gray as her pallid skin.

"What ails you fair demon?" I asked, venturing a guess as to what she was.

"I am kept here, captive to my own duty," she said.

"What is your duty?" I asked her.

"To weigh the souls of the dead," she said. She closed her eyes and a tear slithered down her cheek. "I was given this duty, and though it is a duty of great importance, here I sit, chained to my throne, a slave to the souls."

"Is there nothing you can do to get out of this duty?" I asked her.

"I am to remain in this duty for eternity," she said. "My soul was weighed, and I became this monstrosity before you," she shifted in her chair. "I was once a beautiful woman, a princess. I was killed on the eve of my wedding, by poison," she wiped a tear from her cheek. "I became this, and my love, my prince, he walks the land looking for me, not knowing that I am right here, for I do not appear to be his princess."

"That's so terrible," I said. And truly it was. "I saw him," I said, even though I really hadn't. "If I brought him here, and told him, or made him believe you are the princess, will that do anything?"

My heart was racked with sorrow when she sighed again. "He will not believe that I am his fair princess. He will think of me only as a monster. He will not believe that it is me."

"If it was true love," I said. "He will know it is you as soon as your eyes meet." I thought for a moment. "If this is true, will you give me back to the mortal world?"

She nodded. "You have an hour," she said.

I looked frantically at first for any sign of a prince who looked lost and wandering. There were very few beings wandering around. The area was small and surrounded by a murky river; the River Stix. Charon brought a boat load of souls and they wandered single file down the path to be weighed.

At last I found him. He was sulking under a crooked tree. Every so often he let out a long wail.

"I know where your princess is," I said. I had only seven minutes left.

"How do you know of my princess?" he asked.

"Follow me, and you will see her," I said.

The line of souls was short, so I stood behind the last one and waited.

"Where is my princess?" the prince asked.

"Look into her eyes," I said, pointing up at the demon before us.

"Does she know where my princess is?"

"Look into her eyes," I said again.

The prince reluctantly turned his gaze upward. I watched his face. As soon as their eyes met, his face lit up.

"It is her," he said.

"Mortal," the demon said. "You have brought me my prince, and in return I shall send you back to the mortal world." She snapped her fingers and a boat appear before me. "Do you have two coins to pay for passage?"

I did not.

SOUNDS OF TERROR

THE ALBUM COVER READ *SOUNDS OF TERROR* IN blood red, dripping letters. It also featured a black and white drawing of a haunted house in the background with barely intelligible figures lurking in the windows. Bruce sat down with a paper cup full of whiskey—he had recently moved and it was all he could find—and popped the CD into the player. He leaned back against the sofa and flipped over the case. The first two tracks were called "Blood and Guts" and "Torture." He shuddered, wondering what they would sound like.

Bruce wanted to listen to a sampling of the sounds the CD had to offer for the annual Halloween Haunted House contest that year. He had read about the contest in the local paper and all the folks on his block participated. He figured it was a sign for him to participate when he found the CD in the box that held the paper cups. Bruce felt his haunted house had to be spectacular. He had to prove he could play with the big kids in this department.

It was a way to prove he could live in the neighborhood. That he was worthy.

"Spook-tacular," Bruce chuckled to himself. He took a sip of whiskey.

Bruce pushed play on the sound system remote and the CD whirred in the machine, making clicking and gurgling sounds while the eye tried to read it. Barely audible voices hissed through the speakers; it sounded like an old vinyl record crackling under the needle of a phonograph. Bruce turned up the volume. They were merely whispers, snickering, talking about something. He leaned close to one of the speakers, nearly pressing his ear against it, trying to understand what the voices were saying, what they were discussing. He felt uneasy—cold but hot at the same time, like a warm wind kept wafting over his body. He swallowed the dryness out of his throat and held his breath, listening.

Suddenly, a man's screams filled the air. Bruce jumped back, hitting his back against the coffee table. He fumbled with the volume control and turned it down, heart hammering. He laughed, then looked at the coffee table and groaned. The cup of whiskey had tipped over. The amber liquid formed a puddle around the cup.

A familiar voice on the CD yelled, "No! Please!" jerking Bruce's attention back to the speakers. Heavy footsteps crossed the room, the slither of a knife unsheathed. "Please! Don't hurt me!" the voice was panicked. Bruce's heart beat hard in his chest. His ears pricked at each new sound that issued from the speakers. Eyes wide, he stared into the black mesh covering the front of the speaker. Where did he hear that voice before?

"Don't worry," a raspy voice said with a malicious laugh. "It won't hurt . . . for long . . ." there was a lengthy pause. The only sound was the victim's heavy, short bursts of breath, peppered with whimpers. "Bruce."

Bruce's heart skipped a beat. His mouth dried up and he tried to swallow and gasped at the same time, inhaling some spit. He coughed, trying to clear his windpipe. He gripped this throat, eyes locked on the speaker as if he could see what was happening in that room on the CD.

He couldn't believe his ears. Did the voice really just say his name? Surely it had to be a different Bruce. He jumped, flinging the remote across the room as the man's voice burst forth with a loud shriek accompanied by the sloppy sound of liquids and thrashing limbs. It sounded like someone hacked open a pumpkin, ripped out the insides and threw them onto a floor covered with newspaper.

The cackle of the attacker filled the air as the man's screams subsided and wet sounds continued, interspersed with raspy grunts. The whispering continued, this time in hushed, stifled laughs. A peanut gallery for the macabre.

The lights flickered. Bruce looked with wide eyes at the lamp in the corner, his only source of light. It flickered again and finally went out. All was silent and dark. Bruce's heart beat hard. He hated that first moment when the lights went out. It was always so startling. He fumbled in a box for a flashlight, trying to remember which box he might have put it in.

Whispering voices cut through the silence. Bruce looked through the darkness toward the CD player, but the power was out. The CD player operated on electricity. It was dead, yet the voices continued to whisper. He swallowed his heart, which had crept into his throat.

He started as heavy footsteps crossed the hall outside the door. Bruce's breath quickened, coming in short bursts. The footsteps continued through the door and into the living room. A knife slithered from its sheath.

"Don't worry," a raspy voice said. "It won't hurt . . . for long," a malicious cackle ensued.

WORSHIP OF TOOLS DAY

MARCH 11TH

THE GOLD HAMMER SAT UPON A PLUSH PILLOW OF deep purple velvet, trimmed with gold frills and tassels. Josh carried it carefully toward the altar where other Worshippers had placed their tools. There was a screwdriver on a green pillow, a pair of pliers on a red pillow. The hammer was the most important tool, as it represented strength and integrity. He was put in charge of placing it upon the altar so the ceremony could begin.

He walked carefully, painfully slow, down the aisle, careful not to drop or let the hammer slip from the pillow. His palms were sweaty, and he was relieved that the pillow was velvet instead of vinyl. He set the pillow carefully upon the altar, and the Grand Master nodded at him. Josh took his seat in the front row, which was reserved for Those Who Carried the Tools. They didn't get any special name or anything, but they got to wear a gold rope around their robes. Everyone else had black, so it blended with the robe.

Josh sat through the meeting staring at the golden

hammer on the deep purple pillow. His brow tingled with sweat. What if he dropped it on the way out? What if it touched the floor while he carried it out of the altar room to the display case? He swallowed hard and looked at the Grand Master who was gesturing to the tools before him and reciting the Rites of the Tools. When he got to the hammer Josh saw his eyes shift quickly to his face and then back at the congregation. Did the Grand Master know something?

Josh looked over his shoulder toward where the Grand Master had glanced after looking at Josh, but everyone was intent on the Grand Master's words.

Those Who Carried the Tools had to memorize a bit about the tool they carried. When it was Josh's turn, he stood up and stumbled. His heel was caught in the hem of his robe. He laughed nervously and steadied himself, cleared his throat, swallowed past the lump in it, and spoke his part.

"I carried the hammer," he said in a steady voice. "The strength, the power, the integrity of the Tools." he almost forgot his next line, but it came to him after a second's pause. "Should the hammer touch the ground on the way in, it will result in a bad year for those who use tools. Should it touch the ground on the way out, it will result in death by hammer."

Josh never read too much into the recitation because he never thought he would be chosen to carry the hammer. In his two years as a member in the Cult of Tools, he never saw anyone drop it.

After he recited his part, he sat down and stared at the hammer. What if he dropped it? Someone would die by hammer this year. He didn't know if it meant someone in the Cult or any random person that might use a hammer.

Before he knew it, the ceremony was complete, and the all members said the final prayer to the Tools. One by one, the other tools were carried out. Finally, all that was left was the hammer. The Grand Master nodded to Josh, and he thought he saw some sort of glint in the Grand Master's eye. A knowing glint and something in the half smile that played around the left corner of his mouth.

Josh approached the altar after tripping on his robe again and cursing himself silently. He carefully picked up the pillow. The golden hammer shifted slightly, and he steadied his hands. A drop of sweat slithered down the side of his face as he looked up at the Grand Master.

Josh turned carefully and started down the aisle. Half way there, he heard a snicker. He felt something against his leg. Before he could stop it from happening, he fell forward, stumbling, trying to catch himself to no avail. The entire time his eyes were locked on the golden hammer. The gleam it held with the low lights and flickers of the candles around the room. His chin hit the floor. His arms were stretched before him. The hammer lay precariously on the edge of the pillow, and he sighed with relief. The hammer wobbled gently, his eyes widened. It tilted up and down like a see-saw, and then slid off the pillow and onto the floor.

"Sinner!" The Grand Master shouted with the gasp of the other Worshippers. Josh looked over his shoulder and saw the Grand Master pointing at him. Some of the other members had risen to their feet. They had hammers in their hands.

"Should the hammer touch the floor on the way out," the Grand Master recited. Everyone joined in, except Josh who stared at the Grand Master's dark eyes. "It will result in death by hammer." They came closer, hitting their hammers against their palms, their faces malicious and intent on Josh.

He could hardly hear his own cries over the sick thumps of their hammers striking his head and body.

TEDDY BEAR'S FEAST

Mama always sang that teddy bear song to me before bed. I imagined my teddy bears coming to life at night and waddling down into the forest to dance and play. I wished I could join them as a kid, but I was too young. No matter how long I tried to stay awake, the teddies never left my room, and when I woke up, they all sat exactly as I had left them.

She sang that song to me every night until I was thirteen. Then she became ill and couldn't get out of bed. I ended up singing it to her.

Mama was sick for five years. I took care of her that whole time. Then one night, when I sang the song, her eyes didn't open.

I was nineteen when she died. In her last breaths she warned me never to go into the woods. Her eyes grew soft, and then she was gone. I cried until the sun went down. When I stopped crying, I sat and pressed my face against her hand.

I fell into a shallow, dreamless sleep, and was awakened by a shuffling sound. I looked up, my cheeks stiff with dried tears, and watched as the teddy bears from my room waddled by. Their movements were quick and jerky as if walking was an abnormal movement.

I followed them. They marched across the lawn, single file, and into the woods. I paused at the edge of the forest. Clouds covered the moon. The trees rattled in the wind, their branches swayed, beckoning me forward. Despite Mama's warning, I entered the woods.

After I had forced my way through the lower bushes, I saw a light ahead. In the delirium of my recent loss, my thoughts reverted to when I was a child. I imagined the bears playing and dancing, feasting on cakes and pies. I licked my lips, anxious to taste those succulent treats.

I entered the lighted clearing and gasped. The bears weren't dancing and playing. They stood in a circle lit with candles. When they saw me, they turned and stared. Their eyes glowed red. They leaped forward, attacking. They knocked me down and dragged me into the clearing.

Tied down with stiff, biting ropes, I could hardly move. They started with my hands and feet, little bites, gnawing up my arms and legs. I chanced a look. My arms were raw. Bone showed in places, my hand was a mess of tattered skin and blood.

The largest bear sat on my chest. For a moment he looked almost normal, like the bear sitting on the shelf in my room all those years. Suddenly, he leaped forward and bit into my throat. I screamed as little, sharp teeth tore my skin. I tried to struggle, but he was heavy on my chest.

My screams ceased abruptly as the teddy ripped through my trachea. I gasped for air. The last thing I saw was a sharp claw coming toward my eye.

ROSES ARE RED

THE VASE OF ROSES, DECORATED WITH A GREAT, RED ribbon, sat in the center of the table for Magritte to find when she came home. Tucked deep inside the stems, a white envelope waited. The card was from Franz, her lover. He sneaked into the house using the key Magritte had given him. Casting furtive glances, he left the vase on the table. He made sure to push the card deep within so her husband, Dr. Grim, would not see it.

When Magritte woke the next morning, she was delighted to see the roses. She looked for a card, and when she saw the white envelope tucked deep into the stems, she knew it must be from Franz. He always hid the card. She reached inside, not checking to see if the florist had removed the thorns. Franz always bought her roses without thorns, for he believed that by giving a lover a flower with thorns was detrimental to the relationship. Thorns were for enemies. As she pulled her hand out of the stems, however, the thorns gripped her skin. Magritte jerked her hand with a gasp and looked at it. Deep scratches adorned her fair skin. She watched as blood oozed from the wounds. A tiny bud that had not yet bloomed peeled open slowly to full bloom right before her eyes. Magritte, intrigued by the flowers, and in desperate need to see who had sent them, shoved her hand deep into the stems to retrieve the card once more. The stems tightened around her hand, the thorns dug deep into her skin, puncturing it. She stifled her screams by biting her other hand until it bled. The pain became unbearable, and as she bit harder on her hand, she glimpsed her husband. She screamed for him to help her.

Dr. Grim stood in the doorway, watching. He saw Franz bring the flowers. He knew what his wife was up to. He switched the flowers with those of his own design. As a botanist and a scientist, he was able to create a hybrid of rose and Venus fly trap. A plant with beautiful flowers that needed protein in order to grow and prosper.

As he watched her futile attempts to extract her hand from the carnivorous flowers, he chuckled and came nearer. He crouched by her and lovingly pushed the hair from her eyes, tucking it gently behind her ear.

"This is what you get," he said in a whisper.

Magritte's eyes opened wide as the stems tightened even more, the thorns pressing further into her skin. She willed herself to ignore the pain, it wasn't real. How could beautiful roses be eating her hand?

All sound became muffled. She could hear her heart pounding in her ears. Her vision blurred, and finally, blackness overtook her, and she no longer felt anything.

Dr. Grim dragged her into his basement laboratory where he conducted all his botanical experiments. A place Magritte never went. She didn't care about his science, his experiments. All she cared about was being beautiful, and having tea with her busybody friends, and secret rendezvous with her lover.

He dropped her onto the floor. Blood oozed from the tattered remains of her hand.

"Now my babies will have plenty of food to sustain them," he rubbed his hands together. "Hello, my pretties."

The plants in the incubator pressed their blooms against the glass and rattled their stems, eager for their next meal.

Dr. Grim turned and stepped toward the corner where Franz sat, bound and gagged, a puddle of blood around the chair he sat in, blood that dripped from his ragged shoulder and foot. Dr. Grim stepped closer, pulling something from an instrument tray. A large lily snapped at the doctor as he moved closer to Franz, it shook its spiny leaves when it missed his shoulder. Dr. Grim looked at the lily with scorn and it shrunk away from him. He turned his attention back to Franz, whose scream was muffled against his gag as Dr. Grim picked up a shiny scalpel from a tray.

"Just an eye," he said. "That's all they need. Full of protein, the eye. They will be larger than my last bouquet."

Franz struggled against his bindings, his eyes wide. As the scalpel neared, Franz closed his eyes tight.

With a malicious cackle, Dr. Grim said, "It won't hurt, for long," and dug the scalpel in.

SECOND FLOOR FACES

THE TEN-FOOT TALL MIRROR STOOD AGAINST THE wall in the hallway, looming over anyone who passed it. The frame, made of mahogany, had two-inch long, intricate and smiling faces carved into it. Christine hated the mirror.

The entire house gave her creepy feelings. Her husband, Roy, bought the house on a whim, as it was cheap and everything they ever wanted and more. Christine couldn't help but think of "The Amityville Horror."

"What happened to the previous owners?" Christine asked the real estate agent.

"What do you mean?" The agent asked with a fake smile.

"Why did they leave?" Christine asked. She noted the discomfort in the agent's eyes. "Or were they killed?"

Roy stepped close and squeezed Christine around the shoulders. "Don't mind my wife," he said. "She has an active imagination!" He smiled. Christine crossed her arms and scowled.

After Roy had convinced Christine the house was perfect, they signed the papers.

"I don't like that mirror," Christine said. "I feel like I'm being watched."

"Don't be silly, Chris," Roy said. "It's just a mirror, it won't hurt you."

Roy went to the hardware store to get a few things. Since she was alone, Christine wandered around the first floor.

"We don't have near enough stuff to fill this house," she said in a room with wispy white curtains. A breeze fluttered through the room, lifting the curtains, but the windows were not open.

Christine turned to leave the room and stopped. A girl stood in the doorway.

"Follow me," the girl whispered, motioning with her finger. She turned and disappeared. A distant giggle floated down the hall.

Christine peered into the hallway. The girl was nowhere to be seen. A shiver ran up Christine's spine. She pulled her sweater tighter.

"Come upstairs," the girl's voice came.

"Who are you?" Christine called. "Where did you come from?"

"Come up here," the girl's voice called. "I'll show you."

The mirror was upstairs. Christine put her hand on the rail and paused before going up. Her heart pounded.

When she reached the top of the stairs, the girl stood by the mirror.

She giggled, and stepped inside, her hand gripped the frame. She poked her head out and smiled at Christine.

"It's okay," the girl said. "It's fun in here!" She giggled again and disappeared.

Christine saw nothing but her own weary reflection in the mirror. A hand darted out and grabbed her arm. She struggled, but the grip was tight. Her hand went numb with cold as it passed through the surface of the mirror. Her breathing came in panicked bursts as she leaned back with all her weight. Her eyes searched the hall for anything to help her. She looked at the edge of the mirror. The faces had looks of terror on their carved features.

Christine's foot slipped, and she tumbled into the mirror in an icy blast.

Roy came home and called to Christine, he searched for her. As he passed the mirror, he failed to see her little carved face among the others.

THE HOUSE WAS ONCE A PRISTINE WHITE, BUT AGE and moist air had weathered it into a slumping, peeling gray mass with dark, gloomy windows and an air of misery. It was enveloped by a thick forest of willow trees and other foliage that loved the wet environment.

The house gave Louise the chills, and as her parents pulled their car up to the front steps, jostling over potholes, a window in the foundation caught her eye.

"You're looking awfully skinny, deary," Grandma said with a grin. She squeezed Louise's arms and pinched her cheek.

After depositing her bag in the guest room, Louise went outside to the window she saw. She crouched down and looked in at the cellar as a light clicked on, and footsteps thudded down the stairs.

A man with a large, knotted head entered. He disappeared into a dark corner, and when he reappeared, he hefted an irregular-shaped bag onto a slab table. He pulled a knife from a sheath on his belt and wiped it on his soiled leather apron. He opened the bag and reached inside.

"Louise!" Grandma's voice came. Louise started and jumped to her feet. "What are you doing?" Grandma asked.

"I was, I saw, there's a . . ." Louise stammered.

"Come inside, it's chilly out here, and the damp air will give you a cold!" Grandma gripped her arm and squeezed it rhythmically.

Later that night, Louise crept through the house. She finally came across a hidden door. Whoever last entered neglected to latch it. Louise opened the door slowly, holding her breath against any creaky hinges.

It opened on a stone staircase. Someone down below mumbled in short groans, interspersed with loud *thunks*. She went down a couple steps and squatted. The lumpy man was there at the table, cleaver in hand. In smooth motions he chopped and hacked at something. He tossed aside a handful of fingers and Louise gasped. The man paused, head tilted, listening. She covered her mouth and bit her fingers, stifling a scream. Tears burned in her eyes as the man hacked and discarded more body parts. Grandpa appeared in the light, some slimy organ in hand. He took a lusty bite.

The door creaked, and Louise looked up. Grandma stood at the top of the stairs, smiling.

"We've been waiting for you to plump up," Grandma smiled. "But time has grown short."

She lifted her foot and shoved Louise down the stairs. Louise landed on her back. Gasping for air, her head swam, and her vision blurred.

"Lump, do her next," Grandma shouted.

The man nodded and shoved the remaining body parts into a thirty-gallon, bubbling, cast iron pot. He gripped Louise by a wrist and ankle and flung her onto the table.

Before darkness overcame her senses, Louise watched Grandpa take another bite from the human heart. She screamed as the cleaver come down on her arm with a sick, wet, chop.

THE FORK IN THE ROAD

THE MONSTERS TOWERED OVER THE CITY, AND WHEN Jan and George had seen the first one devour an entire bus full of people, they thought it best to get out of there. The beasts were usually invisible, but they had seen a pair mating behind a building. George nearly threw up. Weak stomach. It was the female—they think—that chased them into the woods, lashing her nine tentacles. Perhaps mating made them angry.

They now stood at the fork in the road, half a mile into the woods. Light filtered in through the thick evergreens dappling the path with white spots of sunshine, though the moment warranted overcast skies, maybe an occasional crack of lightning.

Their breath came in quick bursts. George looked at Jan. A laugh laced with hysteria burst from his lips. She smiled weakly and reached for his hand. As their fingertips met, George's body lurched. His smile disappeared, and he flew into the air.

"No!" Her voice tore from her vocal cords.

His body dangled among the trees, struggling at the unseen bindings. Jan couldn't hear him gasping as the tentacle tightened, constricting his organs. With a whoosh of air, his lungs expelled any chance of breathing. Sweat broke out on his face, hot and prickly. His eyes bulged, threatening to pop from their sockets. In a final struggle, the capillaries in his eyes burst, and he was gone.

Jan picked up a rock and threw it as hard as she could with an angry grunt. It hit something. A hiss issued from high above her. George's body dropped to the ground. She turned and ran down the left path. She fought to contain her fear with anger. She pumped her arms as fast as she could, her lungs screamed for mercy, her calves burned, tears leaked from her eyes. Trees thrashed behind her, trunks snapped, branches crashed. The maelstrom of the monster's movement made her stomach tighten. She had to get out of this place. She had to find safety.

Jan looked over her shoulder. A tentacle lashed out at her out of nowhere. She ducked, and her shoe caught on a tree root, flinging her forward. She landed hard on her stomach. Gasping, she struggled upright. Helpless defeat overwhelmed her.

"I'm going to die," she whispered. Visions of the fight she had with her lover, the promotion she received at work, the positive pregnancy test flashed through her mind. "No, no you're not," she said through gritted teeth. She turned around to face the monster.

The woods were quiet and still. The only thing Jan

could hear was her gasping breaths. She held her breath and heard her pulse booming in her ears. Had she outrun the monster? Was she safe? She wiped her hand across her brow and bent over to catch her breath as a tentacle snaked through the underbrush inches from her foot.

THE FACE IN THE WINDOW

 the attic window. "I swear I saw it, someone's up there."

"Don't be silly." Marsha said, pulling a suitcase from the trunk. She looked at her husband and placed a hand on her back. "Could you help?"

He glanced at her bulging belly and pulled out the rest. Marsha's cell rang, and she put it on speaker.

"It's mom, I saw the pictures. You should have waited to get married until after you had the baby, you look like a beluga whale after a seafood buffet."

"Thanks, mom." Marsha rolled her eyes. Jones grabbed the luggage and hauled it inside.

He left it in the entry and looked around. Marsha wanted to have a hideaway honeymoon, far from technology and people. Though the closest town was thirty minutes away, her cell phone magically still worked. Jones went upstairs and looked around. Another stairway stood halfway down the hall, he stopped at the bottom.

"The attic," he muttered. "Someone's up there."

He crept up. At the top stood a door unlike the rest of the interior. The other levels had rich mahogany. This door looked weathered like it had been beaten by harsh rains and wind. He reached for the doorknob and jerked back. Heat radiated from the metal, not hot enough to burn, but hot enough to give him a start.

Suddenly aware of his pounding heart, Jones swallowed hard.

"Jones!" Marsha yelled. "Where are you?"

He let out the breath he was holding and turned around.

"Upstairs," he yelled. The door swung open and Jones turned around. Gray-green hands crawled from within the too-dark depths. Ligaments showed where the skin had fallen away. They crawled closer to him. Jones stumbled backward. His breath caught in his throat. He groped for the railing as he fell. His head struck the stairs, and all went dark.

He awoke at the bottom of the stairs. His head felt like it had exploded, his neck shrieked with pain. He rubbed his sore spots and got to his feet. Looking out the window, at the long shadows, he realized a few hours had passed. The door on the third floor had closed.

"Marsha?" He called. Why hadn't she come when he fell?

He limped down the stairs, hissing against pain in his ankle. The door at the end of the hall stood open. Marsha lay on the bed, very still. Jones limped down the hall and stopped in the doorway. The bedspread by her legs covered in blood, Marsha's eyes stared, glazed and vacant.

He watched her round belly as it pulsed, like the beat of a heart. The skin split like an overripe tomato and a dead hand poked its fingers through. Jones gagged and stumbled back against the wall. A scraping sound came from the hallway. He chanced a glance as dozens of hands crawled through the door, searching. He looked back at Marsha as the hand from her belly, covered in blood and tissue, leaped at his throat.

BRAIN WITH TENTACLES

"Hm," the doctor said. "I've never seen this before." The stereotypical blood-curdling scream issued from the television.

Louise groaned. "Another doctor horror flick," she muttered. "Oh, wait," she said, her voice thick with sarcasm. "This one has a man whose head turns into a giant brain with tentacles. Awesome," She turned off the TV.

Darkness seeped around her, enveloping her in a discomforting quiet. She hugged a pillow to her chest and peered through the dark. Rain tapped at the window and forceful winds whistled against the window panes. She hated being home alone.

Lightening flashed in the distance followed by a boom of thunder.

With a squeal, Louise ran upstairs to her bedroom. "You're twenty-seven—you should not be afraid of the dark or storms or . . ." she gasped and ran to close the closet door. "Open closet doors." She leaned against it.

She heard a door slam and jumped, then breathed a sigh of relief. Her husband was home.

"You'll never believe how silly I am!" She yelled. But her husband was nowhere to be seen. "Honey?"

The bathroom light was on, and the hiss of running water and splashing came from within.

"Honey? Are you okay?" She pushed the door open slowly and screamed.

Her husband stood at the sink, running water in his hands and splashing it on his face, only, he no longer had a face. In its place, waving slime-covered tentacles, sat an oversized brain. The tentacles probed the toothbrush holder, grabbed at the roll of toilet paper, and hand towels on the racks. One of them reached toward Louise as he turned.

"I don't feel so good," he said. He took a step forward then fell to the ground. The brain splatted against the floorboard as it hit, the tentacles twitched, and slithered, leaving behind smears of slime. Louise screamed and backed away.

"Tsk, tsk," a voice said. Louise jumped and looked up, eyes wide. The doctor from the movie stood at the end of the hall. A scalpel gleamed in his hand. Something large and round hung from the other hand. "Poor thing," he said. He tossed the round thing at Louise. It landed on the floor with a thud and rolled into the light from the bathroom.

Her husband's face stared at her, an expression of fear and shock frozen on its features.

Louise screamed. Heart pounding, she jumped to her feet and turned to run to the back door. One of her husband's tentacles grabbed her around the ankle. It pulled her toward him. She scrabbled at the floor trying to grip something, anything, to pull herself free. She chanced a glance over her shoulder as her foot entered a gnashing maw full of teeth.

She cried in pain as the teeth gnawed on her foot. A hand stroked her hair. She looked up at the doctor as he crouched next to her.

"He's hungry, you see," the doctor said. "He needs," he paused and stroked her cheek. "Fresh meat."

MOZZARELLA BALL

Cindy looked at the calendar. Two more days and her month-long dairy-free diet would be over. She opened the fridge to gaze at the carton of milk, and there, on the top shelf was a ball of cheese. Not ordinary cheese. It was fresh mozzarella. Cindy licked her lips, her stomach growled. She figured the housekeeper stuck it in there, knowing Cindy loved cheese.

"Two more days," she muttered. "You will be mine." She scolded herself for talking to a ball of cheese, closed the fridge and sat at the kitchen table to read the newspaper. She looked up and jumped. The refrigerator door stood ajar. The cheese stared out at her, tempting her. She laughed at the thought and closed it.

Later that day, Cindy went to the kitchen again to daydream about eating the cheese with tomato and basil. Licking her lips, she paused in the doorway. The fridge door was wide open again.

"I know I closed that door," she said. Two more days, but she couldn't take it. It had been too long since her last bite of cheese. She lunged forward, grabbed the ball, and bit off a mouth-filling chunk.

Mozzarella-goodness caressed her palate. Creamy, subtly salty. She closed her eyes and moaned, savoring every bite. She chewed long and hard, extracting every bit of flavor, unaware that the cheese in her hand began to melt. The cheese boiled, burning her. She dropped it and ran to the sink to run cold water over the burns.

Behind her, it bubbled on the linoleum. Expanding and stretching, it mounded up into the crude shape of a seven-foot man in a fedora. A single feather stuck from the hat.

"You bit me," the cheese said. Cindy gasped, backed away, staring up into the eyeless face of the Cheeseman.

"I-I'm sorry," she said gripping the edge of the counter as the cheese loomed over her. "I had two days left, I should have waited," she stammered, as if it mattered.

A cheese slicer gleamed from the Cheeseman's hand. Cindy's heart pounded. She glanced from his face to his weapon-wielding hand.

Cindy reached out. "Please," she said. "I didn't mean any harm." She noticed a missing piece from his face. The piece that now sat, a hard, cold lump, in her stomach. Bile rose to her throat.

In a movement too quick for a man made of cheese, he slashed at her with the cheese slicer, lopping off her outstretched hand.

Cindy screamed. The Cheeseman plucked her hand from the floor, brushed it off against his leg, leaving a smear of blood on the smooth white surface, and sat at the table. Cindy dropped to the floor, wrapping a kitchen towel around her stump. Sweat beaded on her forehead. She retched, and blood soaked the towel. Her heart pounded in her throat, her vision blurred, and finally, she blacked out.

As Cindy lay on the floor bleeding to death, the Cheeseman enjoyed slices of her fingers and hand on buttery crackers.

LITTLE MUMMY CAT

Jake saw something in the darkness of the interstate and slammed the brakes. He took a deep breath, grabbed a flashlight, and jumped out into the rain, sweeping the light over the road. The object looked like some sort of cloth-wrapped package. He ran toward it and gasped.

Completely wrapped in bandages, the little cat mewled.

"Poor thing," Jake said. He tucked it inside his jacket. "You look like a miniature mummy."

Once home, he decided to change the cat's soaked bandages. He started unwrapping. When he was finished, he stared in disbelief.

He had expected a soft, furry kitten, but in front of him sat a hairless cat, shrunken and thin. A skeleton with a sheet of leathery flesh tossed onto it and pinned into place. The eyes were clouded. The cat mewled and purred, rubbing against his hand. The skin was stiff and dry. Jake jerked back in disgust.

I have to get rid of it, he thought. The cat stared through him. He grabbed a spare pillowcase and a brick, stuffed the cat inside, tossed in the brick and drove to the bridge. He dropped the sack over the side and rushed back home to bed, heart pounding.

The next morning, he was sick. Skin pale, eyes dull. He shuffled into the kitchen for medicine and gagged. The smell overpowered his senses: Old musty dirt. There on the kitchen table, staring, sat the cat. Its skin looked pliable and soft. Jake thought perhaps the water had done it some good, but how had it found its way back? And, God, the smell. He gagged and retched into the sink.

He stuffed the cat into another pillowcase, set it behind the back wheel of his truck, backed over it, then dug a hole and buried the whole thing. He went back to bed with a groan, trembling with weakness, and broke out in cold sweat.

Jake woke, heart pounding. His clothes clung to him. The bed moved slightly, and he heard licking. He clicked on the light, and there, with tufts of long white fur shooting out at various spots, clouded eyes staring, lay the cat. With all his remaining strength, Jake grabbed the cat, and dragged himself and the mongrel into the living room. He opened the woodstove and tossed it inside, squirted a whole can of lighter fluid on it, and threw in a match. He closed the stove and went to bed.

His sleep was disturbed by yowling. He felt hot and itchy. He got up to pee and looked in the mirror. His face was gaunt, his eyes sunken. His skin was dry and leathery. He fell to the floor as muscle fatigue overcame him. He stared out into the hall, unable to move, when a beautiful, white cat prowled into view. It turned to look through him with clouded eyes.

As the cat stared, Jake felt his body shrivel, felt his skin tighten against his bones. His vision clouded. The last thing he saw before he went blind was the cat's now green eyes penetrating his soul.

THE TINIEST ENCHILADA

Evan stared out the window, random thoughts roving through his idle mind. He remembered seeing a video of a hamster eating a tiny burrito one time and wondered how small the smallest enchilada in the world would be. Would it even be enough to feed this hungry little hamster? How did the chef even make tortillas that tiny? Was there even a baking dish small enough to bake them?

These were the types of questions that filled Evan's mind on a day to day basis. Trivial ponderings. Nonsensical nonsense. Things that didn't matter. Not when the world was ending.

The plague hit about a month ago. It started in Barrow, Alaska, where a research team thought the cold climate would keep it contained. Kill it if it got out. But the thing had evolved fast until it was indestructible. Invincible. The Superman Plague. Fast as a speeding bullet and all that.

Then, it spread. All over the world.

I need to see the world's largest teddy bear. Evan thought, as he gazed out the window of his seventh-floor apartment, sipping a cup of cold coffee. After all, his mom, who passed a year before, named him after that sixty-one-foot-tall stuffed animal. She said it was that or Theodore. She would have called him Teddy. He was glad she named him Evan.

But, he really needed to see that bear.

There were a lot of things Evan needed to see.

A crowd of Plaguers shuffled by on the street below. They moved in packs now. Before long they'd learn to use tools as weapons to take down their prey. If there was any prey left. Evan glanced straight across from his apartment at the building next door. A woman stood on her balcony.

What is she doing?

The air was rife with the virus. He watched as she climbed up onto the railing. She looked up, and he swore their eyes met, even though he could hardly see her face.

He waved.

She jumped.

He looked away.

The pack below must have heard her land. They changed direction and rushed toward her fresh corpse.

There were so many things he needed to see, but that was *not* one of them.

Evan closed the blinds. He needed to anyway, before the sun came pelting in, heating up his apartment like . . . he tried to think of some clever metaphor, but only came up with a pizza oven. His stomach growled.

When the virus had gone airborne, he'd turned off the thermostat and covered all the vents with garbage bags and duct taped around the doors and windows. Anywhere outside air might get in, he sealed it up. He was surprised he could still breathe. The fact that he could made his skin crawl. Air had to be getting in from somewhere. Air carrying the virus.

So far, he hadn't shown any signs or symptoms.

Maybe that woman had.

Evan sighed. His mind went back to the world's largest teddy.

I'm not big, though.

He looked down at his stomach, which had shrunk substantially over the last two weeks. He ate his last sleeve of stale saltine crackers that morning. His last ration. No more food. Just this cold cup of shitty coffee. He took a sip. Grimaced.

Before the plague, he'd had an impressive gut, akin to a hippo. Well, maybe an average-sized hippo. Regular-sized hippos were much larger. His double XL shirt size had to be considered average . . . for a hippo.

A knock came at the door. Evan dropped the cup. Cold coffee splashed all over the carpet. Another knock. Steady. One, two, three. Gentle. Three, two, one.

He always thought if anyone knocked it would be loud and frantic banging. Or the scrape of fingernails. Fingernails with old blood caked beneath.

"Hello?" a woman's voice called through the door.

Evan didn't respond. He crept to the peephole and peered out.

It was his neighbor, Gloria. Always beautiful, Gloria, even though her shoulder-length blonde hair was stringy and greasy from not washing it.

Evan never thought about the water. He glanced over his shoulder at the spilled coffee, made with water from the tap. Water from out there.

Son of a bitch.

"Evan? Are you in there? It's Gloria."

"Go away Gloria," Evan said, his voice rough from disuse. She'd broken his heart before. They had a one-night stand. He was in love. She was not.

"I'm hungry," she said. He watched her through the peephole. She turned around, and her head slid out of view. Evan sat on the floor with his back to the door and pretended the hard surface was Gloria's back.

"You shouldn't be outside," he said.

"I know." He heard her shift on the other side of the door. "I'm sick."

Evan sucked in a breath and held it. He scrambled away from the door and pulled the collar of his shirt up over his nose. His eyes darted around the door frame. Every scrap of tape was still in place.

Go jump off your balcony, he thought, then took it back, surprised at how easily he'd forgotten what humanity looked like, sounded like, felt like. He suddenly yearned for human contact. To hold her hands, to run his fingers through her grimy hair, feel the press of her lips on his. Her arms around him.

Would it feel like a hug to be mauled by a Plaguer?

What a stupid question.

Gloria was still talking on the other side of the door, her voice laced with hysteria. She stopped and began whimpering, then sobbing, then growling.

The virus was quick.

Her fingernails scraped down the door.

Evan moved to the window again. Opened the blinds and looked out. His stomach rumbled. He ran his hands over his belly.

An average-sized hippo.

Even the tiniest of tiny enchiladas would be good right now.

Narration available on YouTube (with illustrations)!
Go to:
https://clairelfishback.com/stories-and-books

THE TIME MACHINE SAT IN THE CORNER OF THE basement covered in a thick layer of dust and speckled with cat pawprints. The machine was spherical in shape. Strange appendages with knobs on the ends jutted out in various locations along its exterior. It had a similar appearance of a sea bomb, only it sat on planks of wood, giving the impression that it sat *on* the water, not *under* it. The thing hadn't been used in over two decades, not after the ban on time travel that was enacted in 2266.

Benjamin straightened his vest and cleared his throat, preparing himself to approach the machine, as if it might suddenly turn on, snatch him inside, and send him into the past. He looked at his wrist monitor, noting his elevated heart rate. The mechanism also recorded excited levels of perspiration. He cleared his throat again and touched his neck over the small, sickle-shaped scar where his GPS chip had been implanted thirty years ago when he was born. Would They know that he was standing next to a time machine?

They, as the New Government called themselves, did everything they could to keep the general public safe from harm, and in turn keep humanity under strict control. This included banning alcohol (to become inebriated was to cause harm to many), tobacco (to smoke was to cause many to become sick, and therefore harm many), agriculture (to grow food is to show a lack of support to local grocers, and therefore, harm many), and eventually, time travel.

The time travel ban, like with the other bans, came with a statement: To change time was to change the lives of many, and therefore harm many. The statement was supposed to be profound, and indeed, to some it was, but to the major organizations behind time machine manufacture, it was preposterous. No one used time machines to change lives. According to a survey done by the Time Travel Administration, the most common use of a time machine was to visit dead relatives; the *second* being to right a wrong, not wrong a right.

The ban was viewed with renewed interest after the trial of Mercy vs. Lewis when Cynthia Lewis traveled back in time to object to the marriage of Gloria Gray and Frederick Mercy. Upon doing so, she unknowingly started a series of events that would ultimately lead to the assassination of the 100th president, Wilhelm Wundt (the twenty-first century "father of psychology" who managed to travel *forward* in time by—as he put it—hitching a ride), in 2245.

Benjamin cleared his throat again and took a step forward. The sound of his foot on the wooden floorboard made his heart jump. He paused and listened, noting nothing but a deafening silence that was punctuated by with the pounding of his heart in his ears. He breathed a heavy sigh, rubbed his forehead and stepped next to the machine. He didn't know how to work it, though his grandfather used to let him sit in it. He should have shown more interest all those years ago.

He touched his vest pocket where he had tucked his copy of his grandfather's will, along with a note: The only thing in the lockbox willed to him. The note was simple:

I was so close! Get back to March 3, 2245 and stop her!

Benjamin didn't know who *her* was, but he had a good idea. He swallowed hard past a lump in his throat. The hatch to the time machine opened with the press of a button labeled *open*.

Inside was a schematic of the machine, clean and crisp as if it had just been printed. The interior was decorated sparingly, but the cushion on the seat was a plush velvet in cranberry. Benjamin climbed inside.

A warning tone buzzed in his ears and a polite female voice said, "Benjamin Mode, you are in close proximity to a banned substance. Please step away at once."

When he ignored the tone and the warning, they became increasingly loud every second until it was unbearable. He jumped from the machine and went to the drawer where he grabbed a pair of needle-nose pliers. He held his left finger on the scar, and with his right hand, eyes closed tight, dug the ends of the pliers into his neck, shouting in agony. He twisted the skin open, feeling with his opposite hand. When he felt the hard metal of the chip, he gouged it with the pliers. With a final jerk, he pulled the chip, roughly ⅛ of an inch square, and crushed it.

He didn't have much time. They would know he removed it in a matter of seconds. He jumped into the time machine, closed the hatch, and looked at the instructions. His hands fluttered over the buttons and knobs indicated in the drawing. Pressing, toggling, pulling.

The machine started with a bang. Benjamin frantically turned the dials to the date his grandfather mentioned. The machine vibrated at such intensity, his legs became numb. With a shotgun blast, the machine stopped vibrating and the hatch opened.

There stood a woman with dark auburn hair and startling green eyes. Benjamin looked around at his grandfather's basement, now immaculate and clean.

He jumped out of the machine and gripped the woman by the shoulders.

"Don't do it," he said, breathless.

"What?" She asked, touching her lips.

"If you leave him, you will kill him."

Benjamin jumped back into the machine and with a pop, he was back in 2266.

When the hatch opened, his grandfather stood in the now immaculate basement of present time, his arm around a woman with familiar green eyes and auburn hair shot with white.

"I've done it, Ben," his grandfather said with a grin.

"Done what?" Benjamin asked.

"After all these years," he said with a grin, "I finally married your grandmother!" He kissed the woman in question and squeezed her gently around the shoulders.

AN ODD JOB

George awakens on this particular Monday morning knowing that great things are going to happen. He is going to start his hunt for a job.

He optimistically brings in the morning paper and settles down at the kitchen table. Flipping to the classified ads, he takes a sip of hot coffee and a bite of toast. Nothing sparks his attention at first. The regular things a guy might want to be. A janitor . . . mechanic . . . electrician . . .

But then, there below an ad for an administrative assistant with a great smile and good fashion, is an ad that blows his mind.

Wanted, it reads. *One pet sitter. Pay exceptional. Benefits. No experience. Must love dogs.*

He is instantly reminded of a movie his ex-girlfriend made him watch, but realizes this is a job listing, not a personal ad.

He circles the ad and picks up the phone. Within minutes he has a job. They apparently need no resume or an interview at this particular place. All he has is an address, some easy directions, and a time to come in to start.

When George pulls up to the front gates, he is startled to see a large, stone castle looming above him. He never thought there were such structures in this town. The gate swings open slowly, with a long, low sound, and he pulls up the drive way.

He is greeted at the front gate by a woman all in black. She has pale skin and ruby-red lips. She is very attractive, in a startling, *Adam's Family* way.

"My name is Morganna," she says.

"I'm George," he says. "Nice to meet you."

"Rubix is inside," she says with a half-smile. "I believe you two will get along quite well." Her eyes dart to his hair, which he realizes he forgot to comb.

When he enters the castle, he looks around, eyes wide. It's furnished like a castle would be. Tapestries hang from the walls, and there is a suit of armor pushed against a corner. An iron chandelier with lit candles hangs above his head.

"I will go and fetch Rubix," Morganna says.

George nods, and she leaves him in the foyer.

There is a roar from somewhere within the castle, and a shriek. He sidesteps to an adjoining doorway and peeks through. Just a dining hall. There is a set of stairs straight ahead of him and he peers up into darkness. It's almost as if the stairs lead nowhere.

"Here is Rubix," Morganna says. George turns with a start and shouts, jumping back.

Morganna is draped across the jaws of a massive alligator, crocodile, thing.

"It's quite alright," she says with an uncharacteristic laugh. "This is how we play." She grimaces as he shifts her in his mouth with his prehensile tongue, then places her on the ground. She brushes her dress down.

"I'm supposed to pet sit ... *him*?" George asks slowly, gawping at the dragon before him. Rubix is panting, and with each pant of hot breath comes the foul smell of sulfur.

Morganna nods her head.

"The ad said must love dogs," George says dubiously.

"Oh," Morganna says with a laugh. "He's very much like a dog." She looks at Rubix with love and places a hand on his large jaw. "I will be leaving in about fifteen minutes." She pulls out a wad of cash and hands it to George. "This is payment in advance."

He counts out one thousand dollars with wide eyes.

After Morganna leaves, George looks at Rubix who has stopped panting and has a strange gleam in his eyes. He licks his chops, and George swallows hard.

"Hey, hi Rubix," he says. He can't keep his voice from shaking.

Rubix lets out a low growl. He licks his massive chops again, and George glimpses a row of sharp, stained teeth.

MORGANNA ENTERS the castle after a day out. She has a satisfied grin on her face when she looks at Rubix who is lying on his side sleeping, belly bulging. Next to him lies the one thousand dollars she had given the nice young man who so willingly volunteered to be Rubix's lunch. She sits down quietly by the telephone and calls the newspaper.

"Yes, my ad worked wonderfully," she says. "Will you please run it indefinitely?"

PART III

GOITERS

CLOWN IN THE CLOSET

Published in Predicate Literary Journal

Brian Waterby, age 35, was crying. He always cried, and he always talked about the clowns. His childhood was one of terror, he told me. This was the third time I'd heard the story.

"My parents were terrible people, Dr. Melissa," he said, gulping air to gain control of his emotions. He was on the couch on his back, his knees bent. He had taken his shoes off, and his pristine white socks were bright against the cool black leather of the couch. "They plastered every surface of my room with these terrible beings, these clowns," he shuddered.

"What was so bad about the clowns?" I asked. "Clowns are fun and joyful, they make us laugh."

Brian turned and looked at me, his face contorted in disgust mingled with disbelief. "No," he said. "No, they aren't." He sniffled hard and sat up, his face still in that grimace. "Clowns are terrible beings meant to frighten…"

he trailed off, mumbling into his fists as he rubbed his eyes. "My parents never came when I screamed," he said. He dropped his hands into his lap and stared at them. He lay back down and sighed deeply. "They never came."

A tear dribbled from the outer corner of his eye and dripped onto the couch.

"Why did you scream?" I asked after giving him a few minutes.

He turned his head, his eyes wide. "I can't," he said. He shook his head vigorously. "I can't go there."

Every session went this way. It wasn't until session six that I mentioned hypnosis.

"Brian, this is Dr. Ceruthers. He's a doctor, like me, only he specializes in hypnosis." I looked at Brian who stared with wide eyes at Dr. Ceruthers. "I need to know what happened, Brian," I said. "That way I can figure out what I can do to help you."

Dr. Ceruthers smiled at Brian and held out a hand. Brian flinched and pulled his hands away.

"That's okay, Brian," he said, smiling again.

"Don't do that," Brian said.

Dr. Ceruthers frowned. "Do what?" He asked.

"Don't smile like that." Brian started to breathe hard through his nose. His chest rose and fell heavily. "Don't smile like that," he repeated, though Dr. Ceruthers wasn't smiling. "It's like them, it's just like them," Brian turned to me, eyes wide. "He's one of them," he said in a panicked whisper.

"Brian, it's okay," I said. "He's a doctor. He's going to hypnotize you, so I can find out what happened when you were young." I helped him lay down on the couch, but he kept his eyes on Dr. Ceruthers, his eyebrows furrowed with worry.

Dr. Ceruthers moved closer and Brian recoiled and reached for me. I pulled away and sat out of his view. Brian fought the hypnosis for a few seconds, but finally he fell in deep. I only asked one question, and he began to unfold his childhood.

Brian was only five when his parents decorated his room with a clown theme. They believed it would bring him great joy to see all the smiling and happy clowns before he went to sleep. They believed the clowns would make him dream of the circus and fun. Brian had only nightmares.

It was two years later, and night after night of nightmares about clowns choking him in his sleep or attacking him with balloon animals that stung like bees, that he started to hallucinate. He had the same hallucination every night at the same time when the closet door creaked open and the tips of two oversized shoes appeared. The clown was over six feet tall, he had red hair that stuck out at the sides. He had a big red nose that he honked to make Brian laugh, but it never made Brian laugh. It made him cry. Brian's tears only enraged the clown.

"You don't think that's funny?" he shouted. "You don't think Chuckles is FUNNY?"

After that, the clown's face contorted, his teeth grew to razor-sharp fangs, his white gloved hands sprouted thick claws that tore through the fabric with a flesh tingling rip.

Brian covered his head with the blankets and breathed heavily. He could see the silhouette of Chuckles pacing at the end of the bed, coming closer and closer. He felt the claws caress the blanket where Brian lay under the covers.

"It was always painful," Brian said in a weak voice laced with intense lethargy. "He stabbed me straight through the stomach with his claws." At this, he lifted his shirt to show me eight scars on his stomach, each one poorly healed and obvious puncture wounds with lumpy scars.

I shuddered at the sight of them and rubbed my arms to get rid of the gooseflesh.

"I was afraid to show my parents, they never came when I screamed," his breathing quickened. "They never came when I screamed and every night Chuckles, oh God," he started to whimper, and tears streamed from his eyes. "He did this to me every night until I stopped sleeping in that room . . ."

"We need to wake him," Dr. Ceruthers said. "He's going into shock."

"One more question," I whispered to him.

"Dr. Mantovia," Dr. Ceruthers addressed me. "Melissa," he said.

"One more," I looked at him. "What happened when you stopped sleeping in the room?" I asked Brian.

Brian tossed his head from side to side, his eyelids twitched, agitated.

"I could hear him laughing," Brian said. His feet kicked, his hands twitched restlessly. "I could hear him laughing and calling my name, but he couldn't leave my room."

"Why do you think he couldn't leave your room?" I asked.

Brian didn't answer and Dr. Ceruthers stepped in and woke him gently with a three, two, one, snap.

"What happened?" Brian asked, sitting up. He rubbed his eyes. "Why am I all sweaty?"

"You told me about your childhood," I told him.

He looked at Dr. Ceruthers and brought his knees to his chest.

"I don't like him," he said.

"I'll leave," Dr. Ceruthers said.

"You showed me your scars," I said after Dr. Ceruthers had left.

Brian put his feet back on the floor and held his head in his hands, leaning on his knees. He rubbed his eyes with the heels of his palms.

"How did you get those?" I asked him. I wanted him to tell me what he thinks happened, not what his brain remembered.

He remained silent for a minute as if processing the question.

"I got them when I was young," he said. "I don't remember."

"Did either of your parents, or perhaps a sibling, do that?"

"No," he said. "No one ever harmed me." He avoided eye contact. When he finally looked up, there were tears in his eyes. His lip trembled when he spoke again. "It was the clown," he said. His face twisted briefly, then he gained control. "Chuckles," he said. "That man, that doctor that was here, he smiled like that clown."

"How did Chuckles do that to you?" I asked.

Brian's chest heaved a couple of times, he looked up

at me and yelled, "He stabbed me!" His shoulders shook, and he crossed his arms over his chest. "He stabbed me with his claws!" Tears poured from his eyes and he started to wail. I sat next to him and held him while he cried against my shoulder.

I requested his medical records later that day only to find that Brian was a very healthy kid. There was mention of the wounds, a description of them revealed they went all the way through to his back, but somehow missed his organs. His response was noted when asked about them. There was a referral to a psychologist, the one whose office I took over. There was also a letter to child protective services that looked like it was never mailed.

The medical doctor had the same questions I did. If the wounds appeared to go all the way through, how was there no internal damage? What really caused these injuries?

I went home that night feeling drained but satisfied with my findings. I felt like I was making a real breakthrough with Brian. When I got home there was a package on my stoop. I brought it inside and opened it. Among the hundreds of Styrofoam packing peanuts there was a figurine. I chuckled at sight of it.

"How appropriate," I said, placing the figurine on my dresser. It was a porcelain clown who looked in the midst of dancing. He had a huge smile on his face and held a bouquet of balloons. There was no card.

I curled up in bed and fell to sleep.

The closet door creaked open, and I opened my eyes. It opened more, and I sat up, waiting. Two long shoes came through the doorway, followed by a tall clown wearing red and white. He had frizzy red hair that stuck out from the sides of his head, and a red ball for a nose. He honked it, but I didn't laugh. I trembled all over, a cold sweat slithered down my back. I pulled the covers close.

"You don't think that's funny?" His voice came. It was a grating sound, like the sound of a car driving on gravel while the fan belt squealed. "You don't think that's funny?"

I ventured a weak laugh that turned into sobbing. I looked from Chuckles to the bedroom door, gauging if I could make it. He was at the end of my bed, and when I looked at him again, he was smiling, exposing a row of sharp fangs. He held up his gloved hands and I watched as claws ripped through the fingers.

"Please, go away!" I said. "You're all in my head, you're a nightmare, you can't hurt me!"

"Go away, go away," he mocked. He came closer. All I could do was cringe and will him away. He wasn't real. He was a frightened boy's imagination, a grown man's fear. I closed my eyes and when nothing happened, I opened them in time to watch him bring his claws down upon me.

A loud bang woke me up. I struggled against the sheets that had wound around my legs as I slept. I scrambled to lift my shirt and looked at my stomach. I sighed with relief when there were no puncture marks. I sat up, breathing heavily and rubbed my temples and forehead. I looked at the dresser and the clown figurine was gone. My heart hammering in my chest, banged a staccato rhythm against my ribcage. I peered over the edge of the bed and saw it lying on the floor, broken. It was three in the morning.

I went to the kitchen and started the coffee pot. While I waited for the gurgles that meant fresh, hot coffee, I grabbed the broom and dust pan to clean up the clown figurine. When I got to the bedroom, it wasn't on the floor in pieces, it was on the dresser where I had placed it before I went to bed.

"I could have sworn," I said to myself. "Come on, Melissa, pull it together," I gripped the handle of the broom so hard my hand hurt. "You know it was on the floor, right?"

I decided it was probably a good idea to get out of the house. I grabbed a cup of coffee to go and went to the office. My first patient wasn't until nine, but I could catch up on some paperwork and maybe get a few more zs on the couch.

When I got there, I felt so exhausted that I curled up on the couch and fell asleep. I didn't dream of anything, but I was woken up when someone knocked on the door. It was my receptionist. She said Brian was there and he had to see me. It was eight.

"Brian," I said, opening the door after I straightened myself up. "You're early."

He pushed past me and sat on the couch panting. "I know," he said. He swallowed and tried to catch his breath. "I know I'm early, but I had to come to see," he said.

"See what?" I asked.

He looked at me like I should know what he had to see. "Did he get you?" He asked.

My heart skipped a beat, but I kept my poise. I sat down across from him.

"Did who get me?" I asked. My voice sounded high, pinched, and I cleared my throat.

"Chuckles," Brian said. "He came to me last night, the first time in over a decade, but he left through the window," he said. He was shaken but remained as calm as he could. "He said he was going to find who I told, what happened yesterday when I was here?"

"Um, oh," I thought for a moment. "Chuckles left you?" I said. "That's good news!"

"What happened?" He asked again, undeterred.

I thought of a million things I could tell him, but they would all be a lie.

"You were hypnotized," I said after a long sigh. "Dr. Ceruthers hypnotized you and you told me everything about your childhood."

"That's not what was supposed to happen," Brian whispered. "He's loose, he can get anyone, any child!" He rambled on about this for a moment. "He's out," he said. "At least you're safe."

"I got a present yesterday," I said. "It was a figurine. Do you know anything about it?"

"No," Brian said, his face was blank, and his eyes scanned back and forth as if reading something in his mind. "He's out. I have to stop him."

"He came to my house," I said.

Brian's head jerked up. His eyes were wide.

"He was going to stab me with his claws, but I woke up and it was just a nightmare," I told him.

"It was no nightmare," Brian said. "You woke up before he could stab you? That just means something distracted him. There must have been something in the room that bothered him enough to pull him away from you."

"The figurine," I said. "It was a clown that looked like him, holding balloons and dancing. I woke up and it was on the floor, broken, but when I came back in to clean it up, it was fine." I suddenly felt silly confiding in my patient something that could have been my own mental lapse.

"A clown figurine? Where did you put it?" He asked.

"In my bedroom, on the dresser," I said.

"That's it," he said, nodding his head. He suddenly got up. "I have to go," he said.

"Where?" I asked.

"I have to find something, you want to come?"

"I have patients," I said. "But I guess can reschedule them."

A few minutes later, I couldn't believe what I was doing. Was I, a professional who dealt with people that are mentally unstable, slipping into that very niche of people myself? I asked my receptionist to reschedule all my patients that day. They could wait. Brian had me convinced I was in some sort of trouble and wherever it was we were going would help to figure out what was going on. I was sitting in the passenger seat of his Volkswagen beetle, an old one. It jostled and lurched down a cobbled street and he parked outside the library.

"I remembered something," he said with a grin that was unusual for his gloomy façade. "It was this book that a co-worker showed me a long time ago to freak me out. He knew about my aversion to clowns," he shuddered, but continued. "He told me there was a clown in this book that came from a figurine, just like our clown."

I wasn't too keen on his lumping me together with him in reference to the clown I saw in my nightmare.

He dragged me into the library and pulled me to the fiction section. He scanned the titles until he found the right one. He pulled it from the shelf. On the cover was Chuckles the clown complete with sharp teeth and claws.

"That's a work of fiction," I said. "It won't have any facts about what this figurine is."

"That's where you're wrong, Doctor," he said. He opened the book and flipped to a glossy page amongst the acid-free pages. "See?" He showed me the picture. It was the figurine. "This book is about the very figurine from my past, and now your present."

"I can't believe this," I said. I was skeptical, but a few minutes later I was checking the book out to read further into it. Perhaps it was some kind of group hallucination.

Brian and I parted ways at the office and I went home. The first thing I did was remove the clown figure from my bedroom. I placed it back in the box it came in and set it by the front door. Then I took the book and settled on my own sofa and started to read.

The book was fascinating. It recapped several stories of the very thing that Brian said happened to him. Children with bleeding wounds that went all the way through yet were superficial. The main story of the book was about a man who had a story very similar to Brian's. In fact, you could say it was the exact same story as Brian's. In the very end, the clown attacked one of the grown children, but he was able to fend him off. He trapped the clown's soul in the figurine and the clown was never seen again.

I grabbed the box and took it to the post office.

"Is there any way you can tell me who sent this or where it came from?" I asked the postmaster. "I found it on my doorstep, but there's no return address, and I don't want it. I need to know where it came from."

The postmaster examined the box. "It looks like there was a delivery confirmation," he said. "I might be able to look the information up that way. Give me just a minute."

When the postmaster came back out, he told me he couldn't tell me who sent it, but where it came from. He told me it was sent from the post office in a little town called Morrisberg. The town was familiar. I went straight to the office.

I searched my computerized files for any references to Morrisberg. Only one came up. Brian Waterby. I couldn't assume that he sent me the package, though. I read through his file, noting that each session he spoke about clowns. I listened to the recording of his hypnosis, listened hard for any variances in his voice.

I finally decided to go home and get some rest. I put the box on the table and started a bath, lit a few tea candles, and placed them around the tub. When the tub was full and bursting with bubbles, I slipped out of my dress and into the hot water. I placed a rag over my face and drifted off.

I woke up to a loud bang. It sounded like the front door slamming shut. The candles had burned so low the wax smothered the flames. The bathroom was enveloped in darkness. The water was lukewarm.

"Hello?" I called into the darkness. I had left the bathroom door open, so it wouldn't get too steamy. "Is someone out there?"

It was times like this that I wished I had a dog to warn me. Or a man to protect me.

I heard footsteps. My heart quickened. I swallowed a dry lump in my throat and slowly got up, eyes wide against the darkness. I strained to hear, but all I could hear was my own heartbeat pounding in my ears. I pulled on my robe. I looked around the dark bathroom for a blunt object, but all I could find were bottles of various cleansers. I grabbed the largest one and held it like a club.

The footsteps continued. I heard a shuffling sound from the kitchen. Someone was going through the box with the figurine in it. The footsteps went across the living room. A bang, a hiss of pain; the coffee table. I ducked behind the bathroom door and held my breath; I could have sworn whoever was out there could hear my heart beating. I held the bottle against my chest and waited. I heard another door close and let my breath out slowly. I peeked my head out and looked around. My whole condo was dark, but I knew it well enough to navigate. I went to the kitchen slowly, making sure to avoid the coffee table. I pulled a knife slowly from the block and put it in the pocket of my robe.

"Hello?" I called out. "Is someone here?"

No one answered. The box with the Styrofoam peanuts was spilled over on the table. The figurine was missing. Did the perpetrator come in and steal the figure? I went to the bedroom, senses still on high alert, my heart still pounding but slowing. I turned on the small lamp on my bed table and gasped. The figurine was on my bed. The clown's face smiled up at me. I shuddered and grabbed it. I took it into the kitchen and wrapped it in a towel, then threw it on the floor as hard as I could. I threw it over and over again, until I knew the clown was in pieces. Then I put it in the garbage disposal and listened as the porcelain was beat against the blades and was merely a tinkle of tiny fragments.

I was exhausted at this point. Fear was very wearing. I slipped between the sheets, careful of the knife in my pocket, and went to sleep.

Once again, I woke to the sound of the closet door creaking open. I jerked awake. I hadn't checked the closet before I went to bed. My heart hammered again. My eyes searched the darkness. I reached to flick on the bedside lamp, but the closet door swung open and hit the wall. Chuckles the clown stood inside. I could see his eyes glinting in the light from the window.

"You threw me away," he said. "You grinded me into pieces."

"Get out of my house," I tried to yell, but it came out a whimper. He came closer. I trembled and pressed myself against the headboard. He was at the foot of the bed. I slowly reached into my pocket and pulled out the knife. He came around to the side, claws clicking together. I gripped the handle of the knife and gritted my teeth. He lunged. I swung the knife up through the sheets. It plummeted into his chest up to the hilt. I felt hot blood on my hand and released my grip and jumped from the bed. I turned on the light and gaped.

Brian lay on my bed, dressed as a clown. Like a fish, he gasped for air. I must've hit a lung. I called an ambulance and the police. The ambulance took him away while the police questioned me.

I explained to them that he was one of my patients and that, until now, I found it hard to figure out what was wrong with him.

"He had a delusional disorder and a personality disorder," I said. "He read this book so many times that he believed he was the main character." I took a deep breath. "He also believed he was Chuckles the clown."

The next day I got a call from the police. It had been a few years since a murder, and usually the victims were children, but it was confirmed that he was the killer known as The Clown. His trademark was the clown figurine.

It was about eight months after Brian was taken away when I arrived home and saw a box on my front stoop. I picked it up carefully and examined the box. I shook it, but only heard Styrofoam peanuts moving against the sides. I took it outside and threw it into the dumpster.

OLD O

He dreamed though he never slept. Cloudy eyes stared at nothing, saw nothing. His massive form, once powerful with thick muscles, sat atrophied by lack of use. Nothing perked his attention anymore. Not even Trisha.

Trisha, wearing gray leggings under a short black skirt—an outfit too young for her middle age—sauntered into the lab scowling. She unlocked the door to her office, went inside and slammed it. Throwing her messenger bag into a corner, she slumped into the chair behind her desk and placed her face in her hands. Her black hair fell around her cheeks. She took a few deep breaths.

"He did it again, Cornelius," she said aloud to the bird in a cage hanging from the ceiling. "He did it again. He does it every fucking day." She pushed herself back in her chair and looked up at the budgie, who had his head cocked at her. Trisha deepened her voice and puffed her chest, "Hey Trish, they're going to kill him, you know . . . Gah!"

A knock at her office door made her compose herself. She didn't bother to plaster on a fake smile, "Come in."

Dr. Sylvia Andrews, the only scientist who understood Trisha's distaste for the lab, stepped inside. "We want you to be there," she said, flipping her long auburn hair over her shoulder. "We need you. Old O needs you."

"*Old O* doesn't know who I am," Trisha said. Sylvia stepped closer to Trisha's desk.

"I know it doesn't seem like he does, but I believe, deep down, he's still the same guy he once was."

"He hasn't been the same guy for eight years," Trisha said through gritted teeth. The burn of tears in her nose made her close her eyes and hide her face behind her hands.

"Please, Trish," Sylvia's soft voice pleaded.

Trisha sat back and crossed her arms. She stared at the picture on her desk. A picture from what seemed like another lifetime ago. The photo depicted a lovely young veterinary scientist, lighter hair, no dark liner around her eyes, pink polish on her fingernails. Trisha looked at the chipped black polish on there now and huffed. Old O's dark eyes stared directly at the camera, penetrated the lens and gazed deep into the soul of anyone who looked at the photo. His orange fur fluffed from his head and body, his tongue stuck out. She smiled, remembering that he could never keep that thing in his mouth. He blew hundreds of raspberries, as well as kisses, over the course of their relationship. Back then his name was Owen, and he was the best behaved, most intelligent orangutan in the lab.

"It's all my fault," Trisha whispered, picking up the picture.

"Trisha," Sylvia said. "It's time. Will you come?"

Trisha nodded and followed Sylvia down a corridor to the sleep lab.

The left side of the room hosted computers analyzing data retrieved from wires. The right side, a multitude of test subjects ranging from rats to chimpanzees. All of them slept peacefully.

In the center of the room, in a circular holding pen, sat Old O. His once fiery orange fur looked dusty and dull. He sat slumped, his face drooping. His eyes shocked her the most, as they always did upon seeing him these days. The sight of him made her take in a shaky breath. She cleared her throat and stepped toward the pen, keeping close to Sylvia.

"Why do they want me here?" She asked Sylvia in a whisper.

"Because you've known him the longest."

"What does it matter?" Trisha's voice rose with emotion, and she cleared her throat again. She turned to the other scientists, gathered together like a flock of sheep. "I'm here, now what?"

There were three of them: A man with a thick shock of highlighted blonde hair, a woman with a severely pointed face, much like the rats, and an assistant who moved to a computer when she saw Trisha.

"We wish for you to be present for some of the testing we have scheduled today," the male doctor said with a sneer. His nametag read Dr. Quota, and his eyes looked Trisha up and down. The sneer turned to disapproval.

Trisha looked at Sylvia, who gave her a weak smile in return.

"What do you want me to do?" Trisha asked.

"Touch him," Dr. Quota said.

Trisha looked at the great orangutan before her; his breathing suggested he was asleep though his eyes were open. Years ago, she would have been excited to pet or hold her primate friend, but now? He wasn't the same ape. He didn't even resemble the Owen she once played games with, teased, tickled . . .

Trisha reached out, pulled her hand back slightly, then, swallowing hard, pushed forward. Her fingertips brushed the coarse fur on his forearm.

"No change," the harsh, monotone voice from the assistant said. Trisha looked at her through eyes slit with annoyance.

Dr. Quota cleared his throat. "Touch his face," he said, licking his lips.

Trisha moved her hand and, leaning out as far as she could over the rail that served as the holding pen, touched Owen's cheek.

"Hold on," the assistant said. "There is a change."

Trisha's heart thrilled. Did Owen remember her?

"Owen," she whispered. "It's Trish."

Dr. Quota grabbed her hand and swung her away from Owen. "You are to touch, not talk," he said, gripping her wrist tight.

"Doctor," the woman said. "Brain waves suggest he is in REM. Dreaming."

"Damn," the doctor said, throwing Trisha's hand at her. She clutched it to her chest. "If only we could *see* what he's dreaming." Dr. Quota hit the rail with his hands.

Trisha saw the change, but the doctor did not. Owen heard what happened. He heard it in Trisha's voice, heard it in the clang of palm against rail, heard the doctor's aggression.

Old O didn't move to the untrained eye, but to Trisha, he exhibited the slightest twitch of anger. The hair on his arms rose slightly, his cheeks puffed just enough. Yet, his brain still registered REM sleep.

Trisha smiled, but then she saw it. The blood. His scalp had blood on it where wires jutted from the top of his head.

"This is so inhumane," she said. "His head is bleeding!" She tried to step close, to comfort her Owen, but a large, burly man came out of nowhere and grabbed her by her upper arms and held her back.

"Let her go immediately!" Sylvia shouted.

In the foray, no one heard Old O grunt, no one saw him bare his teeth ever so slightly. No one, except Trisha.

"WE'VE DONE IT!" A man in a plaid shirt and holey jeans scrambled up the hall waving papers. "We've done it!"

He ran past Trisha and into the sleep lab. She glimpsed Owen as the doors swung shut, considered going inside to hear just exactly what they'd done, but went back to her office to look at her schedule for the day.

Several appointments glared at her from her

appointment book, but none of them interested her. She had to dress burns on a dog, euthanize several rats—her job sucked. When she went to veterinary school years and years before, she didn't realize this was the work she would fall into. She wanted to help animals in need, not animals that were forced to need her because of scientific testing. Her only reason to stay was Owen. She thought of how he chose to sign 'mom' when talking about her and addressing her. Right hand on his chin, fingers extended.

Selliria Laboratory, a privately-funded research lab, was the only lab left in the United States that still used animals for research. No thought about how the testing would damage the animals ever went through the scientist's minds. They were animals; thus, they were expendable.

Trisha glanced at the rat euthanasia appointment.

"Poor guys," she said. "I bet they didn't know they would be shot up with rabies."

As Trisha made her way to the exam room and the rat appointment, Sylvia stopped her in the hall, just outside Owen's door. Her faced beamed with a giant smile.

"We've done it, Trish," Sylvia said. "We can see his thoughts." She gripped Trisha's hands and looked into her eyes. "All he thinks about is you!"

Trisha's heart swelled, and hammered in her ears, flip-flopped like a gymnast on the uneven bars. "You can *see* his thoughts? How?" Her voice came out high. She swallowed.

"The guys in IT have been working on a way in which to view the thoughts of test subjects for years.

They've finally done it. We have preliminary software—" Sylvia stopped talking when she looked at Trisha's face. "Trisha, are you okay?"

Trisha's head reeled. Black spots danced in front of her eyes. Her stomach rolled over and the contents sloshed around like wet clothes in a dryer.

"Did you hear me Trish?" Sylvia's voice sounded like she was standing at the far end of a tunnel.

"I need to lay down." Trisha backed up to the wall, slid down, and sat on the floor. She put her face in her hands, elbows resting on her knees.

"This is great news, isn't it?" Sylvia crouched next to Trisha.

"I don't know," Trisha said. Thoughts ran through her mind a thousand miles an hour. "I don't know."

Sylvia left and returned with a cold bottle of water and a bag of Reese's Pieces. "This is all the vending machine had that I thought you would like," she said with a chagrined smile.

"Thanks." Trisha took the water and gulped it but didn't touch the candy. "I don't know what to think about this," she said. "This is good, right? I mean, you guys can see what's going on in his head, and maybe the testing will stop soon so he can live the rest of his days in a habitat somewhere warm with other orangutans." Trisha dropped her head and looked at her hands, at the class ring she still wore, the hangnail threatening to snag on something.

"Why don't you come on inside now. Maybe seeing this for yourself will help," Sylvia said, touching Trisha's shoulder. The overhead fluorescents sparkled in the doctor's huge engagement ring. "He's thinking only of you."

Trisha gulped the remaining water and nodded. Taking a shaky breath, she got to her feet and prepared herself for what she might see inside the lab.

Owen sat the same as usual: Unmoving, unaware. A monitor close to his enclosure showed blurred pictures on it. Trisha fought back tears as she watched his thoughts of her unfold on the screen.

Trisha, pushing him in a swing, like a child. Owen asking for more fruit in the sign language Trisha taught him. Trisha hugging him, holding him, swinging him around in circles while his strong hands gripped her forearms. Memories she dreamed about every night, wished she could have with him again.

She covered her mouth. A tear escaped and glided down her cheek, betraying her tough façade.

"Can this be over now?" She wondered aloud in a whisper.

Dr. Quota laughed, a harsh and raw sound among the quiet whir of machines, and Owen's rhythmic breathing. She closed her eyes.

"*Can this be over?*" Dr. Quota mocked, stepping too close to Trisha. "We've only just begun."

She could smell his stale deodorant and cheap aftershave. When she opened her eyes, he was walking away toward a control panel.

"If only the images were clearer," he grumbled. Trisha leaned forward toward Owen.

"Owen," she whispered. "I'm here."

Brilliant colors displayed on the screen, though the great ape didn't move.

"What happened, what was that?" Dr. Quota asked, hitting the side of the monitor. The colors faded to dark, slashed with red. "What is this?"

"Doctor," the severe-looking woman adjusted her glasses. "It seems as though those are his emotions registering on the screen. Watch," she motioned to Trisha. "Say something."

Trisha leaned in again. "Hi Owen," she said.

The brilliant, bold, and full-forced hues swept across the monitor.

"Now you talk," the woman whispered to Dr. Quota.

Dr. Quota cleared his throat. "Owen, this is Dr. Quota."

The screen darkened and jagged rays of red and brown smashed into the black. An angry thunderstorm.

"He obviously doesn't like you," Trisha said under her breath, through gritted teeth.

LATER THAT EVENING, when nearly everyone had left for the day, Trisha tried to get into the sleep lab. She peered through the small window on the door before trying the handle. Of course, it was locked, and, of course, she didn't have access. Owen's form sat hunched in the shadows. The screen continued to play the memories. Suddenly, his form jolted, and the images became frantic, full of blurred forms.

Trisha wanted to get in. She wanted to see the memories that made him move. He hadn't moved in months, maybe over a year. She pulled on the door, frantic. Her heart pounded. Owen was in distress. She could see it. She could sense it.

A firm arm pushed her away from the door, swiped a card, and opened it.

"Hurry, before anyone sees," Sylvia hissed. They slipped into the lab and watched in horror as the events of Owen's life unfolded.

Small. So small. His mother cared for him so well, did so much to protect him from the dangers of the Congo. His father, so large, an emblem of strength, cunning, and beauty all at once.

The poachers came quick. Owen's mother hid him among a pile of large leaves. He never saw her again.

The bright sun. Piercing bright through the leaves of the canopy. Lifted, coddled. Human smells, human hands. Introduction into a new home, a new habitat. A lonely mother, bereft of her baby took him in, cared for him as her own. Owen took her for his mother.

Owen's head jerked, his eyes squeezed shut. His breath came as sharp grunts.

More hands. Strong hands. His new mother fell, asleep. He was taken away.

A lab. The first of many. Still young. Easy to manipulate. Testing. Memories lost. Memories regained. Strange smells. Wires, plugs, tapes, monitors. Beeps, Whirs, Clicks. Dr. Quota. Wires digging, gouging. Harsh hands, strong hands, pain. Trisha . . . Trisha . . . Trisha . . .

From there, the Trisha memories started over. Owen's face relaxed. His breathing returned to normal.

Trisha, eyes wide, looked at Sylvia. "He can't know this happened," she said, speaking of Dr. Quota.

"He will know," Dr. Quota's voice came from the shadows. "I knew you would come here," he said. Owen's breathing remained the same, though the jagged and dark colors pierced the blackness of the monitor. "Thank you for that display."

"It wasn't a display," Trisha said. She reached out and touched Owen's arm. "It's okay Owen, I'm going to get you out of here."

Dr. Quota grabbed her wrist. "You'll do nothing of the sort," he said through his teeth. "He belongs to this lab."

"He is a living creature. He belongs to no one!" Trisha wrenched her arm loose and backed away from Dr. Quota. "Don't ever touch me again," she said. She looked at Sylvia's helpless expression and ran from the lab.

All Trisha could think about on her way home, was Owen. His memories, his sad and tortured life. She cried and hit the steering wheel with her fists.

"It isn't fair!" She screamed. "It isn't fair . . ." Her cell phone buzzed. Sylvia Andrews. She let it go to voicemail, then listened to the message when she got home.

Trisha, it's Dr. Andrews—a deep sigh—*I think it's best if you don't come into the lab anymore. I wish it didn't have to be this way, but Dr. Quota didn't like what happened. I'm sorry. I'll watch over him for you.*

Trisha gripped the phone hard. It was all she could do to keep from hurling it against the wall.

"I have to get him out of there," Trisha said. "He isn't safe." Tears rolled down her cheeks as she slid to the floor, still holding the phone. "What am I going to do? What *can* I do?"

She went to bed and after a fitful night, woke up the next morning feeling nauseous. She decided to stay home until after noon, hoping to feel better by then.

At the lab, after working overnight on the new monitoring device, the monitor displayed Owen's memories in crisper images.

"Perfect! Just perfect!" Dr. Quota exclaimed. "Ladies and gentlemen," he said, addressing the room full of people invested in this new technology. He lifted a bottle of champagne and popped the cork. "This is a great day. Last night, new information was gathered from Subject O's mind and recorded via this new technology."

Sylvia frowned as Dr. Quota pressed a button, and the memories from the night before began to play. At the end of the video, the scientists, doctors and investors cheered and clapped. Dr. Quota's assistant passed around glasses of champagne, as the celebrations began. Sylvia left the lab, unable to stand what Dr. Quota made her say to poor Trisha. She went to Trisha's office and found it empty.

Meanwhile, the monitor linked to Owen flickered to life as new thoughts were recorded. The doctors, in their mindless celebrating, didn't notice the visions on the screen.

TRISHA WOKE UP AT ONE-THIRTY, groggy from deep sleep. She looked in the mirror and found her eyes red-rimmed and puffy. Her skin felt tight and stretched.

"I look like shit ran over twice." She turned on the cold water, splashed some on her face, then went to the kitchen for coffee.

After she showered and refreshed her makeup, she gave herself a last once-over, grimaced at her splotchy cheeks and puffy eyelids, and left for work.

The sky, overcast and ominous, threatened rain. Trisha sighed as she pulled into the parking lot. She got out and went to the front door and scanned her key card. The front door swung open. She stepped inside and paused. The hallway was dark.

The lights were on a motion sensor system. When people moved through the halls, they stayed on. Once movement ceased, like at the end of the work day, they turned off. Trisha checked her watch. It was two-thirty in the afternoon. Where was everyone?

Something didn't feel right. She shivered as a chill tiptoed up her spine.

"Hello?" She called down the vacant hall. A light flickered near the end, near the sleep lab. She dropped her bag and took a tentative step forward. "Is anyone here?" she called out. Then to herself, she said, "Did I sleep through the rest of the week? What the hell is going on?"

A loud clatter followed by a snapping crackle came down the hall. Trisha jumped and clutched at the wall. Her heart beat in her throat as she swallowed.

"Hello?" Her voice lost its strength. Taking a few more steps, her breath quickened as the flicker of a fluorescent light made her think of the other day when Owen just barely twitched in anger at Dr. Quota's irate voice.

"Owen?" The name came out as a whisper as she neared the doorway to the lab. "Sylvia?" Cold sweat broke out under Trisha's arms.

She reached the corridor to the lab and stopped. The door bulged out. A massive dent created a gap. The windows were shattered. The lab beyond the busted doors was dark.

Trisha pushed the door open and cringed against the long, low moan the warped hinges made. She closed her eyes and took a deep breath, then made her way further inside. The door swung shut behind her, banging against the frame. She jumped and let loose a shriek, then steadied herself and looked around.

Trays of medicine and surgical tools lay toppled over. An unidentified liquid created a sheen on the tile. A gurney sat on its side on top of documents strewn about the room. Trisha scanned the area, and gasped when her eyes came to Owen's enclosure. Owen was gone.

The wires, hanging down, frayed where they had been torn at, ripped at, and finally ripped out, dripped blood onto the floor. Those needles were deep inside Owen's head, inside his brain. Trisha took a deep breath.

"Owen," she whispered, her voice catching in her

throat. She turned and a scream caught in her chest. With gagging force, she wretched onto the floor.

Dr. Quota lay in a heap, dead. His arms jutted at odd angles from his body, and blood trickled from his gaping mouth. His assistant and the other doctor were similarly mangled.

When Trisha turned her head to see if Sylvia was somewhere nearby, too, she had to reach out to steady herself. Her vision blurred. Then, she saw it.

A sparkling diamond ring caught the flickering light from outside the door.

"Sylvia, no," Trisha moaned. She ran to the doctor who had shown her so much sympathy and understanding, who'd known her all the years Trisha worked with Owen, who understood Trisha more than anyone else in the lab. She fell to her knees and gripped Sylvia's hand. Her eyes shifted to Trisha, and a gurgle came from her throat. Blood spilled from her mouth.

"I'm sorry," she said. The life left her eyes.

"Oh, God," Trisha whispered, covering her mouth again. "Owen, what have you done?"

She heard a grunt from somewhere deeper in the lab. A soft, friendly grunt. A grunt she'd heard so many times . . . but not for a long time. She stood and sidled to the room full of medical supplies, retrieved a needle of Telazol, and put it in her pocket. It was the same drug she used on the rats with rabies.

"Owen?" She said, leaving the supply room. It was supposed to be a loud, steady shout, but it came out a pinched whisper. She cleared her throat and tried again.

Another grunt came from the shadows. Owen's form

lumbered slowly into view. A spark of electricity popped in front of him. He reached up and pulled a light fixture out of the ceiling. Sheet rock and ceiling tiles rained onto his head and around him. He growled and swung his arms. The debris settled. Owen calmed.

Though he could not see, he could scent, and he sniffed at the air, searching for Trisha. She stood still, afraid to move.

Owen came closer, his hulking form so much larger than any orangutan Trisha had ever worked with. When he was an arm's length away, she took a deep breath.

"There's my boy," she said with a tear-filled voice. Owen's strong arms encircled her. He snorted against her head, breathing in her scent. He made happy sounds and pawed at her. He signed, "mom," and Trisha let out a sob.

"Owen, what have you done?" She asked, petting him, stroking his coarse fur. Tears slithered down her cheeks as she smoothed the fur over the wounds on the top of his head, his blood staining her sleeves and smearing onto her hands. She didn't care. This was the Owen she missed and loved.

She sniffled hard and couldn't stop the forceful sobs. She rested her cheek against his. His arms tightened around her, but not to harm her. He grunted and sighed, leaning more of his weight against her. "I can't hold you up, buddy. You're way too big now," Trisha said through her tears. "Everything will be alright."

Pulling from his tight embrace, she gripped his hand and led him out of the lab, down the hall to a safe and calm room. A room where toys littered the floor: Large balls sat in the corner, and stuffed animals claimed shelves on every wall. A younger Owen loved this room.

He sniffed around. His milky eyes brightened. Trisha laughed, but began to cry again as she thought about the things he did to the scientists. Part of her felt him right for killing them. They got what they deserved. Karma and all, right? But not Sylvia.

She thought about taking him away to a zoo, a place where he could finally be at peace with others of his kind . . . but he was a danger to himself and the more so to others.

As Owen moved slowly around the room, picking up toys and smelling them, then discarding them, she pulled the syringe from her pocket. Owen reached a shelf of stuffed animals and pulled a stuffed monkey from the group of bears. He cradled it in his arms, carried it around as his mother might have done.

"Owen," Trisha said. Owen stopped moving and turned. "I'm sorry," she said. "I am so sorry any of this had to happen to you," she understood him now. Understood the ever-present nightmares running through his mind, reminding him of his awful past, of his life of testing. Of loss.

Owen grunted and dropped the monkey. He moved toward Trisha and reached for her hand. When he felt the syringe, he lifted her hand to his nose. His breathing quickened, and short, guttural noises came from his throat. She held her hand to his cheek.

"It's okay," she told him. "You'll be safe forever." She gasped as new tears drizzled from her eyes. Owen touched her face, her tears dripping onto his thick fingers. "I love you."

She slid the needle into his neck. He growled in pain, but let the drug take him with little struggle. As Owen weakened, Trisha helped him lay down on a pile of bean bag chairs. She stroked his face and held her hands close, so he could smell her. He held one of her hands against his cheek as he slowly slipped away.

SEVEN NIGHTS OF FRIGHT

Seven Nights of Fright aired the entire week of Halloween, ending on October 31st with the top ten scariest movies of all time.

"I've never even heard of any of these," Sara said to her husband, Jordan, while she perused the listings. "*Who's Afraid of the Big Bad Ghost*? Come on." She scoffed. "Oh, this one's good. *The Night of the Zombies*. What is that? Some *Living Dead* knock-off?"

Jordan, who loved scary movies the most between them, smiled at her. "We'll give 'em a chance, yeah?"

She raised an eyebrow at him. "Okay, fine. But if they suck, we're watching *Buffy*."

"Deal." Jordan left the living room and came back with a bowl of popcorn. He sat on the couch. Sara joined him.

"Porch light's off, right?" She asked.

Jordan nodded and stuffed a fist full of popcorn into his mouth. She laughed and plucked one piece at a time from the bowl. Sara didn't love scary movies the way

Jordan did. They gave her nightmares of the worst kind. Back when they'd had a dog, she could manage through them, sure, but ever since Bumpkin died, she always felt a little more ill at ease when awaking from a fright. She watched the movies for him, because this man would do anything for her, and did.

A scream issued from the surround sound. Sara jumped and almost knocked the bowl of popcorn off Jordan's lap. He steadied the bowl and put his arm around her, laughing quietly. The scream was the intro to the Seven Nights of Fright program.

"You'd think I'd be used to that by now," Sara said. She slid onto the floor to clean up the mess.

"Leave it. The movie's starting." Jordan patted the cushion next to him, and Sara rejoined him. "This one's based on true events," he whispered as the credits in red drippy text appeared and crumbled on a black background. Spooky music crept from the speakers. Electronic sounds with low-budget crackling. Sara pushed closer to Jordan and tucked her bare feet under the edge of a blanket.

WHEN THE MOVIE ENDED, Sara and Jordan stared at the screen, mouths slightly ajar. Though it was only a thirty-minute movie, it had them both trembling.

"That was based on actual events?" Sara asked, breathless.

Jordan licked his lips. "Yeah."

She turned to him. His face was pale. He swallowed hard and looked back at her.

"Where did it take place?" Sara's voice came out small and quiet.

"You don't want to know," Jordan said. His eyes glistened, and for a second, Sara thought he might cry. She'd never seen him cry. Not even after Bumpkin passed. Jordan had always been her rock, and though he was trying to protect her right now, she had to know.

"Tell me," she whispered. Jordan flicked his eyes to the screen, then back to her.

"Here. In this town."

SARA TOSSED and turned all night, unable to shake the chilly grip the movie had on her organs. Every noise of the house settling jerked her awake. Jordan snored gently beside her, apparently unfazed. She lifted herself onto her elbow and watched him sleep, both soothed and angered by his ability to so fearlessly drift into slumber.

If Bumpkin were still here . . .

A loud bang from the kitchen brought her upright. She strained to listen. If Bumpkin were still here she could sleep. He'd let her know if the noises were her imagination or not. She could look down at him, sleeping by her side of the bed. If he was still, all was well. But Bumpkin was three months gone. Sara had to console herself now.

It was nothing.

She turned back to Jordan and gasped. His eyes were wide open. So wide the whites showed all around, even in the dim moonlit room.

"Jordan?" Her voice came out a squeak.

He let out a loud *boo*. Sara screamed, then shoved him.

"You ass. Scared me half to death."

"Can't you sleep?" He asked. "You've been thrashing around all night."

"Just wide awake, I guess." She didn't want to tell him the movie scared her more than any other scary movie they'd seen. If what happened to the couple in the movie happened to them—She couldn't even think like that.

WHEN SARA WOKE the next morning, sleep clung to her whole body. She rolled over, but Jordan was gone. She sat up and tore back the covers. Thoughts of the movie roiled in her mind. She stumbled to the bedroom door, down the hall, pin-balling from wall to wall, doorway to doorway.

"Jordan?" Her voice came out rasping as if she'd been screaming all night. "Jordan?" Panic gripped her heart and stomach, smashing them together to create one organ —a *hear-mach* or a *stom-art*. She searched every room of their small split-level and ended in the kitchen where she shrieked his name.

He wasn't home. The coffee pot was half empty. She glanced at the clock. Noon? Jordan would be at work, of course. Noon. She hadn't slept that late in who knew how many years.

Sara grabbed her phone from the kitchen counter, where she charged it each night and called Jordan. When he answered, she gasped and held back a relieved sob.

"Hello? Sara? You there?"

"Yes," she managed to choke out.

"What's wrong?"

"Nothing." She took a deep, trembling breath. "I didn't know where you were," she said.

"Did you just get up?" He asked.

Sara nodded. "Yes." Her voice seemed thick, now. Like the words had to ooze through her vocal cords. She cleared her throat.

"You must've slept like shit if you just got up. It's lunchtime."

"I know," she said, but the words stuck in her throat. She cleared it again.

"Are you sure you're okay?" he asked. "I can come home."

"No, I'm fine. Really," she said. "I'll see you later. I love you."

"Love you, too. Bye." Jordan hung up.

Sara sagged to the floor and gulped air. Jordan was fine. He was safe at work. He was in the city, not in this town where the bad thing happened. She stood and peeked out the window where birds flitted in the sunshine. Nothing bad could happened if the sun shone so bright. She poured herself a cup of coffee, heated it in the microwave, and sat at the kitchen table. Her hands still shook, but at least her heart and stomach were no longer trying to merge.

The newspaper sat on the table, still rolled up inside the little orange sleeve the paper boy used to fling it at the door. Actually it was a paper man in a creepy brown sedan of some kind. A town car. But Sara liked to imagine it was a kid on a bike, wheeling around slinging papers to make a buck or two for the arcade. Did kids play in the arcade anymore? She suddenly felt old, even though she'd only just turned forty last week.

She tugged at the bottom of the orange bag and the paper slid out. Free from confinement, it unrolled on its own. Sara dropped her coffee mug. It hit the table, splattered coffee all over her nightgown, then tumbled to the floor where it smashed, spraying the tile with brown liquid. She didn't even flinch at the sound of shattering ceramic. Her eyes were locked on the front page where Jordan's face stared up at her.

The headline spoke of a brutal murder. Sara stumbled backward, knocked over her chair, turned and grabbed her phone. She hit the phone icon next to Jordan's name and turned back around.

The picture had changed. Now it was a pic of the three winners of the local Halloween costume contest last night.

Sara hit the end button and stared at the page. No. It had been Jordan's face, speckled with blood, dead eyes staring at nothing.

She pinched the bottom corner of the newsprint and turned the page, then the next, searching for the photo. But there was no mention of a gruesome murder within the tight print.

Jordan sat at his desk, phone to his ear. Sara called again, but he'd missed her, and she didn't leave a message. Poor thing was scared to death. He should know better than to subject her to those types of movies. Every year he gave her an out, but she never took it. After this, perhaps next year she would. Hell, next year he'd give himself an out.

His coworker, George, knocked on the edge of his cubicle.

"Lunch?" George asked with raised eyebrows.

Jordan accepted by standing and grabbing his jacket.

"Did you catch the top scariest movie last night?" Jordan asked as they made their way to the front doors and out into the cool afternoon.

"Yeah," George said, shaking his head. "I can't believe *The Grudge* won first place."

Jordan stopped walking. "*The Grudge?*" Jordan said. "Are you sure?" He didn't recall that movie even being in the top ten. Maybe they watched a different lineup.

"Yeah. Stupidest movie ever."

"Channel twelve, right?" Jordan asked.

"Yeah," George said. "Come on. I gotta get back in an hour for a meeting."

Jordan's stomach lurched. Sweat beaded on his forehead. He closed his eyes and images from the movie flashed through his mind. Only, instead of the actors from the film, it was him and Sara.

"I'm not so hungry, actually," Jordan said. He ran back inside to the bathroom and hurled. Coffee on an empty stomach maybe? Sara would get the I-told-you-so on that one. She always harassed him for not eating breakfast. Sara. He had to see her. He had to make sure she was okay. After her call that morning . . .

Jordan grabbed his stuff and went home.

When he got there, Sara was vacuuming with ear buds in. She bobbed her head and swished her hips in time with the music. He took a moment to observe her tight butt in her jean shorts.

There was no graceful way to greet someone zoned out to white noise and music, so he stepped into the room and tapped her shoulder.

Sara screamed and ran to the opposite end of the room and jumped on the couch. Jordan turned the vacuum cleaner off.

"Sorry," he said. She laughed and stepped off the couch, cheeks flushed.

"What are you doing home?" She asked.

"I ... wasn't feeling well, and I had some pretty horrible thoughts." He opened his arms, and she stepped into them. He burrowed his nose into her hair and breathed in her scent.

"Me, too," Sara said.

"I wish I didn't have to go on this stupid trip to Kansas," he said. A sales meeting at the corporate office. It was a longer trip. The sales manager decided to have a team building activity after their endless reporting sessions.

"How long will you be gone again?" Sara asked.

"Seven days."

SARA DROPPED Jordan off at the airport and drove home feeling heavy and tired. At home, she moped around the house. Whenever he went out of town like this, it made her wish she had more friends. The problem was, even if she had a girlfriend or two to hang out with, she'd rather be home with her worries.

She shuffled around the house, straightening up, rearranging the pillows on the couch several times, pushing magazines into a neat stack, then fanning them out again. Her computer was on in the office with her manuscript open, waiting for her, but she didn't feel like doing anything. She ended up laying on the couch with a book. Even then, her mind kept wandering to Jordan and the movie.

Seven days.

Her eyes trailed across the page of the book and slowly slipped shut.

Sara woke suddenly, heart pounding. Sweat covered her face, neck, and chest. She grabbed her phone and looked at the time, then dialed Jordan.

"Hey, miss me already?" Jordan said when he answered.

"Yes, of course. From the moment I drove away from the airport," she said. "I wanted to tell you I love you, one more time." She smiled and slumped back against the couch.

"I love you, too," Jordan said.

"Call me when you land."

"You know I will."

He hung up. Sara took a deep, shaky breath and laughed. The laugh became a sob. Relief washed over her. He was okay. She was okay. They would be fine.

That's what the girl in the movie thought, too, and look what happened.

Sara shook her head to clear it of such stupid

thoughts, then went to the kitchen to make a cup of tea, more for something to do than anything else. Whenever she drank tea, it usually cooled off too much before she was able to actually drank any of it.

She sat at the table while the hot water heated. Today's newspaper sat on the table, still furled within its orange casing. She pulled it out but held it firm, afraid to see what might be on the front page. The kettle shrieked. Sara jumped. She got up and poured the hot water over a tea bag full of cinnamon spice tea. The scent soothed her rattled nerves.

The newspaper lay open, but the front page featured the Mayor with a group of children at a youth club. She let out a breath she didn't realize she'd been holding and flipped the paper to the comics section.

Noon came and went. Sara putted around the house. She organized the closet in the office for something to do. Avoidance behavior, she called it. Every time she stepped over to the computer and her open manuscript, the flashing cursor at the top of the blank page for chapter thirteen turned her back around to find something meaningless to do. Like organizing the junk drawer in the kitchen. Junk drawers don't need to be organized. That's why they're called junk drawers.

Jordan's flight landed at two. Sara sat on the couch and stared at the clock, cell phone in hand. When two came and went and eased into three, she dialed his number.

"I was just about to call you," he said when he picked up.

"How was your flight?" Sara asked. A nervous energy shook in her hands.

"Turbulent." His voice told her all she needed to know. "How's your day going?"

"Oh, you know . . ." She told him the things she did besides work on the Next Great American Novel.

"Avoider," Jordan said with a laugh. "You have seven days of peace and quiet and a looming deadline. Crack to it, lady."

"It's hard to do anything when you're not here," she said. "I'm so lonely and sad. All I want to do is crawl into bed and sleep through it."

"I know. I miss you, too." An alarm sounded in the background.

"What was that? What's going on?"

"Just the bag carousel letting us know it's about to start spinning. Don't worry."

"I can't help it."

"I gotta go. I'll call you later tonight, okay?"

"Okay."

Jordan hung up. Sara took her tea cup and headed to the kitchen. He was off the plane. That gave her a little relief. Once he was out of the airport and safely in his hotel she would feel even better.

Sara stepped off the carpet, onto the linoleum in the kitchen and slipped. She landed on her rear with a sharp pain that jarred up her spine. Then, she screamed.

Blood everywhere. Smeared across the floor like someone mopped the linoleum with a bucket of it. Red fingerprints smeared the cupboard doors. The sink bubbled, filling with crimson fluid from a backed-up drain. Sara looked at her hands, covered in the sticky stuff and screamed again.

When she dropped her hands, the blood was gone from the room. She looked at her hand again. A shard of ceramic was lodged in her palm. The wound dripped onto her lap.

It'll need stitches, she thought.

The girl in the movie needed stitches. Look what happened when she went to the hospital to get them. That's when it all started.

Sara got to her feet and grabbed a wad of paper towels. She held them against her palm and made her way to the bathroom for the first aid kit, the kitchen covered in blood completely forgotten.

After pulling the shard of tea cup from the wound and cleaning it, she applied five butterfly strips across it to hold it shut. Her dad would have sealed the cut with super glue, but she didn't have any. Besides, she'd likely glue her hands together if she tried that. She wrapped a roll of gauze around her hand and taped it off, then opened the medicine cabinet to find adequate pain killers. Tylenol was all they had. She shook two into her uninjured palm and closed the cabinet.

In the mirror, Jordan stood behind her. Sara jumped again, almost smiled, but he looked so strange. His mouth opened and closed like a landed fish. His eyes were sunken and red-rimmed. The slit across his throat dribbled blood.

Sara whipped around, but no one was there. She let out a whimper. A sad, terrified sound. Blood in the kitchen, Jordan with a slit throat. She looked at her hand.

Blood had already seeped through the gauze. She took a deep breath, but her lungs wouldn't fill. She looked in the mirror again, but before she could see if Jordan still stood there, her vision flashed with black spots and down she went.

JORDAN DIALED SARA'S CELL, hoping to catch her before either of them went to bed. She didn't answer. He tried the house phone. No answer. He left a message at both numbers and crawled into bed. Maybe she'd gone to bed early.

Wouldn't she have called first?

SARA WOKE to the phone ringing. Not her cell. The jangly kitchen phone. A leftover of the previous residents, the yellow, corded phone sat across the kitchen by the refrigerator plugged into an old answering machine. Sara hauled herself up, using the toilet, then the counter, for leverage. She squinted her eyes against the bright bathroom light, against the pain in her cheek where she must have struck the toilet on her way to the floor.

She stumbled down the hall and stopped just shy of the kitchen door. The knock on her head didn't strike the memory of blood everywhere from her mind. She sidled to the entry and peeked inside. No blood. It had all been cleaned up.

It was never there.

She crossed the kitchen just as the old answering

machine picked up. Sara and Jordan's cheery voices informed the caller they weren't home, then the recording began.

Heavy breathing came through the line.

"Help . . . me . . ." Jordan's voice groaned. An electric jolt prickled Sara's skin. "Help." The line went dead.

She grabbed the phone and dialed his cell. Three tones beeped in her ear, extra loud.

We're sorry, your call cannot be completed as dialed.

She tried again. Same result. Maybe it was the landline. She turned and frantically tried to remember where she'd left her cell phone. The living room.

Sara ran to find it, aware of the throbbing in her head. Her phone showed two missed calls from Jordan. She pushed the phone icon and called him back. The phone rang. And rang. And rang. After twenty rings or so, the line died. Call lost. She called him again, panic shuddering its way up her abdomen. Her breathing turned into gasping. A sharp pain dug into her gut.

Every time she called him she got a different result. Three tones. Crackling. The line never connecting. Finally, Jordan's groggy voice answered.

Sara burst into tears.

"Sara? What's wrong? What happened?"

"Oh my god," she whispered.

"What? What is it?" She could see him sitting up in a strange bed in a strange room. Would he get the next flight out if it was serious enough?

"I couldn't reach you," she said. "I passed out in the bathroom. There was blood everywhere. You were dead or dying."

"Blood? Where? Did you cut yourself?"

"No." She looked at her hand where the blood soaked the bandage. "I mean, yes, I did, but . . ." But what? Did the knock on the head rearrange the facts? "I was . . . just scared. I guess."

"We're getting a dog when I get home. A big one." He laughed, but it was mirthless. "You said you passed out. Are you okay? Did you eat today? Drink enough water?"

Sara nodded. "Yes. I just—after all the blood—I guess I got woozy."

"How bad is the cut? Send me a picture."

Sara took her cell from her ear and snapped a picture of the bloody bandage and sent it in a text.

"Jesus Christ, Sara. You probably need some stitches. How did this happen?"

"I can't get stitches, Jordan," she said in a steady, stern voice. "That's how it'll all start."

"What . . . Oh." He swallowed audibly. "The movie."

Sara nodded. "I put five butterfly sutures on it. It'll be fine. I just need to hold it above my head and apply some pressure. I couldn't do that when it first happened because I passed out, but now I can."

"Okay. Well, if it starts to look weird, go to the doc, okay?"

"I will." They said their goodbyes. Sara had completely forgotten to ask him about the weird message he left on the answering machine. She went into the kitchen and pressed play.

"Hey, Sara. Just calling before I go to bed. Early day tomorrow. I love you. Call me back if it isn't too late when you get this," Jordan's voice said.

Sara stared at the machine. She pressed play again. Listened hard for any harsh breathing, groaning, like what came through the line before. It was always Jordan's cheery voice.

THE NEXT DAY, Sara woke with incredible pain in her face. At first, she thought it was from hitting the toilet on her way down to the floor, but her nose was stuffy, too. Sinus infection. A heavy grogginess held her head in a vice-like grip. She could hardly open her eyes. When she did get up, it was only to use the bathroom or to refill her glass of water. She avoided looking in the mirror.

Jordan called her a couple times. Their conversations were brief. He only had a few minutes during the breaks in the sales meeting. In the evenings, he went out to dinners with the executives and clients. Glad-handing and networking. He told her he'd called every night before going to bed, but Sara didn't have a single missed call on her cell phone.

He wouldn't lie to her, would he? He knew she didn't like it when he drank out on the town without her. It's not that she didn't trust him, she just didn't trust other women.

Sara slept through most of the following day as well. She woke at 11:00 p.m. with a face that felt like it had swelled to five times its normal size. She touched it and found it was the same face she always had.

Movement in the corner of the dark bedroom caught her eye. She peered into the darkness.

"Is someone there?" she croaked.

"Sara." Jordan's voice came in a harsh whisper. "Why'd you do it, Sara?" His voice was pleading. A regretful cry.

"Jordan?" She squinted her eyes, opened them as wide as they could go, which still seemed like just a squint. "You're not supposed to be home until Monday."

How long have I been asleep?

"Why'd you do it, Sara?" He asked again. This time with accusation.

"What? What did I do?" She fumbled for the lamp on the nightstand and clicked it on. "I don't unders—" She turned his way and screamed. "No, no, no," she cried, eyes wide, unable to look away.

"Sara . . . why?" Jordan stood at the end of their bed. His neck dribbled blood onto their white comforter. He reached toward her with a gory hand, and his head tumbled from his shoulders. It landed between her feet, rolled once, and settled at her knees.

Sara took in a breath, then another. She seemed only capable of breathing in, not out. When she finally let go of the breath, it came out in a shrill scream. A scream worthy of an Oscar. Except she wasn't acting. She tore back the covers and ran from the room, tripping and almost falling down the stairs. She ran out the front door and onto the lawn. She looked up at the house, at the lighted window, at the front door, waiting for Jordan's headless corpse to follow her out into the chilly night.

"You should be indoors, young lady. You'll catch your death out here in that getup." The neighbor lady, Rosalind, was outside with her small rat-looking dog. Sara shivered in the sweaty tank top and shorts she'd worn the past few days. Her head throbbed. Rosalind shuffled to her front door, threw a grimace at Sara, and stepped inside.

"Wait," Sara whispered. "I need help." She gasped and sobbed and hiccupped. Goose flesh broke out over her entire body, hardening her nipples. Her teeth chattered. She finally gave in and went back inside. She turned on every light in the house. Even the basement light. She considered staying on the couch for the rest of the night, but a part of her had to see.

She slunk up the stairs and peered into the bedroom. No headless husband. No decapitated head. No blood splatters on the comforter. All was as it should be.

Even so, she took her pillow back downstairs and slept on the sofa.

Sunlight filtered in through the windows. Birds chirped outside. Somewhere in the distance a dog barked. Not the annoying yap of Rosalind's rat.

Sara opened her eyes. Her hand throbbed. Her head throbbed. She peeled back the bandage on her hand and winced at the raw redness. At the smell.

She fumbled for her cell phone on the coffee table. Noon, Saturday. Jordan would be home tomorrow. She called him to leave him a message.

A woman's voice answered. A cold stone dropped into Sara's gut.

"Uh, is Jordan there?" Sara asked.

"Oh, honey, you have the wrong number," the woman said.

"This isn't 303-555-2625?"

"Yes, but there's no Jordan here. This is a battered women's shelter." The woman paused. "Say, do you need help? Are you pretending? I heard about a woman who called 9-1-1 to order a pizza once—"

"No, no. I'm fine. Thank you. Sorry to bother you."

Sara hung up. She stared at her phone, at Jordan's contact info. She dialed again. Maybe the wires got crossed. The same woman answered. Sara hung up, dully aware she was gasping air in and out. Hyperventilating.

In the movie, the woman went crazy and saw dead people who weren't really there, but maybe they were. Based on true events, supposedly. How much of it was true?

Sara turned on the TV and DVR. She scrolled through and found the Seven Nights of Fright, found day seven.

The Grudge.

"No," she said in a firm voice. "It wasn't *The Grudge.*" She scrolled through days one through six. Maybe they'd watched the wrong night. She knew they hadn't, but she had to check. None of them were the right movie.

Jordan's dead.

The thought popped into her head.

The movie was based on you.

"He's at a sales meeting," she said in a weak voice.

That's what you told yourself to believe.

"No," she said again. "You don't know anything." A chill shuddered through her body.

His cell phone number is no longer his.

The thoughts kept coming, filling her head until all

she heard was the static of a crowded room. She covered her ears and squeezed her eyes shut against the noise.

The movie title glared at her from the TV screen.

"It wasn't the fucking Grudge!" She threw the remote at the television and screamed. Her cell phone rang. Jordan's name popped up on the screen. Relief flooded over her. Tears, always threatening to build up and fall this week, trickled from her eyes. She answered.

"Jordan?"

"Hi, ma'am?" It was the woman from the battered shelter. "I thought I'd ask, since you called us, if you wanted to donate any blankets or food or anything to the shelter. Anything would help."

Sara dropped her hand.

"Ma'am? Are you there? Ma'am?" The woman's small, distant voice jabbered on. Sara ended the call.

"I killed him," she said aloud. "I killed him and all this time I've been living in a dream. A lucid dream."

She drifted to the kitchen and numbly took a bottle of whiskey from the cupboard. She hated whiskey. She unscrewed the cap and took a swig, winced at the immediate sharpness, then sighed as the liquid warmed her belly. She coughed.

He was gone. How long? A week? A month? Years? He'd just been there what seemed like days ago. He'd just been there hugging her, soothing her after that horrible movie.

The Grudge.

"Not *The Grudge*," she whispered, then took another gulp. Then another. "It was about me. The movie was about me. Sara the Slaughterer." That wasn't even the girl's name in the movie, but it was something like that. "I killed him, then I killed myself." She sat up. "But . . . I'm still alive."

She went into the bathroom where she'd seen bloody Jordan the first time.

"You're supposed to be dead," she told her red-eyed reflection. The front door creaked open. A whining hinge Jordan was supposed to oil when he was still alive. Sara's heart started to pound. She listened as someone stepped into the foyer and dropped something heavy on the floor. She slinked into the kitchen and took a knife from the block. On tiptoe, she made her way down the hall to the entryway.

Jordan was busy taking off his coat and scarf. He looked up the stairs as if expecting her to come down to greet him.

"You're dead," Sara said from the hallway shadows.

Jordan's eyes flicked to her, and he took a step back. His eyebrows lowered in confusion.

"You're dead. I killed you, but I don't remember when, but I did it. You're dead," Sara said in a low voice.

"What? Is this a joke?" He laughed uncertainly. "That's what the woman in the movie said . . ." his eyes lowered to her hand, to the knife. "Knock it off, will you? You're totally freaking me out."

Sara took a step toward him.

"Jesus. What's that smell?" He took a step toward her. "Is that you?"

Sara still wore the sweaty pajamas—tank top and shorts—she'd worn all week, or month, or year.

"You're dead," she said again. "I'll prove it!" She

lunged at him, grabbed a fistful of his hair and slit his throat. The blade ground against his trachea.

Jordan gasped, mouth opening and closing like it had in the mirror when she saw him like this.

"See?" She said.

You're supposed to be dead, too.

Sara dropped the blade. It *thunked* onto the hard wood. She shuffled into the kitchen and picked up the yellow-corded phone.

"Nine-one-one, what's your emergency?" A woman asked.

"There's been a murder . . ." Sara said, her voice wavering. She gulped, took a deep breath, let out a sob, and said, "And a suicide."

MEDICINE MEMORY

Published in Predicate Literary Journal

I T WAS LIKE SLUDGE. HOW COULD ANYONE DRINK coffee like that? I drank it anyway, needed to wake up. I was on medication for my condition, which always made me drowsy. It affected my memory, too. I could never remember when or even if I took my medicine for the day, and if I took more than one, it could be very dangerous. But if I didn't take it, it would be worse. I don't even remember why I must take it. My mother was the only person who knew, and she passed away suddenly of a heart attack three years ago.

"Marilyn?" I called. My secretary bustled in. She was wearing a light purple dress-suit that was stunning. She was gorgeous. I stared at her in awe.

"What is it, Roll?" she asked. I loved it when she called me Roll. My full name was Rolland Jeffrey Franks III, and she was supposed to address me as Mr. Franks, but I allowed her to call me Roll. Looking like that, she could call me 'Shit Head' for all I cared.

"Have I taken my medication this morning?"

"What do you think?" she asked.

"I don't think I did," I said, leaning back in my large, cushy chair. It rocked slightly.

"Tell me exactly what you did this morning since the moment you woke up,"

"I got out of bed, took a shower, got out of the shower, shaved, put on deodorant, got dressed, ate breakfast, and," I smiled at her, "took my pill! Thanks, Mare," I said. She smiled, then handed me a folder of papers I needed to sign. As the president of my corporation, I had a whole lot of paperwork, as well as a bunch of people that ran the place for me.

My corporation, which was passed on to me after my father passed away and my older brother declined the inheritance, he wanted nothing to do with our family, involved about eighty workers who sat at desks and talked to people all day. Some helped set up folks with the paperwork for buying a house, or for buying land to build a house on. My corporation dealt with houses and everything about them. From selling, to renting, to buying, to building, to renovating, to destroying. My grandfather, Rolland Jeffrey Franks I, had founded the corporation and named it Franks Housing Corporation. Our motto was "Everything Houses." I thought it was lame and changed it to "Houses R Us." That was after my father, Rolland Jeffrey Franks II, changed it to "Everything About Homes and More." I'm sure when I have a son and give him the corporation, it will change to something else.

WHEN I GOT home that evening, I looked at the orange pill case sitting on the kitchen counter. Had I taken my medicine? I didn't remember. I reached for the pills, struggled with the childproof cap, and finally shook a small triangular tablet into the palm of my hand. I poured a glass of water and was about to toss the pill to the back of my throat, when Marilyn's voice filled my head.

Tell me exactly what you did this morning from the moment you woke up.

"I did take it," I said aloud. "I did take it. Close call Rolland." I ran a clammy hand through my hair and put the pills on top of the refrigerator, then heaved the door open and brought out sandwich fixings.

The medicine I take has a whole lot of side effects, like migraine headaches, abdominal pains, indigestion, hair loss, weight gain, things like that. I have some of the more severe ones, which include stomach ulcers, heart problems and memory loss. I forget the most trivial things, for instance, putting the coffee grounds in the coffee maker. I end up with hot water on those days, so I just drink tea. I've also forgotten to put ham in a ham sandwich before. When it didn't taste right, I realized what I had forgotten. One thing I'll never forget, though, are my feelings for Marilyn.

Marilyn had been working for me since I inherited the company. She stuck with me through thick and thin, as a faithful secretary, and had always helped me out with difficult situations, especially with my memory loss. She was so understanding, so patient with me. I truly loved her. But she was genuinely professional, and why would she be interested in me anyway? She seemed to like work much more than play, and I don't think she's ever had a serious relationship before.

I grabbed a bottle of beer from the fridge and went into the living room with my sandwich. I sat in my recliner and clicked on the television. The news was on, but nothing interested me, so I flipped to the game show channel and watched old reruns of *Let's Make A Deal*. A guy won three pot-bellied stoves, but only two showed behind the curtain. He asked, where's the third potbelly? And a large man came out and rubbed his round gut. I laughed, the bite of sandwich threatening to fall from my mouth. I continued watching, and before long dozed off.

When I woke up, there was an empty beer bottle in my hand, and a plate littered with crumbs on the end table next to me. I sat up straight and gasped.

"Where am I?" I whispered. "What's going on, whose is this?" I looked at the bottle in my hand. *I don't drink beer,* I thought to myself. I looked at my hands, they seemed foreign. I ran to the mirror and almost screamed as I stared at the vision in the reflection, the dark disheveled hair, the almost black eyes that seemed to go on forever.

My heart began to pound as my gaze shifted to the lips, twisted in a cruel expression of horror. "Who am I? Who am I?" I yelled. "Where am I?" I looked around the house I was in, dazed and in a state of panic. "Whose house is this?"

The room started to spin around me, my head swam with disturbing thoughts, pictures of blood-splattered walls, stained carpets, swollen, purple tongues, and wide staring eyes that would never see anything ever again. As I felt my body hit the floor, my vision blurred, and then went completely dark.

"Rolland," a sweet voice said. I was shaken slightly. "Rolland, wake up," this was my first experience with death. I wasn't sure how things worked, but I thought that maybe when a person goes to heaven, their guardian angel shows them around. I opened my eyes. My guardian angel was beautiful with red hair, and a gentle touch.

When my vision cleared, and I saw my angel more clearly, I smiled, then frowned.

"Marilyn? You died, too?" I asked. "I'm sorry I crashed into a tree," I mumbled. My mouth seemed foreign; my tongue felt out of place. I guess I had to get used to my new form as a ghost or spirit or whatever I was. My head was throbbing. "I wonder if everyone feels this way when they get up here." I sat up, too fast, and my vision blurred. I grabbed my head as it throbbed more intensely. "Do you feel funny?" I asked. I had a feeling in my stomach, the feeling you get when you think of something exciting, like going to Disneyland for the first time. A surge of anxiety, like being tickled deep down, I almost had to laugh, it felt so weird, but my head ached.

"No, Roll, we're not dead," Marilyn said. She stroked my hair; I felt like a cat and even wanted to purr. "Something happened to you, what happened, Roll?"

"I don't know," I said, shamefully hanging my head

and rubbing my eyes with a thumb and forefinger. "I only remember leaving work and coming home. I guess maybe I fell asleep and had a bad dream that you woke me up from," I looked around. "Why am I in the bathroom?"

"This is where I found you," she said, "Did you take two pills yesterday?" She didn't give me time to answer, or even think. "Did you forget and take two?"

"I don't remember," I said. "I, I don't know,"

"Think, Rolland, think, did you take two?" She shook my shoulder, making my head wobble, making me cringe with pain.

"Did I hit my head?" I asked her, reaching back to feel it. She grabbed my arm before I could touch my head.

"Yes, you hit your head, it's bleeding, but I put a bandage over it." she checked the dressing. "Tell me what happened. Start from as far back as you remember yesterday, even if you start from when you woke up that morning." She was deeply concerned about this. I personally didn't really care, as long as I got my medicine before too long.

"How did you get in here?" I asked. "I usually lock the doors before I go to bed." Then I thought again. "How did you know to come here?"

"It's two in the afternoon, Rolland. You hadn't shown up for work yet. I was worried." She looked me in the eye. The front of her blouse was low-cut, and I could see in just a little. She was wearing her red suit today, I loved that one, she looked great in red. "And as for the doors? You probably forgot to lock them." She looked at me with soulful eyes. "Now, what happened? Reach way back and tell me what you did yesterday,"

"I remember leaving work and coming home, but everything after that is a blur," I said, frowning. "I need to take my medicine," I said, starting to rise.

"No, not yet. We need to figure this out." She put a hand on my arm. "Maybe if you see the main rooms in the house you might remember what happened," she said. She helped me to my feet and guided me around the house. Nothing sparked even the minutest thought. When we reached the living room, I sat down in the recliner and looked to my right, right at the dirty plate. I gasped. "What?" Marilyn rushed to my side.

"I came home last night and made myself a sandwich, then sat here with my plate and a beer, and I fell asleep watching television. Was the TV on when you got here?" I didn't give her time to answer, it was as if my mouth had taken over and was spewing out anything that came to mind. "I woke up and was . . ." I trailed off, not sure what was next, but knowing it was on the tip of my brain, ready to come out.

"What happened when you woke up?" Marilyn was crouching next to the recliner to get at my level.

"I-I was horrified," I said in a slow, low tone. "Strange feelings, thoughts, urges." I looked at my hands, which were mine again. "I didn't know who I was, where I was, or even if I was," I said. A tear dripped from my eye and trailed down my cheek as I remembered the incident. "I ran around, trying to figure out where I was." I paused, and Marilyn squeezed my arm, telling me to go on. "When I saw my reflection, it wasn't me," I said. I looked at her for the first time since I sat down. Her gaze was questioning. "I looked, strange, angry," I paused, thinking about what happened next. That was when I began to shake uncontrollably. I remembered the visions and pictures that flashed through my mind when I reached the bathroom. "I ran upstairs to the bathroom, in a frenzied panic. When I got there, I had these visions flash through my mind." I shook harder, trembled all over. The trembling became worse as I told her about the visions. I looked at her when I finished. Her face was distorted in a half-grimace, half-surprised expression.

"What do you think it means?" she asked.

"I don't know, but I do know I didn't take another pill. I almost did, but your voice entered my thoughts and I remembered that I had taken it already." I smiled; my shaking had ceased, and Marilyn smiled at me, a smile that made everything seem so much better. But my smile faded.

"Marilyn?"

"Yes?"

"Do you know the reason why I take this medicine?"

"Why? Don't you?"

"I don't know why I take it. The only person I know that knows was my mother, but she passed away three years ago," I said. "Bless her soul,"

"Well, speaking of your medicine, don't you need to take it?"

"Don't change the subject!" I said through gritted teeth, grabbing her chin and jerking her face toward mine.

"Rolland! I wasn't changing the subject! I was merely

telling you that you need to take your pill!" She was frightened, and I knew then that she did know why I took my medicine. And that was why she was afraid of me.

I pushed her face away and she stood from her crouching position. "Get out," I said. "Go, get out."

"You need to take your medicine."

"Just go," I said, holding my hand up to silence her.

"Fine, but you'll see. You just remember to take that medicine, or you'll regret ever telling me to get out." She straightened her clothing and went to the door. "I don't understand, Rolland. You've always been so nice." She was crying, I heard it in her voice, although she tried to hide it. "I almost loved you," it was a whisper, and the door closed softly after that. I knew she was gone, maybe forever.

"I'll take my medicine, dammit." I said. I got up and went to the kitchen. After the short walk across the living room and into the kitchen, I had forgotten why I had entered. I looked around, trying to remember. I noticed the orange bottle of medicine, and a knife rack with assorted knives, the dripping faucet, and crumbs on the counter, which I must have forgotten to wipe up.

Reaching for a rag, my sleeve caught on one of the knives. "How intriguing," I said aloud. I pulled on the largest handle.

A long, sharp blade hissed, as it was unsheathed from its slice in the wood. I turned it over in my hand, catching my reflection in the shining metal. It was a horrid face, horrid, yet appealing. My black eyes flashed, and my hair, dark and tousled reminded me of a lion's mane. I smiled grotesquely, then went to the front door. I held the knife tight against my leg, then opened the door. Marilyn was sitting on the front steps, sobbing. She jumped when she heard my voice.

"Dear, sweet Marilyn. How could I be so mean to such a beauty?" She looked suspiciously at me, a sidelong glance.

"What's on your mind?" she asked, the hint of suspicion tweaked something inside my head.

"Will you please come in and talk to me?"

"Did you take your medicine?"

I had forgotten, and I didn't want to lie, but I couldn't help myself. I nodded yes, a crude nod where my head seemed to wobble on my neck.

"Okay, I'll come in," she said, rising to her feet. "But you stay away from me until I know you're alright." I stepped aside to let her pass by me. Heaven forbid she should see my bright, shiny knife!

"Sit, you can have my recliner, I'll sit on the couch," I said. I slipped the knife between the cushions of the couch as she sat down and plastered a smile on my face. "I'm sorry," I said through my teeth. I hadn't meant to say it that way, but something else was controlling my actions, and I liked it.

"What's wrong, Rolland?" she asked. I realized that my smile must not have been a smile. Without thinking, I pulled the knife from the cushion to look at my reflection and heard Marilyn gasp. "What are you doing with that?" She jumped to her feet. But I knew she wasn't going to leave. The look I had on my face was one of despair, so I took my time training my face to smile.

"What do you mean? It's my mirror. I have a right to

look at myself in the mirror!" My face felt funny, so I looked at my reflection in knife again and laughed, a laugh that came in spurts, loud and not so funny. But the sound of it made me laugh even more. The look on my face was hideous, but I loved it. Marilyn stumbled backward, heading for the door. "Stop," I said. I tried to relax my face, but it was impossible. "I'm not going to hurt you," I said, but started laughing again.

"What are you doing with that knife?" she stammered.

"Admiring my urbane appearance. If I were you, I wouldn't leave," I said, still looking in the mirror.

"You didn't take your medicine, did you? You lied to me, and now look at you." She gestured toward me.

"What?" I said, looking up at her. "I'm fine, just sit down, and we'll talk," I put the knife down next to me. I had tired of looking at my reflection in it. Marilyn started talking to me, but my attentions were elsewhere. Visions had started to flash in my mind again. There were only three, this time, and they seemed in some sort of chronological order. There was a grisly wound with blood spurting out. Then a bloody knife, and finally . . . my vision was interrupted by Marilyn's annoyingly persistent questioning.

"Rolland!"

"What?" I yelled. The knife handle was in my hand, I suddenly realized.

"Weren't you listening to me?" she asked.

"No," I said, truthfully enough. "I was thinking about your murder." It had managed its way to my mouth, and just came out. Before I knew it, the knife was slicing through the air. I heard a scream, and this crazy sound. It sounded like someone hacking a chicken in half, preparing it for supper. A fleshy, cracking sound. When I looked down, I had blood all over my hand. But it couldn't have been all over my hand because my hand lay on the floor, oozing blood onto the carpet. Blood was spurting from the open wound at my wrist. I cackled uncontrollably, staring at my dismemberment. I looked at the ground where the bloody knife lay, and then at Marilyn who was backing toward the door. I smiled at her, then remembered I had to take my medicine, and went to the kitchen.

THE HEALER

Dedicated to Wissa. I wrote this about a month or so before she had knee surgery, because I wished I could take her pain away.

I REMEMBER THAT IT WAS RAINING THAT NIGHT. I could barely see past the drops dripping from my eyelashes. The gunman's bullet hit its mark.

"I'm sorry . . ." She choked past the blood filling her lungs.

"No, no, shh," I whispered. I smoothed her rain-soaked hair and placed my hand over her heart, over the bullet wound, the other on her forehead.

Her eyes widened. "No," she gasped. "Don't."

I shushed her gently. "I don't want you to die," I whispered, clenching my jaw to keep from crying. "I love you." I took a deep breath and prepared to steal away her pain and take her from death's grip.

. . .

IT WAS A CURSE, not a gift. Those who I helped thanked me and referred to me as a Saint, but I'm just a man with the ability to heal the wounded. I am a healer, but not the kind with herbs and magical chakras. I take the pain of other's and make it my own.

A writer with a broken hand? Cured. Me? Left with a terrible tendonitis in all connecting tendons in my hand. Phalanges to carpals to metacarpals. An opera singer with laryngitis left me scratchy for a week. One of the worst I've healed, until the dark night twenty-six years into my life as a healer, was a torn heart valve.

It was a tough decision; I never know how I'll be affected. Though the pain I receive is far less than the degree of that which I take away, I am always reluctant to heal. I weigh my odds. How serious is this injury, this disease, this cluster of symptoms? How may I come out? I was approached by Mr. Robert Candava's wife a week before he was scheduled for surgery to repair his aortic valve. She was distraught and shoved an envelope full of cash into my arms.

"Heal my husband! One more surgery and I will lose him, I just know it!" She cried.

"I'm sorry, I think you have the wrong person." I didn't advertise, why would I? I'd have every Tom, Dick, and Harry at my front door. I'd be bedridden with numerous ailments all at the same time, all the time.

"I heard your name from a friend," Mrs. Candava said. "She told me I could find you here." She motioned to the steps of the public library I had just come from.

I sat down on a step and Mrs. Candava joined me, eyes full of tears.

"He's going to die." She looked out across the street. I gave the envelope back to her. She looked at me with wide, tear-filled eyes.

"I'm going to help you, I just don't require payment," I whispered.

She pressed her face against my shoulder and sobbed. "Thank you. Thank you."

Mrs. Candava told me the date of his surgery and told me to meet her in the waiting room. From there she would get me in to see Mr. Candava. When I was alone with him, I explained who I was and what I was going to do. He nodded in understanding.

I placed my hand over his heart on the lower-left. My other hand I placed on his forehead. I'm not sure when or why I started doing that, the hand on the forehead that is, but I think I started doing it because I felt it would calm the patient.

I closed my eyes and saw Mr. Candava's heart. I scanned the entire thing, and when I reached the aortic valve I gasped as searing pain entered my chest. I pushed on Mr. Candava's chest until he grunted with the pressure. After that I don't remember. It always happens that way. When I feel the intensity of the pain, it's almost as if my brain shuts down. I open my eyes and there I am, breathless, on my ass on the floor. Sometimes, if it isn't as bad, I open my eyes and I'm still standing with my hands on the patient.

But Mr. Candava's valve was so torn. I saw it in my mind, working so hard to shut tight, but unable to. My chest burned.

Someone came into the room behind me.

"Are you alright? What happened?" A female voice asked.

"I'm, fine." I gasped. "I was just . . ."

"He was visiting and the grief of me going into surgery just shocked the poor lad," Mr. Candava said.

"You aren't supposed to have visitors once you are in here, Mr. Candava," the female said. I looked up at her.

"Are you sure you're okay?" She crouched by my side and felt my pulse. Her touch soothed. I wanted her to keep touching me, but she stopped and helped me to my feet.

"I'm okay," I said. "I just have really bad heartburn." I couldn't stand up straight it burned so bad. "Do you have something for that?"

She smiled. Her nametag said "Victoria, RN".

"I'm sure I can find something for you." She winked. "But you need to go back out into the waiting room." She held my arm and led me out to a seat near Mrs. Candava, who looked at me with wide eyes, expectant.

Victoria, RN left, and Mrs. Candava leaned over.

"Well?" She whispered.

"It's done. I cured him." I gripped my chest. Black spots danced before my eyes. My heart was on fire. "You have to stop the surgery." I gasped and doubled over.

"Are you okay, Mr. Valentine?" Mrs. Candava asked.

"Yes, but it's not Valentine, it's . . ." My head swam with visions of my own aortic valve working overtime to seal tight. But that wasn't it. What was it? I closed my eyes and put my hand on my heart. Everything was in fine condition. I placed it lower. Acid reflux. Bad. Bile rose in my throat.

"Here's some, oh my gosh." Victoria, RN was again by my side pressing a cool hand on the back of my neck, and then my forehead.

After that, it all went downhill. I tried to blurt out to stop the surgery, but instead I vomited on my shoes and on Victoria, RN's lap. She seemed more concerned about my wellbeing than the stains on her scrubs. She rushed a wheelchair into the waiting room and had me whisked to a bed on a different floor.

"I think he's in shock," she told the attending nurse on my floor. "I'll come back after my rounds and check up on him."

She did, too. She came back only an hour later, though. Mrs. Candava stopped the surgery, demanding another EKG, MRI, ultrasound, "Whatever it is you do!" she shouted. The doctor complied and Mr. Candava's heart was just fine.

When I woke up the next morning, heartburn still present, but smoldering softly now, there was a package on my side table full of money from the Candavas.

Victoria, RN, who was really Victoria Knightley, RN, never came back to see me, and when I was released the afternoon the day after I healed Mr. Candava, the attending nurse told me to call her later.

"She seemed real weird about it, son," the woman said, handing me a slip of paper with Victoria's number on it.

I kept the number, but I didn't call her. I knew she was going to ask me about Mr. Candava, about my severe case of heartburn, and what was going on. I didn't have answers that made sense to those of a scientific mindset.

A week later, however, I bumped into her at the market one day while shopping for produce.

"I know you," she said over the onions. "You're the heartburn from last week." She laughed.

"Yes, the heartburn," I said. "I'm Christopher. Christopher Valenteen." I held out my hand and she squeezed it gently. Her hand was soft and warm. The touch of a healer, though not the type I am. "Victoria, RN," I said with a smile.

"I noticed you haven't called," she said raising an eyebrow. We'd moved on to citrus. She put a large orange in her bag and picked up another one.

"I know," I said. "I'm sure I know what you wanted me to call about, and I try to avoid answering questions as much as possible."

"Questions? What questions?" Victoria asked.

"Didn't you have questions about Mr. Candava's miraculous self-healing valve?" I asked her, pausing in the handling of a nectarine.

"No. I figured it was just a mistake. You know, some sort of glitch in the EKG." She twist-tied her bag of oranges and put them in her basket.

"Right." I could see she didn't really believe that. "Then what did you want me to call you about?" I asked.

She flushed and smiled shyly. A smile that gripped my heartstrings and tugged hard. "I just . . ." She looked up at me through her lashes. "I wanted to see if you'd like to go to dinner," she blurted. "But if you don't, that's fine; I know it's kind of weird." She quickly put a bunch of potatoes in a bag and tied it off, then moved to the apples and away from me.

I played coy. I didn't follow her to the apples, but I did watch her from the oranges as she struggled not to look at me or make eye contact. Her face was still flushed. I sidled over to the apples and stood very close to her.

"Yes, I'll have dinner with you," I told her.

She smiled and let out a long breath. "I knew you would," she said. "I could feel you staring at me." She looked up at me and smiled.

"Right. Do you always call yourself stupid when you believe someone will accept an invitation?" I chuckled, and she relaxed.

We went to The Screaming Rooster, a small pub-type restaurant that served mainly fried food, beer, and the occasional plate of wilted salad. Victoria, RN chose the place. Later she informed me she thought it would be relaxed enough to enjoy a first date, without the usual nerve-racking inability to keep the person you're out with enthralled with what you have to say.

After dinner, more of a snack, Victoria had greaseball chicken strips, I had mozzarella sticks that dripped hot oil down my chin, we took a walk to the park and sat on a bench in the moonlight.

"How did you do it?" She asked me after we sat in silence for a few minutes.

"Do what?" I leaned back and put my arm around her. She relaxed against my shoulder.

"I don't know," she said. "You did something to Mr. Candava."

"What do you think I did?" I asked her. Her hair smelled like a summer day.

She sat up and twisted to look at me. My arm dropped from her shoulders. "You healed him," she said, but shook her head, as if she didn't like the way it sounded. "Or something like that."

She was so beautiful in her puzzlement.

"I did heal him." I took her hand and held it gently. "And as a reward I got heartburn."

"Acid reflux." She corrected me, then laughed, then stopped abruptly with her eyebrows furrowed. She pulled her hand away. "Are you mocking me?"

"No, not at all." I held up my hands. "I didn't want to tell you before because I knew you wouldn't believe me."

"And I kind of don't," she said.

"But you also kind of do—Look, I don't usually tell people about it because they don't believe me." I paused and looked at her through narrowed eyes. "But, there's something about you, Victoria, RN, that I just can't put my finger on." I stood. "This is going to sound crazy, but, I feel like I need whatever it is in my life." I laughed. "That sounds like a bad pickup line."

"Yeah. It does," she said. "As corny as it sounds, I have to admit, there's something about you, too."

I sat next to her and she leaned against my shoulder again. "I don't know what it is, but I've been thinking about you since you threw up on me last week."

I laughed. "I am so sorry about that."

We sat in silence for a few minutes, watching the stars twinkle above, the reflection of the moon on the pond.

"I believe you," she murmured.

"I know," I whispered in her ear.

Victoria saw several healings in our short time together. She called me during surgeries that weren't going very well. The surgeon she assisted was always very kind in allowing me into the OR to do what I did best. I usually sat in the waiting room and spoke with the family of the patients first, to tell them what I was going to do. Most of them had never heard of me before, but some of them had. Regardless, their eyes always lit up at hearing what I told them. I'm going to heal your son, your wife, your sister-in-law, your newborn baby. They were always pleased, and I was always injured afterward, but they never saw that part.

After I healed a seventeen-year-old who had been hit by a car, I was hospitalized with several minor fractures that healed quickly, but were painful nonetheless.

"You have to stop," Victoria told me while she changed some of my dressings. "I don't want you to do this anymore." Her voice was stern, her forehead creased with concern, her lips pursed.

"I have to. It's what I'm meant to do." I told her. My voice was dry and raspy. I was drowsy from the pain killers.

Victoria stopped wrapping my wrist and put her hands over her face to hide her crying.

"Victoria, RN," I said in a sing-song voice.

She turned and smiled through her tears. She loved it when I called her that.

"What, Chris?" she asked.

"I can't heal myself," I sang. I jiggled my injured

wrist, the bandage dangling nearly to the floor. She laughed, wiped her eyes and finished wrapping my wrist.

After a time, she said, "I know you can't, and that's what hurts me." Her voice was thick with sorrow. "What if you heal someone and end up dying because of it?"

"That won't happen," I told her. "I'm more careful than that."

"I know, but what if . . . ?"

"I always assess the injury, if it's too severe, I don't do anything but try to calm the patient down, you know that. You've seen it." I was beginning to feel anger seep through the drug haze.

"I know, but there's always the possibility that you won't see how severe it is. Even doctors who've gone to years and years of medical school sometimes can't assess well enough! That's why I've called you for help in the OR, because we didn't see that it was so serious." Her voice raised as she spoke.

I was quiet for a minute, not sure what to say. She was right; there was always the possibility of a wrong assessment. I knew that, she knew that. To be honest, I'd always known that, but I still risked it. I healed people to relieve not only their pain, but the emotional pain of those around them.

"I'm not afraid of death," I whispered. I didn't add what I was afraid of—the pain those around me might suffer should I die.

"I know you're not." She sat on the edge of my bed and placed a cool hand on the side of my face. "That's what scares me."

I reached up with my good arm and caressed her cheek.

"Come here," I whispered. She lay down gently on my chest and I stroked her hair. "I won't do anything stupid, okay?"

"Okay," she said. "Just be careful."

"You know I am."

She sat up and wiped her eyes and said, "Yeah, right. Look at you now, Mr. Always Careful."

"It's not that bad." I said. "I've been worse, trust me."

She finished with me and left the room to see to her other patients. After she left I cringed with pain until tears leaked from my eyes. It had never been this bad.

I went to my doctor, a psychologist by the name of Abrahm Guthry, and spoke to him.

"I think it's leaving me." I lay on a sofa in his office, staring up at the ceiling.

"What is leaving you?" he asked. "Your healing powers?"

"No, my, I don't know what to call it." I sat up abruptly with my elbows on my knees. "I'm feeling more and more of the sufferer's pain," I said. "I recently healed a kid that got hit by a car and ended up hospitalized."

"Well, I'm sure he had extensive trauma . . ."

"No, it wasn't that extensive, but it was almost like I felt the full brunt of his injuries."

"Perhaps you need to take a break with the healing?" Dr. Guthry stated gently. He knew I wouldn't want to hear that. It's what Victoria wanted, too, but I just couldn't. It wasn't in me to give up on something I'd been doing for so long. It was a part of who I was.

"I don't think I need a break," I said, shaking my head. Dr. Guthry didn't say anything, just raised his eyebrows in a way that said, 'suit yourself.'

I have to admit that I did think about it while walking home, and I decided to try it for a week.

"You aren't yourself," Victoria told me over scrambled eggs and bacon the fourth day into my trial period. "You seem distracted and distant." She sat down across from me in her silk nightgown without making eye contact.

"I haven't healed anyone in four days, what do you expect?" I said, a little harsher than intended.

Victoria looked up at me, pain in her eyes.

"I've walked by injured people, sick people, people I can easily help with little consequence and forced myself to look away." I hit my hand on the table. Victoria jumped. I met her eyes and said softly, "I can't live like this. I can't just ignore them."

"I know," she said. "I want you to do what makes you happy." She looked down at her plate and flipped a chunk of egg around with her fork. "I just don't want you to get too hurt."

"Too hurt? What's that supposed to mean?" I wasn't sure what she was getting at.

"I don't want to raise a child alone." A smile played at the corner of her lips.

"A child?" It didn't click at first. I looked at her and she was beaming. "Are you, I mean, we, are you—"

"I'm pregnant," she said. Her smile widened.

"Wha—wow. I don't know what to—you're pregnant?"

She smiled and nodded, then got up and rushed over

to me. She sat in my lap and hugged me tight. She kissed my face all over, excited, so excited to have a baby with me. I cried. The thought of life growing inside her, life that we both poured in, it was overwhelming. I held her tight and didn't want to let her go. She was glowing with happiness.

She was six weeks pregnant when she told me. She wanted to be sure of it before she said anything. We went to dinner to celebrate, an elegant restaurant with a dress code. Victoria wore a long black dress with a slit up the side. I wore a tuxedo. We couldn't help but smile at each other through dinner, a dance, and then dessert.

"So, Victoria, RN, do you hope it's a boy or a girl?" I asked her. I couldn't help but smile when she looked up at me over her glass of water and grinned.

"I don't know. A girl would be nice."

"What would you name her?" I whispered, sliding around the table and sitting next to her. I held her hand and nuzzled her neck. She had never been so beautiful to me.

"Christina," she said with a giggle as I nibbled her earlobe.

"Will you," I started. She pulled away slightly and looked at me, her smile gone, her eyes full of expectation.

"Will I what?" she asked.

"I love you," I whispered. I tucked a velvet box in her hand. "Marry me, Victoria."

She accepted, and we had a second dessert in celebration of our baby and our engagement.

We left the restaurant with spirits high. We laughed about different and odd names we could name our children. She skipped along next to me like a little girl, and I swept her around and kissed her deeply, three blocks from our apartment.

"We should buy a house," I said into her neck as I dipped her.

"In the country," she said. "I want horses and a garden."

"Anything for you," I kissed her again and when we stood up, Victoria screamed.

"Hand it over," the gunman said in a voice laced with insanity. He cocked his gun. "Hand over the purse."

Victoria threw her purse on the ground at his feet. My heart pounded. It was just a decorative purse; she had nothing in it but keys and a tube of lipstick. The gunman emptied out these two items and scoffed.

"Give me your money, credit cards." He looked at her hand that she quickly put behind her back. "Give me that ring."

"Please, sir, we just got engaged, let her keep the ring," I said.

"Shut up." The gunman waved the gun at me. "Come on, missy, hand it over."

Victoria looked up at me, tears welled in her eyes. She pulled the ring off her finger and put it on the ground by her keys and the lipstick. When the gunman bent down to retrieve it, I brought my foot up and kicked him as hard as I could in the face. Victoria screamed.

"Run, call the police," I told her. She turned around and started to run when I was nearly deafened by the sound of the gun going off.

I wasn't hit, but when I turned around, Victoria, my

Victoria, RN, was on the ground. I ran to her side, praying it wasn't bad. Thunder clapped overhead, and it started to rain.

"I'm hit," she said. Tears streamed from her eyes, though she wasn't sobbing. "I'm sorry," she said. I lifted her into my lap and cradled her.

"No, don't. You didn't do anything wrong," I told her. "It was my fault; I shouldn't have tried to be a hero." My tears dripped onto the front of her gown.

"I love you, Chris." Blood trickled from the corner of her mouth and mixed with the rain drops.

I put my hand over her heart and closed my eyes. The bullet was lodged in her left ventricle. When I opened my eyes, she was looking at me.

"I'm sorry . . ." she choked.

"No, no, shh," I whispered. I smoothed her rain-soaked hair and placed my hand over her heart, over the bullet wound, the other on her forehead.

Her eyes widened. "No." She gasped. "Don't."

I shushed her gently. "I don't want you to die," I whispered, clenching my jaw. "You have to have our baby." I held her tight and cried into her hair. "I love you, Victoria."

I took a deep breath, placed my hands, and proceeded to stop death from taking her away.

I didn't only heal to relieve pain; I healed to relieve the emotional anguish, the fears, the trauma of family and friends. I wasn't afraid to die because death would take away the gift I carried, the curse of healing others only to be hurt by their pain.

As I healed Victoria that night, I saw our life together,

how it might have been, with our baby, a girl, at our house in the country. I wasn't left with heartburn; I wasn't left with torn valves. I was left as only a memory to those who loved me. I was remembered as the man who gave his life to heal others.

SOUNDS AND SILENCES

Harold McCreed pulled into the gas station at just after 1:00 a.m., weary from driving all day. When he climbed out of his old Chevy pickup, his back cracked. The truck door mimicked this sentiment and protested with a grinding whine when he slammed it shut.

He pulled his wallet out of his back pocket, but the old pump didn't have the option to use a credit card. In fact, Harold wasn't even sure if the pumps were operational. He'd have to check inside.

Clustered near the entry to the tiny convenience store were a band of shady characters. Two girls just over the edge of adulthood wore short skirts and midriff halter tops. They smoked cigarettes with bright, red-painted mouths. One whispered to the other and pointed in Harold's direction. The pointer wore a short, fluffy fur jacket, despite the lingering heat. The thing might have once been white, but now it resembled the color of an old mattress, slept on by someone with incontinence.

Off in the shadows to the right of the girls, outside the

bright fluorescent lights spilling from the grubby convenience store, three man-shaped figures huddled together. They tossed glances Harold's way every few seconds.

Last, to the left of the entry, a man in a brown overcoat lay on his side. He may or may not have been dead.

The old Chevy didn't really need gas. It still had a quarter tank. It might get Harold to the next town, and even if it didn't, he'd rather walk in the dark than approach the front of the store.

He grabbed the truck's door handle and pushed the button.

"What's the matter, mister?" One of the girls yelled. "Not lookin' for a good time?" She let loose a horrible cackle. Harold glanced over his shoulder just as another scantily-clad girl stumbled out of the bathroom at the side of the building, wiping the corner of her mouth. A man came out behind her, zipping up his pants. Harold grimaced. When he turned back to his truck, the man who'd been laying on the ground stood next to him. Harold lurched backward with a guttural sound, like a thick gasp had stuck in his throat.

The man's eyes were wide and lined with concentric wrinkles. He pointed over the bed of the truck.

Harold followed the gnarled finger.

Across the street, the Sohvi Motel, a two-story, sickly sea-green colored building, sat huddled among the pines. Harold hadn't even seen it on his way in. There was no sign or anything.

The man's lips moved, his throat worked like he was

trying to speak. Strange sounds clicked and creaked inside, but no words came out. Harold saw the man had a gruesome scar on his throat. As if someone had ripped his larynx out.

Harold dug in his pocket and pulled out a crumpled five.

"Thanks," he said, handing the money to the man.

The man grabbed Harold's arm instead. His haunted eyes burned into Harold's mind. He'd never forget them.

"Dammit, let go of me. Take the money. Here, I have more." He flung a ten, a twenty, at the man, and finally shoved him away hard enough to knock him onto his ass.

Harold climbed into the truck and pulled across the street.

The motel looked like the kind of establishment that would offer an hourly rate for the girls in front of the gas station. Right now, Harold would gladly pay for eight hours of sleep.

None of the windows were lit except in the entry. He didn't care if it was shit hotel or the Ritz Carlton. At 2:00 a.m., and fourteen hours on the road on a flat bench seat with springs poking him in the ass, he'd sleep in a coffin *with* a dead body, as long as it wasn't a zombie.

Harold grabbed his duffel bag off the bench seat and went inside. He squinted against the harsh, yellow light. Soft music crackled out of wooden speakers in the corners. Harold cocked an ear. Sounded like "The Girl from Ipanema." He sidled over to a fountain sitting in the middle of the lobby. It could be a lovely feature, if water were running through it. The bottom was choked with cigarette butts and chewing gum. Harold snorted when the shine of a nickel caught his eye.

The only wishes that came from this wishing well were STDs and unwanted pregnancies.

He wasn't usually so cynical, but lack of sleep does a number even on the best folks.

"You want a room, sugar?" A low, sultry voice came from beyond a polished cherry counter, which was the only thing in the lobby that seemed clean.

Harold turned. It was then he noticed the woman standing by the counter, and the smoke coming from the cigarette. She took a drag, then deftly flicked the thing into the fountain where it smoldered before going out. She took a sip of an amber-colored beverage. Harold thought she was already standing, but when he approached, she unfolded herself from a creaky leather chair.

Harold was not a small man himself, at six feet tall. She was just as tall with an additional five or six inches of head-wrapped hair. She peered at him with bottomless, almond-shaped eyes. A smile full of straight but nicotine-stained teeth pulled across her face.

"Is this . . . "The Girl from Ipanema"?" he asked, pointing vaguely at the ceiling. His voice caught in his throat, and he cleared it.

"Indeed, it is." She leaned forward over the counter, and the stretched-out V-neck collar of her shirt hung low. He peered at two cinnamon-colored mounds within. Bra-less. Something told Harold she always got what she wanted.

"Sharzhad Sohvi," she said.

"Excuse me?" Harold asked, unsure if it was a sneeze or another song title.

"My name," she said. "Sharzhad Sohvi. This here is my establishment." She cocked a shapely hip and placed her hand on it. "Now do you want a room or not?"

She had an Angela Basset-type of assertiveness to her that he admired.

"Yes, please. One night." He pulled out his wallet.

"A hundred bucks. Cash only," she said. "There's an ATM across the street."

Harold had just the required amount in his wallet. Thank God he hadn't thrown anymore cash at that homeless guy. He handed it over. She placed a key with a tag the size of his palm in his hand.

"Take the elevator to the second floor, sugar. Your room is all the way at the end of the hall." She pointed to a set of tarnished brass doors.

"Thanks," Harold said. He scribbled his name on the next blank line of her leather-bound register, then made his way to the elevator.

"Can't run," she said in a low voice.

Harold turned. "Wha . . .?"

"Can't run," she said, pointing at the ceiling. "Lee Williams?"

"Oh, right." Harold turned back to the brass doors.

"Don't go to the thirteenth floor." Sharzhad let out a barking laugh.

Harold didn't get the joke, if there was one. The motel only had two floors. He took his duffel bag to the elevator and pushed back the outdated metal accordion door, cringing at the screech of the metal. Sharzhad's cold laughter followed him inside. When he reached to press the button for the second floor, he paused.

There were no buttons. Just a lever with three characters. L, for Lobby he presumed, 2 for the second floor, and written on a scrap of paper and taped to the wall, 13. Ha. Thirteenth floor.

Harold rattled the accordion door shut and moved the lever to the second position. The exterior door sealed him inside.

A chilly draft came from above. Harold glanced up. A missing ceiling tile left a gaping black hole to the elevator shaft. Harold looked at each corner for cameras out of habit, or maybe from a guilty conscience. The elevator had yet to move. His eyes darted to the black space in the ceiling, drawn to it. What was up there in the elevator's cavity?

Nothing but greasy cables and emergency ladders. And cold dark.

If there'd been buttons, he would have pressed the 2 again, maybe several times in a row. He tried to move the lever back to L, but it wouldn't budge.

He looked up again. Sure, this time, something lurked above, peering down at him through the square hole. Harold moved out from under it.

Still the elevator didn't move. It didn't have a red emergency button either. Just the cold brass lever. He tried it again to no avail.

A slight breeze wafted down from the ceiling. The kind of breeze made when someone walks by. His eyes jerked up to the patch of dark. Harold squinted. Was there something there? He swore there was. Something blocking the space now. Couldn't he see a faint light from somewhere in the shaft before?

The elevator doors opened with a ding that made Harold's butt cheeks clench. He gripped the handles of his duffel bag and backed out of the elevator with his eyes on that black hole.

Safely across the threshold, he turned around. Every other light down the hallway flickered. Half of them were out. Perhaps it was an illusion from the strobe effect, but the hall seemed to stretch much farther than the size of the hotel. Harold looked at the tag on his key and made his way down the hall to find his room.

The quiet of the place made his ears yearn for sound. Sure, it was after two in the morning, everyone would be asleep. But there was a complete lack of sound. No hum of electricity. Even the usual susurration of foot on carpet was absent. He looked down at the grimy, chaotic carpet pattern.

The hair on the back of his neck rose and he turned around. The only consistent light on the floor came from the two sconces flanking the elevator, which remained open. A creepy-crawly feeling came over him. There was something there, watching him. He walked backward down the hall, only glancing away from the elevator to check the room numbers by the doors. The flickering lights started to give him an ocular headache. He had to force his eyes to stay open. No blinking allowed.

As Sharzhad said, his room was all the way at the end of the hall.

Harold glanced away from the elevator to stick his key in the lock, then darted his eyes back to it. He turned the knob. The door creaked open on rusty hinges so loud after so much silence. At least he knew, now, he hadn't gone deaf.

The light right outside his room flickered.

Harold backed into his dark room and closed the door. He fumbled for a light switch, found one, and flicked it. The steady light, though sickly, was a relief. He threw the deadbolt and the privacy bar, just in case.

In case of what?

Whatever was in the elevator. The metal bar fell off the wall and thunked onto the threadbare carpet. Well, the deadbolt would have to be enough.

The room smelled of stale smoke. Two double beds took up the majority of the living space, along with a dresser topped with an old tube TV. The remote was nowhere to be seen. Between the beds sat a small table with a phone and a single drawer. Inside, he knew, would be a Bible. He had to check. Harold pulled the drawer open and took a step back.

No Bible.

For some reason, despite his lack of religion, this made his throat go dry. He swallowed hard, and when the dryness didn't go away, he went to the bathroom, turned on another sickly light, and drank directly from the tap. He let the water run for a few seconds, just to hear the sound, then turned it off.

The room was a little stuffy, so Harold pulled back the curtains to open a window, only to find a solid wall.

"What kind of crap is that?" he wondered aloud, if only to hear his own voice. Harold opened his duffel bag and pulled out his spit kit, then a folder, bent and creased and worn. After brushing his teeth—the bathroom was surprisingly spotless—he sat on the bed farthest from the door and opened the folder.

Inside were a collection of photos of women, stealthily taken from the shadows. Women who didn't know they could be seen from their windows. Women who cheated on husbands.

Harold always kept one photo from his cases for his file. For his scrapbook, he liked to joke to himself. Behind the stack of loose photos, in a manila envelope, were three pictures of his own wife. Or, ex-wife, given the circumstances.

Photo number one: Bent over while their neighbor pummeled her from behind.

Photo number two: Her frightened face with blood trickling from her temple, hand held aloft against her attacker.

Photo number three: Her lifeless eyes.

Harold had stowed the crowbar he bludgeoned her with in the traitorous neighbor's trashcan, then got the hell out of there.

"We had you over for barbecues," Harold remembered whispering as he watched the man fuck his wife. He remembered the scorn burning his conscience when the sight of them turned him on.

A single bang on the door brought Harold out of the dark memory with a start. He stared at the door, at the flickering foot shapes under the door. The handle jiggled.

The lights stayed constant outside the door, went out, and when they came back on, the foot-shadows were gone. Harold tucked the photos back into the envelope and folder. He stuffed them into his bag and went to the door. He peeked through the peephole. Only the cracked and crumbling plaster of the opposite wall peered back. He unlocked the door and cracked it open to listen. But all he could hear was the pounding of his own heart.

Harold returned to the bed, pushed off his shoes, and lay down. He rolled toward the nightstand and turned on the radio, tuned it to a non-station for the white noise, and clicked off the lamp.

He awoke to the sound of heavy, rapid footfalls in the hallway and someone pounding on the other doors. A glance at the clock told him it was now three in the morning. Three-oh-nine to be exact. The footfalls sounded again. More pounding. Closer this time. Maybe two doors down. His first thought was Sharzhad was waking everyone up to get them out because of some emergency.

Footsteps. Pounding. Harold turned on the lamp, pulled his shoes on, and gathered his things from the bathroom. If he had to leave at three in the morning it'd be for good. He'd get back on the road and put more distance between that bloody crowbar and himself.

Footsteps. Another loud bang on his door. The handle jiggled again like earlier in the night. More pounding and . . . was that scratching? Were they clawing to get in?

"Now hold on just a minute," he said, anger creeping into his voice.

He unlocked the door, threw it open, and stepped into the hall. A draft blew past him.

"What the hell—" No one was there.

Except the elevator. But elevators aren't *someones*.

Harold looked at the ceiling. Perhaps the sounds came from overhead. He went back inside, locked the door, and picked up the phone to call the front desk.

"Front desk," Sharzhad's sultry voice said. "How may I assist you, Mr. McCreed?"

"How did you know it was me?"

"Caller ID, sugar. Now, how may I help you?"

"Someone upstairs is running around pounding on doors. Hasn't anyone complained?"

Sharzhad's raucous laugh barked through the line. Harold flinched and pulled the phone away a few inches.

"Sugar, you are outta your mind. This motel is only two floors. Now unless someone is on the roof . . . are you sure you didn't have a bad dream or something?"

"What about the thirteenth floor?" Harold asked with a good amount of snide in his voice.

Sharzhad let out a girlish giggle. "I was just playin'. Motel industry joke."

Harold grumbled.

"If you're sufferin' from bad dreams, sugar, I can sell you something to help," she said. He could hear her wicked, nicotine-stained grin through the phone. See her fathomless eyes peering at him. He got that creepy sensation of being watched and glanced up at the ceiling, at the vent. There was a hotel once whose owner was a voyeur and installed boards in the ceiling, so he could spy on his customers.

"That won't be necessary. Thanks."

"Goodnight, Mr. McCreed." The line went dead. Harold replaced the receiver and lay back on his pillow. He stared at the texture on the ceiling until his vision started to double, then darken.

Right as he slipped to the edge of slumber, his cell phone rang. Harold grabbed it and answered.

"Do you have any idea what time it is?"

Ragged breathing replied.

"Very funny. Who is this?" He looked at the phone screen but didn't recognize the number. The line went dead.

Harold took a deep breath through his flared nostrils and let it out. He hung up, then dialed the number. Listened as the line connected. A digital ring in his ear. A real ring right above him. Digital ring. Real ring.

He jumped out of bed, grabbed the key from the dresser, and stomped into the hallway.

The elevator, its gaping black mouth, waited at the end of the hall. Harold swallowed. The anger drained out of him at the sight of that deep darkness.

He clenched his free hand into a fist and strode toward the steady lights flanking the elevator, climbed aboard, and pulled the accordion shut. He looked up at the black maw yawning over his head, then threw the lever to the right. To thirteen.

The elevator didn't move, but when Harold tried to pull it back to two, it wouldn't budge. He left the phone connected but pulled it away from his ear to listen for cables grinding or any indication the car moved.

Ten seconds went by. Twenty. His eyes were drawn

compulsively to the hole in the ceiling. To the darkness beyond.

Thirty seconds.

A full minute. The tinny digital ringing from the cell phone continued.

The collar of Harold's t-shirt seemed to tighten. A cold sweat broke out on his upper lip. He pressed himself into the corner farthest from the hole and kept his eyes on it.

There. Was that movement? The darkness seemed to shift and morph. He blinked hard.

Fourteen hours on the road would make a man crazy. Half of those hours were spent in a blood-spattered t-shirt. Once he got out of dodge, he pulled over at a vacant rest area and changed. He left the t-shirt in the trashcan, headed back the way he came for an hour, then circled around to the west.

A scratching sound perked his ears. His eyes jumped back to the gap in the ceiling. The scratch came again, and Harold realized it was his own finger scraping at something on the leg of his jeans. He looked down. A single drop of dried blood.

Without a ding, the elevator's outer door shuddered open. Harold peered out through the metal accordion. Same flickering lights. Same floor. But it wasn't, was it? The lighting was different. The colors were muted. It was like he'd stepped back into Kansas after being in the bright and cheery Land of Oz. Only Kansas was dead.

Now why'd you have to go and think that? A cold draft caressed his neck.

He wrestled the metal clap trap aside and leaped out.

A few feet clear of the elevator, he lifted the phone to his ear. It still rang. He listened out into the flickering darkness and heard the faint ring of a phone far down the hall.

The lights overhead buzzed in time with the flickers. The carpet shushed against his feet. Harold stopped outside the room where the ringing came from, hung up his cell phone, and put it in his pocket. He hit the door once as hard as he could, then jiggled the knob back and forth. Locked, of course.

But then, the door opened. A cold claw clamped around his balls. Thick darkness filled the room like some kind of living substance.

"Hello?" Harold whispered.

He needed to run back down the hall and return to the second floor, but he stood frozen outside this room with the door open into darkness. He had to leave, and soon. Whatever was in the room was going to come out and yell at him, or pound him to a pulp for bothering it in the middle of the night.

Harold couldn't leave. His legs trembled, and he fought to contain his bladder.

He had to leave. Now. Before it came out. Before—

The lights went out. Harold let out a short scream, then another when they didn't come back on right away. He fumbled his phone back out of his pocket.

The metal accordion rattled down the hall. Harold held his breath. The shudder of the exterior doors closed. Harold flipped the burner-phone-of-the-week open and let out a high laugh laced with hysteria at the insignificant amount of light the minuscule screen provided.

It almost made things worse.

If I can't see you, you can't see me.

The overhead lights buzzed back to life. The elevator was gone.

Harold ran down the hall and searched the wall for the button to call it back, but there wasn't one.

Sugar, this motel is only two floors.

The lights threatened to go out again, all flashing at once instead of taking turns. Harold cringed each time they darkened. He made his way down the hall again in an attempt to find the stairwell to get back to the second floor. Behind him, the elevator dinged. He turned and stared at it just a few yards down the hallway. The doors slid open. The accordion was already open.

The interior was black, like the interior of the room down the hall. A living darkness. His ears strained to hear if something was inside. A soft shifting sound. No. Just his hand again, scratching at the blood on his pants. The lightbulbs in the sconces popped and went out. Harold backed away from the dark mouth.

The set of flickering fluorescents just outside the elevator flickered once, then stayed dark. Something did shift in the darkness. A sliding sort of sound. The sound dragging something through grass might make.

Harold lurched to the first door and pounded on it, tried the door knob. Locked. The next set of lights went out. He moved to the next door. Then the next. Pounding on each one. Testing the doorknobs. All locked. No one was home.

The darkness followed.

When Harold reached the door at the end of the hall, he pounded his fist against it. Someone was inside, he knew, they opened the door before. The lights right overhead flicked out, came back on. He jiggled the doorknob. Locked. The lights went out. Harold clawed at the door, then sank to the floor. He curled into a ball against whatever attack might come from whatever thing slithered down the hall.

The door opened. Harold jumped up and ran inside, despite the darkness within. He tripped over the first bed, fumbled his way around the second, and cowered in the corner. The door clicked shut and locked.

He bit his knuckles to contain the whimper trying to erupt. He pulled his knees to his chest and covered his head with one arm. He rocked in the blackness.

After an eternity passed with no incident, Harold got to his hands and knees. He found the edge of the curtain and pulled it back. No window. Just like in his room on the second floor. He searched his memory for the lighting situation in his room. There was a lamp on the table between the beds.

Harold crawled along the end of the bed, turned the corner, and reached out for the table. His hands found something cold. He jerked back with a gasp, then lunged for the table and the lamp. He clicked it on.

On the floor at his feet was a crowbar. *The* crowbar. On the bed, the pictures from his folder. On top lay the one of his wife's dead eyes.

The lamp flickered.

Harold stared into the eyes in the photo. A sickening

sadness welled within his gut. He sank to his knees and picked up the picture.

"I'm sorry, Lori. I'm so sorry," he said. He had to turn himself in. It was the only way to escape this. He grabbed the phone. It started to ring before he could even dial.

"Do you have any idea what time it is?" His own voice asked. Harold only breathed into the line. Too shocked to say anything. "Very funny. Who is this?"

He dropped the phone back onto the receiver. A second later, the phone rang. A sob erupted from his throat.

The crow bar lay at his feet. He picked it up and touched the hooked end with his thumb.

HAROLD LAY on the ground in front of the gas station convenience store. A vehicle pulled up. He didn't look. He'd stopped looking years ago.

The whores started giggling. Harold turned his head. He sat up. It was finally who he'd been waiting for.

He watched a younger version of himself contemplate going into the store. Harold in the brown coat rolled to a standing position and stumbled over to Harold in the fresh shirt. His eyes darted to the single spot of blood on younger Harold's jeans.

"What's the matter, mister?" One of the whores said to the younger Harold. "Not lookin' for a good time?"

When the Harold from the truck turned, the Harold in the brown coat pointed at the motel. Harold from the truck turned to follow the pointing finger. When he turned back, Harold in the brown coat tried to speak.

The other Harold's eyes shifted downward, probably to the scar on Harold's throat. A mangled mess of a scar. The crow bar hadn't been sharp enough for the job, and he'd lost his will.

Don't go in there. Run away, and keep running, he tried to say. Only clicking and creaking sounds came out.

"Thanks," the other Harold said, and offered him a five-dollar bill.

THE REPLACEMENTS

Published in the Rock 'n' Roll is Dead *anthology by*
Bloodbound Books

MOREY GRIGSBY DID NOT BELIEVE IN BODY replacement. He did not believe a person needed a new body every five to ten years, nor did he believe that his would crap out on him. On his thirtieth birthday, however, he looked like he was ninety.

"Damn pollutants," he muttered, combing the thin white hair over his bald spot. "Stupid planet killers." He stuffed his partial denture into his mouth, clicking it into place. He showed his teeth at his reflection, leaned forward to examine a brown spot on his semitranslucent skin. "Damn stupid ignoramuses."

"Honey," his wife, Celia, now on her fourth body though she was only five years older than him, poked her head into the bathroom. "I think it's time." He knew by the look on her face that she despised him because he looked so old.

"No, never," Morey shook his head. "I refuse," he said. He believed diet and exercise would prolong his body's life, and though he was tired of hooking himself up to machines to live through the night, he did not want to trade in his body for someone else's. Because that's what the replacement was: Someone else's body.

The replacement bodies were harvested by means of cloning aborted fetuses and genetically altering them, so they would not grow brains. With no brain, there is no mind. With no mind, the person technically isn't a person. Just a body. They were hooked up to complicated machines to keep them alive, so the organs would continue to function, and the muscles wouldn't atrophy.

The brain of the person seeking a replacement was removed and implanted into the new body. The old bodies were recycled back into the system, the cells used once again to create clones of that body. Morey did not want someone else's mind floating around in his body, clone or not.

Celia looked at Morey with her large blue eyes filling with tears. He hated her large blue eyes. He missed his real wife. The wife he fell in love with. The dark-skinned beauty with big, round dark chocolate eyes. He didn't like this blonde, tan-skinned, perfect Celia. And though she claimed to be the same Celia, she just wasn't.

"Why did you get a white woman's body?" he asked her, looking at her in the mirror.

She shrugged and sighed when he glared at her. "Hurry home after work," she said. "I have a birthday surprise for you." She smiled at him but didn't meet his eyes and the smile was gone as she turned and left the doorway.

Morey got dressed for work and made his way to the office, daydreaming on the bus ride about his dark-skinned wife who was no more while his eyes scanned the paper.

As usual, he ignored the disgusted looks from the other passengers. He was used to them pointing at him, whispering behind their hands. Judging him. He glanced sideways at a woman who was obviously staring. She looked a little green.

"Take a picture," Morey muttered. He turned his head slightly toward the woman. She leaned away from him, taken aback, then got up and moved to a different seat. Morey chuckled. Served her right to be staring at him like that. He returned his gaze to the newspaper in his lap.

When the bus screeched to a stop, he looked up.

Out the front window, looking at the bus driver through the windshield, waving her arms and kicking the bus was Celia. Not the blonde, tan one, but the original dark beauty. Morey gasped. His heart fluttered, and he feared it would go out on him. He pounded his chest and jumped to his feet, his knees protesting. The bus started to move after the woman, his real Celia, stomped across the street.

"Stop the bus!" Morey called. He gripped the handrail as the driver slammed on the brakes again and turned to look at him. "Thank you," Morey said. He shuffled down the aisle as fast as he could and made his way down the three steps onto the pavement. The bus took off, blasting pollutants in his face. He held his breath until the black cloud disappeared.

The woman was just entering the hotel across the street. He wanted to call out to her, but he knew her name likely wasn't Celia. Instead, he made his way across the street and followed her inside.

She stood at the counter at the coffee stand in the lobby. The same body, the same woman, the same beautiful eyes. When she laughed, tossing her head back, flinging her long black hair behind her, he saw she had the same crooked front tooth, and her eyes crinkled in the exact same way his original Celia's had. His heart pounded, and he clutched his chest.

"Don't give out on me now," he muttered to himself, tapping his breast bone.

She turned, her eyes widened, and she gasped. "I've never seen such an old body," she said, then demurely covered her mouth with her fingertips. "I'm so sorry," she said. "Sometimes I say things without thinking."

"That's okay," Morey said. He cleared his throat when his voice came out scratchy and old, but he knew it wouldn't do any good. His body was old. That was a fact. "I'm Morey," he said, holding out his hand.

"Tanya," the woman replied. She gently took his hand and stared at it as she shook it. "How old are you?" She asked.

"Thirty today," said Morey. "This is my original body."

"Wow," Tanya said. "Happy birthday." She still held

his hand and turned it, examining the hair on his knuckles, the brown spots dappling his thin, loose skin. "Why haven't you gotten a replacement?" She asked.

Morey didn't know how to answer the question.

"I wanted to see how long this one would last," he said with a smile. His partial popped out and fell into his mouth, exposing his three missing teeth. He covered his mouth with his hand while he worked it back into place. He thought Tanya would be disgusted, but she laughed and moved his hand away.

"You have missing teeth!" she said. "That's so amazing. Let me see."

Morey pulled the partial out, cupping it in his palm, and smiled.

"How'd you lose them?" She asked.

"Boxing," he told her with a lisp. It was sort of true. Really, he got in a drunken fight when he was in his early twenties.

The barista behind the counter slid a cup of coffee to the middle of the counter. "Coffee's done," the girl said. "Ten ninety-five."

"Let me get that," Morey said. He fumbled in his back pocket for his wallet and pulled out a twenty. "Keep the change," he told the girl.

"Thanks, Morey," Tanya said, smiling her imperfect smile. Morey thought if he was a cartoon his pupils would be hearts beating out of his eyeballs. She cleared her throat. "Are you busy right now?"

"Nope!" Morey said without thought. Of course, he was busy. He was on his way to work, but he felt like she was going to ask him to have breakfast with her.

"Can you help me with something?" She asked.

"Yep!" Morey said smiling uncontrollably.

Tanya took his hand and led him to the elevators. "I'm starting a business," she said as the car zoomed up five floors. "You seem like the perfect candidate to test my skills on."

"What kind of business?" Morey asked.

"You'll see," Tanya said with a coy chuckle. The doors opened with a ding and she led him down the hall to the right. "This is my room," she said.

"I can wait in the hall, if you'd like." Morey said.

Tanya giggled. "No, please, come in," she said. She slipped the key card into the door and opened it.

The room was a standard hotel room. King size bed, smallish bathroom, a dresser with a television. A round table stood in a corner with a chair that didn't match. Tanya deposited her purse there and turned to face Morey.

"Take off your clothes," she said.

Morey choked on his own spit, flinging himself into a hacking and coughing fit. He pounded on his chest. Good God, she wanted him. This was way better than breakfast. To be with his Celia again? To ravage her like he had when they first got married just five years ago. Oh, to caress her round, firm butt. To gaze into her eyes and know the woman looking back at him loved him maybe more than he loved her.

He could hardly contain himself, but he wasn't sure he heard her right. He coughed again, a long phlegmy, face-reddening cough.

When he had himself under control, he looked at her with raised eyebrows. "What?"

"I said, take. Off. Your clothes." She raised an eyebrow and undid the top button of her blouse.

"What is your business?" Morey asked, reaching for his belt buckle.

"Sex." Tanya said.

Morey's heart fluttered again, and he cleared his throat several times. Was she serious? She unbuttoned the next button on her blouse, and the next.

How many men had she used Celia's body with? Morey's excitement faltered. But, it wasn't really the real Celia, he reminded himself. Just a cloned version. He could pretend it was his real Celia. That would work. He would pretend.

As Tanya undid the last button, Morey glimpsed her beautiful breasts under a thin cotton bra. He fumbled with unbuckling his belt and untucking his shirt, while slipping off his shoes. Tanya giggled again and moved closer. "Let me help," she said, dropping to her knees. She looked up at him as she pulled his belt free and unzipped his pants.

"Oh my," she said with wide eyes. She smiled up at him.

When it was all over, they lay next to each other, silent save for Morey's wheezing. Disappointment filled him. It wasn't Celia. Of course, it wasn't Celia. It was just a clone of her body. Nothing felt the same, nothing even looked the same. She didn't do the things Celia used to do. She didn't move in unison with him, she didn't even look at him. In fact, the more he thought about it, he wasn't even sure she really looked anything like his original Celia. Was her skin that dark? Had her eyes had that slight upward slant?

He stared at the ceiling trying to calm his breathing. Tanya pulled him back to the moment with a breathy laugh.

"I can't believe you're still in your original body," she said. She rolled over onto her stomach and drew circles in his white chest hair. She fingered a withered, saggy nipple. "My body gave out when I was eighteen," she said. "This is my first replacement. It's only a year old but I'm kind of getting tired of it already."

Morey wanted to tell her she looked like his wife, that he wished his wife had never changed bodies, but instead he asked her, "were you black originally?"

Tanya nodded.

"My wife . . ." he started and mentally smacked himself.

Tanya smiled. "That's okay," she said. "You're not the first married client I've had. Most of them are married, actually."

"Oh, right," Morey said. The disappointment flared again. Why did he ever think this imposter in his wife's body would be anything like his Celia? "How much do I owe you?" His voice was small and choked.

"Three thousand," she said, sitting up. "But I'll give you fifty percent off. Consider it a senior citizen discount." She giggled. "Fifteen-hundred." She smiled and held out her hand.

Morey swallowed hard. "Do you take a credit card?"

Tanya nodded.

After the transaction was complete and Morey had his clothing and belongings together, she walked him down to the lobby.

"I'm always here," she said. "In case you get lonely." She brushed her lips across his and sauntered away. Morey sighed, then pounded on his chest again to get his heart beating. He watched her board the elevator.

"I'm an idiot," he whispered.

Later that day after work, Morey stepped into the house feeling heavy like the day was smashing him into the ground. He thought of Tanya, of the sex. Disgust filled him, turning his stomach. His shoulders sagged, and he closed his eyes.

In the designer kitchen, a martini sat on the granite counter. He smiled and took a sip. Perfect. She may not look like the woman he fell in love with, but Celia could make a mean martini.

"Morey, is that you?" Celia called from the other room. Morey sighed and made his way to the living room. Celia lay on the black leather sofa in a white negligee embellished with marabou boas. "This is the first part of your surprise," she said with a wink and a smile full of perfect teeth.

"I'm not in the mood," Morey said. The guilt. He couldn't even look at her. He shuffled past her to the bathroom, martini in hand. Celia followed him.

"But it's your birthday," she said.

"Yeah, and I would like to be left alone." Morey told her, not meeting her eyes. Guilt mingled with the disgust and disappointment.

Celia pouted, stomped her foot, and swirled away

toward the bedroom. He heard her slamming dresser drawers and throwing things. He shook his head and went to calm her.

"I'm sorry, Celia," he said. She was halfway out of her lingerie, sitting on the edge of the bed.

"You don't love me anymore." She crossed her arms. She wiped furiously at a tear.

"Yes, I do," Morey said. He sat next to her and put his arms around her. "I don't love your new body, but I still love you."

She pulled away.

"It's the mind that matters," he told her, trying to convince himself of this. "It's you in there, just not out here."

"Is that why you slept with her?" Celia asked, her voice clipped.

Morey coughed and hacked. He pounded on his chest. "What?"

"You know what I said, and you know what I mean," her voice was all venom. Her eyes cut into him when she looked at him through her lashes. She stood and stomped to the dresser, jerked open the top drawer and pulled out a piece of paper. It was an email. "The credit card company sent me an email about a suspicious charge," she said. "Hookers Anonymous? Really, Morey?"

"I-I'm sorry?" He didn't know what else to say. His whole body flushed, heating him. He felt hot and sticky and slightly tingly.

"I knew it was true. How could you?" Celia shrieked. "Fifteen hundred dollars?" She threw the paper at him, but it drifted to the floor. She turned away. Morey sat still, feeling stupid and horrible. Her shoulders trembled. He thought she must be crying, but a wicked laugh cackled from her throat. When she turned around, she was smiling.

"Drink up, Morey," she said. He looked at the martini, nearly gone, the olives not even covered by the clear liquid. "Your other surprise is waiting." The smile disappeared. Her eyes tightened and took on a malicious gleam.

Morey dropped the glass. Not on purpose. His hand stopped working. His arm dropped to his side. A numb tingling spread up his arm and across his chest. His heart, oh God his heart was finally going out. But no, it was still beating. He could feel it in his pulse points. He fell backward onto the bed, then slid off when his legs gave out. He crumbled onto the floor, frozen in place. Only his eyes could move. He looked up at Celia standing over him. Her cell phone was at her ear.

"Come and get him," she said. "Bring the ambulance, I'll pay extra for expedited service." She left the room.

"Celia!" He cried. "What did you do to me?"

Celia came back in and crouched next to his head. "I'm getting you a new body for your birthday," she said, petting his hair. "You see, I don't love this old disgusting thing anymore," she stuck her lips out, cocked her head. "But that shouldn't matter, right?" She patted his head and stood up. "It's all about the mind, not the body."

"No," he croaked. "No, I don't want a new body, this one is fine!"

The doorbell rang. Celia bent and kissed his forehead

and ran to get it, tossing on a silk robe on her way out the bedroom door. Two men came in with a stretcher.

"His body just gave out, but his mind is still good," she said. "Let's get him to the hospital."

"No, I'm fine!" Morey shouted. "She drugged me! There's nothing wrong with me! I'm drugged!"

"There, there, sweetheart," she said.

Morey cried and shouted, he struggled to even just struggle but his body would not move.

"You have to believe me," he yelled. "She drugged me! There's nothing wrong with me!"

"Don't listen to him. His body is old. It's affecting his mind, he's out of it!" Celia shouted. Her perfect brows were low and brooding.

"We'll get him into a new body as soon as we can," one of them said. As they wheeled Morey out to the ambulance, he overheard Celia say, "No, that won't be necessary" before the doors slammed shut.

What did she mean it won't be necessary? She said she was getting him a new body, had she not? He tried to scream but his vocal cords broke. He called out to Celia, to anyone who would listen, but no sound came from his throat.

At the hospital, Morey was wheeled into a room. The doctors gave him a sedative. He fought with all his might to stay awake, but they pumped more into him and finally he passed out.

When he came to, he was staring at their four-poster bed. Celia lay asleep. Everything was very quiet. Silent. She rolled over and sat up. No sound. No rustling of sheets. Good Lord, was he deaf? He tried to move an arm to wiggle a finger in his ear, but he couldn't move. Perhaps the drug hadn't worn off yet. He wondered what his new body looked like and wanted to cry. There was nothing wrong with his old body.

Then it hit him. If he was staring at their bed, was he sitting on the dresser? He tried to look around to figure out where he was, but again, nothing came of it.

Celia got up and stretched. He tried to speak, but no sound came out. In fact, he couldn't feel his lips. She approached the dresser, her mouth moved but no sound came out. She laughed. He knew it was that fake, high-pitched laugh she did because she held her hand against her chest. She bent over slightly, her eyes on whatever her hands were doing. Morey could see down her nightgown into her cleavage.

When she stood up, she held a note up to his eyes.

"I hope you slept well," it read. She reached toward him, and he started to move, his vision jostled about. She was taking him somewhere, but . . . how? She wasn't strong enough to carry him. She stopped and walked around behind him. His line of sight turned ever so slow. The edge of the bathroom came into view. The doorway, the towels, the mirror.

If Morey had a throat and new vocal cords he would have screamed. Celia wasn't carrying him. Oh no, she wasn't. She was pushing him on a cart. All that remained of Morey was a square container with a brain and eyes. The eyes were held steady with hooks attached to the mouth of the container, which sat in the center of a cart inside fluids to keep it supple. Positioned around the jar were machines pumping oxygen and blood into and out of his brain.

Celia held up another note. "I thought about cutting off your dick," it said. "But decided this was a much better alternative."

She tossed her head back and laughed.

Morey heard silence.

GLORIA'S TEARS

I was in love with Gloria Marks, the girl from Wednesday night art class. I never really talked to her much, because she wore head phones in class. Sometimes I nodded to her when she looked at me. She usually smiled and continued painting.

She was gorgeous with long, luminous auburn hair and sparkling green eyes. She was short, and slender, and always wore knee-high boots of some variety. One night she looked like Robin Hood, wearing green tights and worn, brown leather boots. She always wore a scarf, no matter what the weather was like outside, and she carried a large, slouchy purse where she stowed her art supplies.

I felt like we belonged together. Some cosmic pull that guided me to sit next to her every Wednesday. It took me almost six months to ask her, I mean, who would want to date me?

I'm the nerdy kid in art class that paints impressionistic art that sucks. Finally, one night before class I asked her if she wanted to go for coffee afterward.

"Class ends at eight, I'd be up all night!" She covered her mouth with her hand as she laughed. I took her hand.

"Don't cover it, you're—" My voice caught in my throat, and I cleared it. "Beautiful."

We went for coffee after class, and yes, we were up all night, sitting on the plush carpet in her living room, talking about art, love, relationships. We even talked about death, of all things.

"I'm not afraid to die," Gloria said, handing me a plate of chocolate pie. "Not at all."

"Why's that?" I dug into the pie. It was heaven.

"Well, I feel that I live every day to its fullest, so if I did die, I have no regrets." She smiled with chocolate in her teeth. "What about you? Are you afraid to die?"

I was terrified of dying. "No."

We finished our pie in silence. Gloria took the plates to the kitchen and when she came back, she dropped to the floor next to me and kissed me. She tasted like chocolate pie.

The next morning, Gloria was gone before I got up. She left a key on the counter with detailed instructions on what to do with it.

1. Pick up key
2. Go to door
3. Open door
4. Walk out
5. Turn around, close door
6. Put key in lock
7. Turn key
8. Put key in pocket
9. Call me later

I smiled.

When I called her later, she didn't remember giving me the key or our night together.

THE FOLLOWING WEDNESDAY, I saw her in class. She approached me with a confused expression on her face.

"You didn't call me," she said.

"Yes, I did," I told her. "You didn't remember me." I handed her the key to her place.

"What's this?" she asked.

"The key you gave me."

"What does it open?" She asked, turning the key in her hands.

"Your front door." I should have checked my tone. Her mouth fell open and her eyes grew wide. She shook her head slightly and regained her composure.

"What did we do?" she asked in a small voice. She looked at her hands, fiddling with a hang nail.

"We stayed up most of the night talking," I said.

A tear dripped onto her hand. I raised her chin with a finger and wiped a second tear from her cheek.

"What did we talk about?" she asked with a thick voice.

"Tons of stuff," I said with a smile. "It was the best night of my life."

"I'm so sorry." Her face contorted with sadness. "I shouldn't have done that."

"Shouldn't have done what?" I asked.

She sniffled hard and took my hand. "Let's go sit down somewhere." She pulled me into a closet in the art wing and sat on an overturned bucket. I sat on a step stool.

"I black out," she said. "Whenever I have strong feelings, I black out and I don't remember things that happen."

"Oh." I looked at the toes of her boots.

"I don't know what happened the other night, but I remember writing a note for you to call me," she said. "I must have felt something powerful or the situation caused some sort of stress, and my brain blacked it out."

"But you were still moving, you were still conscious." My heart beat hard. She didn't remember, she really didn't remember our kiss, or . . . the other stuff. It was all a blank space in her mind.

She shrugged her shoulders and looked down. Her face contorted again.

"I don't feel anything," she cried. "Because whenever I start to, my brain blocks it from my memory." She full out bawled into her hands at this.

I held her close and pet her hair that smelled like raspberries and champagne.

"We'll get through this," I said. "I still want to be part of your life."

I did some research and told Gloria that I thought maybe she couldn't remember because a lot of memory has to do with the emotions we feel when experiencing them. I didn't find anything on why her brain seemed to turn off when she experienced the feelings but tried to link emotions back to her childhood. Gloria couldn't remember much of her childhood, she thought because it was so full of good emotions. She was wrong.

A letter came from her mother a week after. It was a note that explained everything. It was one that started: *If you're reading this, I am dead.*

Gloria let out a small gasp as she started to read it, and one by one, tears began to slip down her cheeks. I was in the kitchen chopping vegetables for a stir-fry, but I could see her on the couch. Her hand went to her lips.

When she was done, she crumpled the letter and threw it hard, then fell back against the couch and cried.

I rushed to her side.

"My mom . . . Is dead." She gasped for air. "I was—" Tears started anew.

"What?" I asked, once again.

She pointed to the letter. I picked it up, straightened it out and read.

Her mother explained that Gloria was adopted at birth. I read further and gasped, just as Gloria had.

I knew he was doing it, and I didn't stop him. If he could get it from you, it kept him from asking for it from me.

My stomach turned, and anger burned in my heart. How could a mother, adoptive or not, allow a grown man to molest a young child? I didn't know what to say, so I crumpled the letter and threw it against the wall. Then I picked it back up and burned it.

"Where is your adoptive father?" I asked her.

Gloria was quiet now, her head shaking back and forth slowly, her eyes red-rimmed. "Dead," she said in a whisper, staring at nothing.

After about an hour, in which tears continued to slide down her cheeks, she finally looked at me.

"Why am I crying?" She wiped her eyes, took a deep breath, and stood up. "Aren't you making stir-fry?"

I didn't tell her about the letter, but it explained everything.

A year went by. We moved in together after three months, talked about marriage, but Gloria didn't want to get married.

"I won't remember it anyway." She plucked a grape from a vine and tossed it into her mouth. "Besides, we're happy like this, aren't we?" She held up a journal that I told her to write in. She could look back and read about the high emotional incidents we shared. Sometimes I wrote them for her, so she could read my viewpoint. I got the idea from a movie with Adam Sandler and Drew Barrymore. She flipped open the book, and I watched her eyes scan across the page. They got wider and wider, and then her mouth dropped open again. She looked up at me.

"I remember this," she said. She turned the book toward me. It was an entry from a month ago when I asked her to marry me.

I laughed. "You crushed me, Gloria!" I said. I had written that entry for her. The ring I had given her sparkled on her ring finger.

"I said, a lifelong engagement would suffice," she said. That wasn't in the book. "I love you," she said suddenly. After a year, she had never said it, telling me she didn't know if she did or not. Finally, she knew.

I grabbed a pen and started writing down what had just happened. Gloria gave me things to say, her feelings, how it was all so overpowering. Then she stopped talking.

I looked at her. Her eyes were glazed over, she looked through me, not at me. Suddenly, they rolled up into her head and she dropped to the floor.

"Gloria!" I shouted. I went to her side and held her while she trembled in my arms. "Oh, God, Gloria!"

The ambulance came, and I followed it to the hospital. Waiting during a time like this was torture. What happened to her? What was going to come of it? Would she remember me? The event we just shared?

A doctor came out of the ER and approached me.

"She's stable," he said with a grim expression. "It won't be long, though."

"What?" I asked. "What won't be long?"

"She has a tumor in her brain," the doctor explained. "You can go in and see her."

"Can't you do surgery?" I asked, flabbergasted. I didn't know what to say. I felt a panic welling in my chest, causing my heart to beat in my throat. My breathing quickened. My nose burned with tears. "Well?"

The doctor's lips tightened, his brow creased for a moment, and he shook his head. "We did everything we could, but it's in a place that is too dangerous to get to. We would have to sever connections in her brain that would leave her in a vegetative state the rest of her life." He touched my shoulder. "She doesn't want that. I'm very sorry." He walked away.

I went to Gloria's side. She looked like she had aged twenty years in an hour. Her skin was pale, her hair has lost its luster. I sat down and took her hand.

"I love you." She gave me a weak smile.

I squeezed her hand, trying to control my tears. "The doctor said you don't have long."

"Shh," Gloria said. "I know." She took a deep breath and swallowed hard. "I can feel, now." She said. "I can feel the emotions of my past welling up inside." A tear leaked onto her pillow. "At first, they were all bad feelings, they must have been from my childhood. But now," she smiled and caressed my cheek. I pressed my face into her palm. "All I feel is happiness." Her eyes twinkled. "And this overwhelming feeling that I don't know what it is, but it has to be love."

I cried against her hand.

"Don't worry," she said to me. "I'm not scared."

"I know," I said. "You told me a long time ago you aren't afraid to die."

"I know." She smiled. "I remember."

A SICKNESS LIKE NO OTHER

I AM SICK. THIS SICKNESS I SPEAK OF ISN'T SOME incurable disease, like cancer or the common cold. It is beyond that. It's like, well, let me give you an example.

I was walking down the street one day, and a thought occurred to me that the rubbish bins were conspiring against me. They weren't talking out loud, but telepathically, and somehow my brain had been transmitted over into their telepathic channel. They were talking about rejecting anything I tried to throw away or tipping over as I walked by. They snickered and snorted, and when I covered my ears and tried to clear my mind they got louder and louder. The laughter penetrated my brain.

Someone touched my shoulder, a youngish looking woman, and said something, but the trashcans were so loud, I didn't hear what she said, and she scrambled away as if I were bleeding from my eyes. And indeed, I was.

I'm not sure why these episodes occur, but it wasn't the first time and it wouldn't be the last. The telephone booths and newspaper stands did the same. Laughed at me, threatened to get me into trouble. Giggle, snide, and jeer until my spleen felt as though it would burst and spill precious fluids onto the ground.

I remember, in horrific detail, the first incident in which the chortling and remarks came from the objects around me; I was at the bank.

I had a check in hand ready to deposit, and I heard someone to my left comment on the style of my jacket, and another about the way I walked. They all made fun of me. I turned and addressed a young man with a pierced lip and asked him to repeat himself. He told me he had asked if I wanted to go ahead of him. I smiled awkwardly and thanked him. Then it came again, only from the other direction.

"Look at that styoooopid hat, Aha! Aha ha ha ha ha!!!" A vicious cackling that set my teeth grinding. I looked at a small, mousy woman who smiled at me. She couldn't possibly have said that. It was a deeper, masculine voice, rough and obnoxious. A voice and a laugh that made me want to beat my skull against the counter.

"Over here!" I heard and then a whole chorus of them. No one around me was talking, and that's when I knew. It was the chairs, the pens, the piles of goddamned deposit slips. I grabbed my ears and they kept on. They laughed at me as I ran outside. Then the telephone booths joined in, and the traffic lights and the trash bins and everything!

People's briefcases, newspapers, they all laughed, and I dropped to my knees crying and screaming, deafened by the incessant jeering. I looked at my hands, covered in blood and I thought I was dying. I was convinced it was seepage from my bleeding brain.

The shrieks of hideous laughter did not cease until I reached my lightly furnished apartment three blocks away. As I closed the door, a few jabs at my masculinity ensued from a lone armchair, which I hastily threw across the room. My own furniture had turned against me.

My apartment was void of furnishings by morning, and at last, my aching skull had a silent break from the insanity of the streets. The only thing I kept were the appliances, which hadn't started in on me yet. They didn't seem to hate me as much, or at least they didn't tell me. Perhaps they would stay faithful.

My sickness, as anyone can clearly tell, isn't quite the type of sickness one might think of when the word is used. My doctors tell me to get more sleep or take a vacation. How can I when my seat on the plane would laugh at my very existence? And sleep, I only wish I could. My back is tormented by the hard wood floor. I'd tossed my bed out, you know, and I haven't the courage to purchase an air mattress. It would most likely taunt me in my sleep, if I could indeed sleep knowing an 'outsider' was inside my apartment. That's what I called *them*. Outsiders. And knowing they could not get in was the greatest comfort.

It happened about two weeks after I had been locked inside what I now refer to as my sanctuary. I heard a titter, a giggle, and before I knew it, the blender and coffee pot were in on it too. I tried hard to ignore them, I tried to tell them to shut up, but it made them double their efforts. Mocking me with shrill, taunting voices.

I ran to the bathroom, certain there would be blood pouring from my eyes, I could feel it. But there was none. My face was perfectly normal, aside from the dark circles under my eyes and weeks forth of beard growth for lack of shaving. I rubbed my eyes and looked at my hands, blood. Blood all over my fingertips. I snatched a look in the mirror again, no blood. Was my mirror, too good for words, distorting my own image of myself in the reflective surface?

I laughed at myself. The whole thing was ludicrous. Inanimate objects couldn't talk, or laugh or shout, "Hey, you stupid fuck face!" as you scuttle down the sidewalk.

I laughed, and it felt good to laugh. I threw my head back and opened my mouth as wide as I could and out poured the loudest laugh that could ever exist. My soul was insatiable, I kept laughing. I laughed so hard I had to sit on the floor. I laughed until I pissed my pants, and then kept on laughing at having done so.

I laughed at how I laughed, I laughed at how suddenly I didn't feel so alone, that maybe *I* was one of *them*. I crawled, laughing, into the kitchen and placed my hands on the counter and laughed into the faces of the blender and then into the coffee pot and then the microwave, and the stove.

I laughed until I realized I was laughing alone, and when I stopped, just as abruptly as I had started, they were whispering.

They whispered that I was crazy. That I needed help and they should call someone. They whispered about how they didn't realize I was like them, one of them. They whispered and whispered until their whispering was an unbearable hiss in my ear. I screamed at them to shut up, and for once they listened. I told them how it was going to be. How they would shut the hell up and quit bothering me. I screamed, nothing really, just yelled as loud as I could, and not a peep from them. They had been silenced.

I got the nerve to go outside after the appliances in the sanctuary had learned that I was in control. As I stepped out of my apartment, I heard a single voice.

"Excuse me."

"SHUT UP!" I screamed into the face of a lovely young woman. She cringed and started to hurry away, but I stopped her. "I'm sorry, I'm under a lot of stress." I tried to keep it simple to avoid having to explain everything, although I wanted to tell everyone about my accomplishment. How *I* was now in control of *them*!

"I heard you screaming, are you all right?" she asked me, standing halfway down the hall.

"Yes, I am just wonderful!" I clicked my heels and started down the hall as well. As I passed her, I tipped my hat and grinned. A grin that would soon fall flat. For as I stepped outside, there was not a soul on the street. Not a car, not a sound. It was eerily quiet, and very still. No breeze at all. A gray sky blotted out the sun.

A panic welled inside my chest. My heart pounded, and my breath quickened.

"Where is everyone?" I yelled as loud as I could. Then they started up again. Yes, *them*. The ones who took away my sanity. They all spoke at once, like one giant rehearsed 'surprise!' for someone's secret party, but they didn't yell surprise.

The people didn't jump out with streamers and pointy hats. They didn't even sound excited, but morbidly harsh. They, all at once, screamed, "they are dead!" and then they laughed.

They all sounded different, it was a jumble of mixed laughter. Crazy loud laughter, giggles, chuckles, chortles, my head was full of laughter, and I could do nothing but stare at the emptiness of the streets and sidewalks. I ran back inside and there she lay.

The wonderful woman who asked, who cared, if I was all right or not. The stranger from somewhere inside my building. A stranger who cared. Lifeless on the maroon carpet of the hall, her golden curls caressing her face like angel wings.

She was dead.

Nothing brutal, nothing hated, but dead as if the life was sucked from her lips. I ran to the other apartments and beat on doors, yelling to let me in. I kicked open a couple and saw the inhabitants all lying mercilessly dead. I was the last one. I was the only one left. *They* had done this. The inanimate objects. I ran back inside the sanctuary and called a random number. No one answered. I tried another, again, no answer. I called 911, and a voice picked up.

"Hello, Horace," it said. "They are all gone." and the line died, too. I slammed my phone down and no sooner had I done so than it rang.

"Hello?" I asked abruptly. "Who is this? Hello?"

Nothing, silence. But whoever was on the other end

was breathing, so I knew they were there. "Are you all right?" a voice asked. It sounded like the woman who lay in the hall. I dropped the phone and ran into the hall once again. She was gone. I ran to the fourth door down, taking a wild guess that that would be her apartment. I knocked greedily, and the door opened.

"Can I help you?" It was her. She was alive.

They all had to be alive again. I laughed hysterically and grabbed my hair. I knew my eyes were bleeding but didn't care because I wasn't sure if it was visible on the outside or not.

I wandered aimlessly down the hall, bumping into the walls, stumbling and almost falling. I went outside, and it was all normal.

Everyone was there, the cars, the street kids, the businessmen. They were all there, but not *them*.

The ones who taunted me were silent. I started to laugh again, a laugh that pasted 'lunatic' across my forehead in bold, capital letters. Someone had called an ambulance and the paramedics pushed passed me to get inside. I stayed on the front steps of the apartment building, and when they came back out, the stretcher had a body on it, sheet covering the thing and all.

A gust of wind picked the sheet up and flapped it back. I screamed.

I screamed as loud as I could. I screamed and clawed at the body, at the paramedics. I screamed until my throat hurt and I couldn't breathe.

They were loading *me* into the ambulance.

They were taking *me* away.

I was dead. Dead and gone. Just like everyone else.

THE INTERRUPTED AUTOPSY

"IT WAS JUST A DOG BITE," DR. MORRISON'S VOICE said.

"So, why did he die?" Dr. Worthing asked.

They spoke in hushed tones. Dr. Clempta listened and wondered why he couldn't see them. He was laying on a cold, hard surface. Who they were talking about?

"Poor Dr. Clempta," Worthing mumbled.

Clempta tried to sit up. He tried to open his eyes. He tried to tell them he wasn't dead.

Something drew a cold line from shoulder to sternum on both sides of his torso, and one long line down to his pubic bone, he screamed inside telling them he was alive. In his mind, he bucked and knocked the doctors away, but really, he lay still in the icy room, panic gripping his insides and twisting them together.

"I'm hungry," Worthing said. "Should we break for lunch?"

"Break?" Morrison asked. "We just started!"

"I know. But I haven't had anything since breakfast."

"Fine. Help me spring the ribcage first."

Spring? Ribcage? His body vibrated as the blaring whir of a saw touched down and forced its way through his sternum. He felt pulled apart as his ribs cracked in protest to the rib cage spreader. But he felt nothing.

"See you in a few," Worthing said. The door shushed open.

Clempta heard the metallic clinking of surgical tools. He yelled out in his mind, shouting as loud as he could for Morrison to stop. He managed a small grunt.

He heard Morrison jump, chuckle, and then say, "Just the gasses releasing."

"Where . . ."

"Just gasses," Morrison repeated in a high voice. Clempta felt an indiscernible tug as Morrison sliced open the pleura encasing his organs. Each organ he snipped free felt like pieces of Clempta's soul set loose. Individual tugs within his body.

If organs had tactile sensation, Clempta would have felt a large and tender hand cradle his heart.

"The lifeline," Morrison whispered, his voice thick.

Clempta had to move, had to do something to keep Morrison from clipping his aorta. He pushed hard, straining.

His body jolted. A loud clatter and squeak of wet shoes. Morrison grunted as a loud *thunk* sounded. He hissed with pain.

Clempta groaned. He twitched and lifted his hand toward his throbbing head. Barbed wire pain wound its way around his skull, piercing into his brain.

"I . . . am . . ." The words *whooshed* with air.

"Oh god," Morrison whispered, breath coming in quick, shattered gasps. Clempta stopped to listen.

Morrison's shoes squeaked on the floor again, frantic sounds like terrified mice running for cover.

"He was dead. I know he was dead. He was gone. He was dead." Morrison whispered. Clempta struggled to sit up, to get his bearings, to understand the situation. His head ... so foggy.

He swung his feet over the edge of the table. They struck the floor with a wet smack. Like hinges, the flaps of skin meant to cover his insides flopped shut. Morrison's gagging sounds came from nearby as Clempta's organs pushed through the flaps of skin holding them inside.

A sort of pressure released and Clempta thought of a cystic zit being popped. He opened his eyes to a blurry, brightly lit room void of warmth and furniture. He stumbled forward, slipped and reached out, sending a tray of surgical instruments clattering to the floor. His intestines, partially held within by the flaps of skin, hung to the floor in a neat pile. He coiled the visceral organ around his hand like a length of rope.

Morrison covered his mouth with bloodstained surgical gloves and looked at Clempta, trembling, eyes wide.

Clempta groaned, trying to tell Morrison it was okay, that he understood proper procedure was in order after any death. Frustrated, he closed his eyes. When he opened them, Morrison lurched toward the door. Clempta's abandoned lung squished grotesquely under Morrison's shoe and let out a squelch of juices and air.

Morrison's foot slid out from under him. He fell to the floor. The lung shot across the room.

Looking at his colleague, Clempta thought about tasting him. It came from nowhere and made him gag. The desire was so overwhelming. He licked his lips and moved closer. Morrison struggled on the floor, shoes sliding, slipping, unable to find purchase to propel him forward. Morrison screamed. Clempta's torso skin swung open and shut, like the doors of a Western saloon.

Clempta fell to his hands and knees over Morrison. He spotted his own heart dangling like a nauseating Christmas tree ornament between the branches of his rib cage. It flopped around as he tried to keep Morrison pinned to the floor. Morrson's shattered breaths flung snot from his nose. He made a weak and pathetic sound that didn't make it from the room. Clempta eyed the bare skin on Morrison's neck and imagined the sinewy muscles under that tanned flesh.

Tears leaked from Clempta's eyes at the thought of biting Morrison, but he could not stop. He gasped with a sob as his teeth dug into Morrison's neck.

Footsteps echoed down the hall. Clempta licked his lips and fingers and had one last bite of Morrison before looking around and spotting the observation room. He slipped inside and watched out the window with wide eyes.

Dr. Worthing sauntered into the room, sandwich in hand.

"Hey, Morrison, I saved half for you, in case you—" He stopped, looking at Morrison lying prone on the floor. Clempta followed Worthing's gaze to the organs littering the floor like discarded hamburger wrappers in a college dorm room. The intestine trail ended at Morrison's body. Worthing swallowed audibly.

"Morrison?" he whispered. "Are you okay?"

Clempta stifled a chortle despite the severity of the situation, then gasped and sobbed at what he'd done. Did the man not see the blood all over the floor? Worthing knelt down and scanned the room as he reached to feel for a pulse. He jerked back, eyes wide. Clempta didn't have to see that the man's fingers were greased with blood. Clempta retched, remembering the rubbery tear of flesh, the snapping tendons. His head hit the window on the door and Worthing jumped to a standing position, eyes locked on Clempta. A cry started from Worthing's throat.

The hunger drove Clempta forward. He flung the door open and moved toward Worthing. The man backed against the wall, whimpering.

A few minutes later, Clempta stumbled down the hallway, the skin folds slapping sickly with each step. Under his arm, a surgical coat from the morgue. He paused to pull it on and fumbled with the buttons. He looked at his hand. His left thumb: Gone. Everything came back, smacking into his memory and forcing him to lean against the wall.

The dog. 501.

"What's wrong girl?" He said to her in a soft voice. "Are you sick?" He rubbed her ears through the cage door.

Rodge came in. Distracting Clempta. He took his eyes off the dog.

The dog growled. A deep sound rumbling from her chest. She lashed out and bit off his thumb.

"Oh my god! Gus!" Rodge cried.

"She bit my fucking thumb off!"

Blood. So much blood.

"I'll get some help," Rodge said. He rushed away before Clempta could stop him.

Clempta felt hot, then suddenly chilled to the core.

Falling to his knees. Gasping, choking, unable to get a breath, unable to breathe. His vision blurred, distorted. Pain in his chest made him pant and shudder.

Muscular spasms, lurching heart. Blackness. A thick darkness. Still conscious. Still . . . aware.

Consciousness fluctuating in and out like undulating waves in a calm sea. Fingers pressing his neck; someone checking for a pulse.

Shrieks for help. Loud, piercing. Painful to his ears

Heels tapping out an urgent message. Awareness fuzzed and fading.

An overwhelming desire to sleep. Voices. Muffled and distant.

Clips of conversation spelling out an impossible story.

Dog 501. Dead yesterday . . . alive today. Bit him. Couldn't have. Did

Clempta. Dead.

"I'm not dead!"

Screaming inside. Urgent. Panicked. Final darkness. The morgue.

He gripped his head, clawed at his temples and ran down the hall, the garment flapping about his knees.

His skin itched. A deep pulling and tugging, like his

flesh would stretch and split. He scratched all over, never finding the right spot. He stopped and gripped the skin flaps hanging open like doors on a dilapidated barn. Perhaps they were the cause. He pulled and tugged hard to a pinching sensation that alleviated the itch, but only momentarily. He tried to rend the flaps from his body with little success, and finally gave up, exhausted from the effort. The itch continued.

And the hunger. He didn't know which was worse: The hunger, or the itch. Whenever he thought about what he did to doctors Worthing and Morrison, he wanted to gag, but also wanted to go back and have another bite.

"Nooooo," he moaned. He leaned against the wall, defeated. He scratched his arm, dug his nails in. The pain alleviated the itch, but only for a moment. Insane hunger, wild itchiness, Dr. Morrison . . . he heaved and reached for his stomach. His hand slipped through the flaps and he looked down, taking a few awkward steps backward. No organs, save for his heart.

"Heart," he said, cradling the organ in his hand. Lifeless and still. "Dead."

He groaned again and started to run down the hall, banging back and forth against the hallway doors, a pinball racking up points.

A young woman stuck her head out a door. "Are you okay?"

Clempta stopped.

"Nooooo," he moaned taking two stumbling steps and turning around.

The girl screamed. So shrill to his ears. He grabbed

them and shrieked. He had to silence her. He charged forward and fell against her, on top of her. Still she screamed. She hurt his ears.

He stared at her pale flesh, the fear in her eyes. A voice in his head told him eating her would cure the itch.

"No!" He shouted, holding the girl's throat with one hand and hitting himself in the side of his head with the other. "No . . ." he sagged onto her, his face close to hers. Tears leaked from his eyes. The girl's breath came in spasmodic gasps. She whined for him to let her go, to get off her, but he couldn't. He ached for something he did not want but could not resist. He sunk his teeth into her cheek and ripped a piece of flesh off. He gagged as the tangy, metallic taste of blood filled his mouth, but he bit her throat before he swallowed the first piece.

Clempta crunched through her trachea. Her body squirmed against his. Her jerking knees jabbed repeatedly through the flaps and against his spine. Her choked screams became gurgling coughs. He tore at her throat again, tugged at it, feeling the sinewy snap of veins against his cheeks and chin. Her screams subsided. Everything he bit off and swallowed fell through the dangling skin flaps back onto her.

Footsteps pounded down the hall. Someone must have heard her screams.

Clempta jumped up and charged into a broom closet, tumbling among buckets and mops. After making sure his heart remained unscathed, he opened the door and lurched toward an emergency exit. A shrill siren sounded when he opened the door and ran outside into a cool evening.

Making his way toward town, Clempta crossed several farmlands, ripe with corn or pluming with lettuce. At one point he stumbled across a sod farm, the soft grass tickling his feet with cool fingers, making him high-step to avoid the feeling. He scratched his arms through the thin coat and shook with a chill at the incredible and fierce itch that spread over his limbs; an itch that penetrated deeper than his skin. It made his brain yearn to roll in a bath of broken glass.

He trudged across a barren field, tripped and fell forward into the dirt. The dry earth caked the splayed skin flaps with soil. A dried leaf clung to his heart. He stood and looked at his only remaining organ.

"Heart," he groaned, covering it with his hands. He closed the grimy flaps over it protectively and looked up. Vision blurry, he could just make out a house in the distance.

When he reached it, he wrapped an arm around a tree trunk, finding comfort in rubbing his face against the rough bark. He watched a family load into an SUV; giggling and squealing children jumped inside. They would be tender, soft, easy to chew. He licked his lips in desperation as the car drove off. He looked at the house. Perhaps someone remained inside.

Staggering toward the door, he heard a horse whinny and changed direction. He stopped and stared at the horse. She squealed and bucked in her corral at the sight of him, her reddish coat glistening over taut muscles in her neck, her nostrils flaring. She tossed her head, her black mane tangling and whipping with her startled movements.

"Horse," Clempta groaned. He clambered through the fence and fell again. The horse ran past him, squealing, unable to stand still. She bucked, and Clempta scrambled to get up, her hooves dangerously close to his head. She reared up and came down on his back. Clempta cried out at the thick snap of his backbone. He managed to get to his feet, but his body bent backward, his spine broken through.

The horse bucked again, rearing in front of him. He covered his heart, his lifeline. Her front hooves came through the air and pummeled him to the ground.

He reached out for something to help him to his feet as the horse galloped around. Despair pulled a tormented moan from his lips.

The horse reared over him, her hooves pawing the air. She came down on his shoulder, dislocating it. His arm lay lifeless at his side. She galloped around the corral. Clempta cried out each time her hooves stomped his legs, arms, anything in her wild rampaging way.

Out of the corner of his eye, Clempta knew the end had come. She reared up for the final time and came down on his head, splitting his skull like a squeezed grape.

He was dully aware of her warm breath on his cheek, her nervous wicker graced his ears. He opened his eye, wanting with everything in him to touch her soft nose, to feel her coarse whiskers against his palm, to bite into that large and flaring nostril, so close. He twitched. The last thing he saw was her hooves rushing toward his face.

REMEMBRA

Previously published in Found, *the 2017 Colorado Book Award winner in the anthology category, by Rocky Mountain Fiction Writers.*

Dedicated to my mom, May Brouhard, and my grandma, Cynthia Gibbon (rest her soul).

MOM

The woman in front of me seems familiar, but I can't find her name in my mind.

"Mom . . . do you know who I am?"

I shake my head and close my eyes. They all think I close my eyes to block them out. I've heard them say that. But it's not true. When I close my eyes, I remember.

We, the woman who called me mom, and I, twirl in the sunshine. We pick flowers in a meadow. We laugh by a tipped-over Christmas tree while the naughty cat who tipped it watches from the couch. We bake cookies in a kitchen clouded by flour. They are good memories.

There are also bad. The arguments of teenaged youth. But she always came back to me. She is my daughter. Her name is Cora. There are others, too, in the memories. Jamie and Ben, my twin sons. A mutt called William. And Albert. Oh, Albert. My one and only true love.

I form the words on my lips. *Yes. Yes, I know you. You are my daughter. My little Cora. My butterfly.* But when I open my eyes, it all disappears.

CORA

Cora's mother looks at her with dewy eyes set deep within fleshy lids. Her face, once full of a vibrant light, is now drawn and gray.

"Do you know me?" Cora asks. Mom closes her eyes and for the briefest moment, the light returns. A youthful glow rises in her cheeks and a small smile tugs at her lips. Cora sits up a little straighter and moves to the edge of the chair. She reaches for her mother's hands. Mom opens her eyes and it all fades. Cora grips her own knees instead.

She hoped to catch her mom on a good day. Her heart aches as she pats her mother's shoulder and rises to leave. She remembers a time when her mother was her best friend. A time when taking turns reading *Harry Potter* to each other filled the afternoon. They'd done so in the shade of a tree that was torn down last year and replaced with a sapling. A time when she and her mom sat up late at night sharing secrets. Cora could tell her anything, everything. Her mother never judged her, never told her she was wrong or being stupid, never chastised her for her bad decisions.

You learn about life by making mistakes, she once said to a heartbroken Cora.

Cora's phone rings. She looks at the screen, then steps through the glass doors and onto the stone walkway outside.

Doug. Just what she needs. She swipes her thumb across the screen.

"Hello?" She can't mask the weariness in her voice.

"Hey," Doug says. He always says that. *Hey.* Like he's calling to shoot the breeze with no indication of the hell he put her through. The hell he still puts her through. "I'm at the house. I need to get into the garage to grab the last boxes."

Last boxes. She'd put the last boxes in there and asked him to come get them. Three weeks ago. Next, it'll be something else. The lawnmower or some other forgotten thing he needed to claim as his own.

"I'm not home." Obviously. "Can you come back tomorrow?"

"I can't," he says. Deep breath. He wants to share why, but at the same time he doesn't. She has to give him a little credit for that. "The baby is getting baptized tomorrow. Full day of activities. Where are you?"

The baby. A product of his infidelity.

"Next week then," Cora snaps.

"What time will you be home?"

"I'm up north." That's all she should need to say.

He knows what's up north. He picked out and helped move Mom into the home. "It could be hours with traffic."

He sighs the grumbling sigh he always used to get his way with her. Cora wonders if he used the same sigh on what's-her-face to get her into bed.

"We can wait," Doug says.

We. So she's there, too. Probably the baby as well. Cora looks at the front door of the home, back at her car, up at the window where her mother's room is.

"I just got here," she lies. "Mom's having a good day." She hangs up and heads back inside.

Sitting with a mother who's forgotten her is far better than seeing an ex-husband and his perfect little family parked in her driveway.

MOM

A woman sits in the chair next to me and sighs.

"I wish I could talk to you about things," she whispers, almost as if she doesn't want me to hear. "Doug is . . . Doug."

I close my eyes, and everything is stormy. Black clouds eclipse Cora's joyful happiness in dark shadow. I feel my brows crease. Cora is crying here in this dark place. I don't like Doug.

"He's making me miserable," Cora on the outside says. "He's at my house with his new family, flaunting them. There's always some reason to come back. I just want him to go away."

"Don't," I say, without opening my eyes. The words

are difficult as I don't speak much anymore. "Don't let him . . . see your pain."

"Mom? Mama?" Cora says. "Are you here with me?"

"He makes things dark here," I say in a whisper. I open my eyes and for a moment I see her. The child, the teen, the young woman from the memories. "Butterfly."

The woman's eyes light up.

CORA

As quickly as the moment comes, it vanishes. One uttered word, Cora's nickname from her childhood and always. Mom's eyes glisten, then fade. She's gone again. But her whispered words stay with Cora.

Don't let him see your pain.

Cora rises and pulls *Harry Potter* from her mother's bookshelf and opens it to page one. She reads all the way to Harry's arrival at Hogwarts. Mom listens, her misty eyes on Cora the entire time. Cora smiles at her. She smiles back. And when it is time for Cora to go, her mom asks her to keep reading.

"I'll come by tomorrow to read some more," she says and pats her mother's shoulder.

"You are so kind, dear. Your mother raised you well," Mom says.

Cora lets out a cool laugh. "Yes, she did." She kisses the top of her mother's head and takes the long way home. The back route on a two-lane county road. It takes twice as long and she's fine with that. Perhaps Doug and his new family will have grown tired of waiting. It has been hours since he called.

When she pulls up, the garage is open. The light on the garage door motor illuminates the barren space. A searing hatred burns through her. There's a note on the door leading into the house. She snatches it.

You should change the code on the garage door – D.

Cora rifles her phone out of her purse, hands shaking. The violation lashes at her. The boxes are gone. And that's all. Small miracles. Instead of calling, she sends a text.

Never contact me again.

He replies with, *OK*, which irritates her even more.

Cora calls Ben, the more rational of her two brothers, but he doesn't answer. She leaves a message.

"Hey, Benny. Just seeing what you're up to." She doesn't know what else to say, so she hangs up and tries Jamie. Same result.

Doug destroyed her life. He estranged her from her family. But that's not true, is it? She chose Doug over her family, even when they tried to warn her. Family is funny like that, and love masks faults.

Instead of going inside, she sits on the front porch, too weary to step into the time capsule of the house. The home she and Doug built. Too many memories live there. Most of them bad, dark. Even the good ones are tarnished by the pain and suffering she put up with.

He makes it dark here. Mom had said at mention of Doug. Yes. Yes, he does. Her phone rings. Cora answers. It's the home.

"Your mom has taken a spill, but she's okay," a man's voice says in a gentle voice. "She has a couple bruises but nothing more serious than that. She tripped over the flagstones in the garden. We already have plans to smooth out the walkway."

"Thank you for letting me know." Cora looks up at the sky, toward the higher power some people preach about. A lone goose flies by honking with such despair she scans the sky for the V of his family, but none are there.

She hangs up and stands. She examines what was once her dream house, now a residence full of dread. Doug picked Mom's home up north, claiming it was the best and most reasonably priced. Cora knows it was another way to separate her from her family.

In the divorce, he gladly signed the house over to her. At first it was a relief. Where else would she live? She couldn't bother Ben or Jamie. They gave up on her years ago after their warnings went unheeded. After she sold Mom and Dad's property.

Cora calls her real estate agent.

"I don't care about making money on it. Sell it as is, furniture included."

MOM

I'm awake and it's night. I know where I am. A home. I was put here because . . .

My daughter reads *Harry Potter* to me in the shade of a tree. Jamie and Ben run around with water guns. Albert prunes the rose bushes. He brings me a fully bloomed flower. Pink with darker edges. My favorite . . .

Albert is gone. My heart aches for him. For his smile. His touch, so gentle despite rough, working hands.

Where is my family? Where are Ben and Jamie and my little butterfly?

Cora is sad, but I don't know why. I must go to her.

CORA

Cora tosses and turns, trapped in a dream that makes no sense. The kind that changes point of view, location, and companions at an unsettling rate. People yelling. A sense of hopelessness. Driving a car from the backseat at night and the headlights keep going out. A dream in which there is fear, but nothing real to be afraid of.

Her ringing phone pulls her out so abruptly she's disoriented and can't make sense of where she is.

She gropes the nightstand. It's the home calling at two in the morning.

"Hello?" Her voice, though groggy, is full of fear of the worst. The fall must have been worse than they thought. She broke a bone and is bleeding internally. They couldn't stop it in time. Cora shakes her head.

"I'm so sorry to call so late." It's a man's voice, and he identifies himself as a staff nurse.

"It's fine. What's wrong?"

"Your mother is gone."

Cora can't breathe. No. She's not ready for her mama to be gone. Tears flood her eyes. A sob builds in her chest.

"When? How?" she manages to choke out.

"We aren't sure, but we think she must have sneaked out during the shift change. We've searched the premises but can't find her. We have the sheriff's department looking for her."

"Oh, my God," Cora says. She touches her forehead and relaxes. "I thought you meant she was dead."

"Oh, I am so sorry. That is completely my fault," the nurse adds, his voice sincere. "No, she's missing. I guess I should have said that."

Cora lets out a breath, stands, and struggles into a pair of jeans.

"Do you know where she might have gone?" the nurse asks.

"I . . . I'm not sure what she even remembers." She slips into a blouse. "I'll think about it on my way there."

Once in her car she calls Ben and gets his voicemail. She leaves a message: "I'm sorry it's late. Mom snuck out of the home. She's missing." Cora doesn't expect her other brother to answer her call either.

Cora had been the closest to Mom out of the three of them. She was the youngest and the first to get married. She was too young, she knows now. Doug was an older man. Made promises he failed to keep. Though she came out okay in the divorce settlement, she could never get those years of her life back. She'd missed out on precious moments with her family. With her mom.

Off the freeway, she scans the sidewalks, on the lookout for a little old lady in a nightgown and slippers, thankful it's summer and still warm outside.

She arrives at the home. Ben is already there. She falls into his brotherly embrace.

"Thank you," she says.

"Jamie's in New York," he says. "He wants hourly updates, and if she's not found before morning, he's getting an earlier flight back."

"Any news?" Cora asks.

Ben shakes his head. "When was the last time you saw her?"

"Earlier today, well, I guess it would be yesterday now," Cora says with a glance at her watch. "She called me Butterfly after I told her . . ."

"What? What did you tell her?"

"Doug was making me miserable. I just wish I could talk to her." Cora realizes how selfish it sounds as soon as she says it. She looks up at Ben's pained eyes and reads the same thing. "She said he makes it dark here."

"What does that mean?" Ben asks.

"I don't know," Cora says. "I can't decipher everything. When was the last time *you* saw her?"

Ben dismisses her question. Cora's shoulders slump. Ben walks away while tapping at his phone. Texting Jamie, probably. She watches his back, desperate to reconnect with him.

Instead, she goes into Mom's room and looks around. Nothing seems out of place.

The stuffed kitty Cora gave her when she first moved in sits on Mom's chair. The books on the shelf are a little crooked. She scans the titles, then rushes to the nurse's station.

"I think I know where she went."

MOM

A truck coasts by, giving me a wide berth, then pulls over onto the shoulder. Tires crunch on the gravel. The driver's door opens, and a nice, elderly gentleman climbs out.

"What are you doing out here?" he asks. "Are you okay?"

"I'm going home," I say. "Will you take me home?"

He nods and helps me into the cab. I set the book on my lap.

"Are you at St. Mary's Assisted Living, or that other one, what is it, Sunshine Estates?" he asks.

"Neither. I live up the street here." I point in the direction the truck is facing.

"Tell me the way," he says.

I laugh. "Albert, you know the way."

"Name's George," he says. Maybe it is a game Albert is playing. I humor him and tell him the directions. He pulls up to the curb outside a park. I close my eyes and see our old house. The kids playing outside, the shade tree towering over everything. Watching over us.

When I open my eyes, it all disappears, replaced by a gaudy playground. The shade tree is gone. A blank space in the night sky.

"Albert," I whisper. "Where is the house? The tree?"

"Sorry, ma'am. Name's George. House that used to be here was torn down when the city bought the land."

"Our children grew up in that house." I look at him, but he isn't Albert. I cringe away from him, grope for the door handle, slide out, and hurry across a lawn more immaculate and landscaped than Albert ever could have kept it. But that's not true is it? Albert had the greenest of green thumbs. A panic builds in my chest, quickening my breath. I'm confused by the jumble of memories and thoughts. I turn around in a circle.

A truck idles nearby. I don't recognize the vehicle, nor the driver. Maybe he means me harm. Where is my Albert to protect me? Where are the children? Why am I here at night in—I look down at myself and gasp. A nightgown and slippers? At least I had the wherewithal to remember a shawl. With one hand I pull it tight and press it against my breast. My other hand holds a thick book.

Another car pulls up, parks behind the truck. Before they can make a plan to attack and kidnap me, I back into the shadows. A pathway leads to a stand of young evergreens.

"Mom?" A woman yells. I know her voice.

CORA

Cora turns on her high beams and drives as fast as she can to the park named after her family. Guilt at selling the house and land to the city settles heavily in her chest. She wanted to live there but she let Doug talk her into selling. Ben and Jamie didn't care as much as she did, preferring the city and foothills to the farm lands. If she'd fought Doug on it, she could have lived in the house now, closer to Mom.

Cora had asked Ben to stay at the nursing home in case Mom turned up. She pulls up behind a truck, idling outside the park, and cuts the engine. She approaches the truck and knocks on the driver's window. The driver rolls it down.

"You here for the little old lady?" He asks, as if he isn't a little old man himself.

Cora's apprehension flees in a released breath.

"Where is she?"

"She wandered off into the park. Was about to call the police to come help. She seemed awfully confused. Called me Albert even though I told her I'm George."

"Thank you," Cora says. She rushes off. "Mom?" She calls. "Where are you?" Fear that her mother won't trust her sours her gut. Cora ducks onto the path through the trees.

"Cora?" her mom says from up ahead. A street lamp shines its light onto the path. Mom is sitting on the ground beneath a sapling that, Cora realizes, is in the same place the old shade tree used to stand.

"Mom," Cora collapses on the ground next to her. "What are you doing here?"

"Reading *Harry Potter*," she says, though the light is too dim and the book isn't open. She sets the book aside and peers at Cora.

Oh no, here it comes. She's gone again.

"Cora, dear," she says. "My butterfly."

Cora's throat tightens. Tears blur her vision. She pulls her mom's frail form into her arms. Mom laughs. The sound chases away Cora's recent anger and depression and fear.

"I'm sorry I sold the land, the house . . ."

Mom pats her back, strokes her hair.

"Oh now, butterfly. It's okay." Mom pulls back and looks into Cora's eyes. "You were so sad. It was so dark and cold when I last saw you."

"It was? What was?"

"Let me show you." Mom takes Cora's hands and grips them tight. "Close your eyes."

MOM

I don't know if it will work but I have to try. I can sense my tremulous grip on the here-and-now slipping. I hold my daughter's hands and close my eyes. We stand together under the shade tree in the warmth of a summer day, a look of awe and wonder on Cora's face. It reminds me of when she was young, experiencing things for the first time. Sometimes she had that look even if she had experienced something over and over. Like petting the rays at the Aquarium, or the first crocus in spring. Bird footprints in the snow.

"What is this place?" she asks.

"Remembra," I tell her. "A place of lost minds. A place full of memories forgotten." I smile and pat her hand. "I never forgot who you were. I only had to close my eyes."

William, the mutt Cora grew up with, runs by with Ben and Jamie chasing behind. Cora laughs and watches them circle the shade tree and bolt into the corn field.

"I want to show you something," I tell her.

CORA

Cora can't fathom what is happening, but a great peace fills her. It's the feeling only a mother can give her child. Protection and love. Security.

Mom points. A montage of memories flash and flicker before her as if on an old movie reel. Her young self on a stage.

"I want to be a ballerina . . . zoo keeper . . . candy store owner . . . when I grow up."

The image of herself matures with each rendition. Candy store owner becomes veterinarian becomes archeologist becomes veterinarian again becomes writer becomes . . . darkness.

A dark cloud drifts over Remembra. Cora looks up at the sky, then back at her mom.

"You met Doug," Mom says. "You wanted to be his wife. Deep down you knew this darkness. I know you did." Her smile doesn't falter. "Love is blind that way, isn't it?"

Cora nods. She did know. Looking back like this, the voice in her head urged her to follow her dreams, her passions. Instead, she chose a man who didn't appreciate or support her creative pursuits.

Doug told her he'd read everything she wrote. He told her she was the best writer. He never read a word of hers other than texts and emails. He promised to take care of her while she wrote her first novel, and when it took longer than a month, he complained about having to work so hard to support her. She never went to college mainly because she couldn't decide what she wanted to study. Writing was her passion. Until Doug. Doug became her life.

"You wanted to travel and write about the world," Mom says. High school senior Cora on the screen confirms this. Cora told Mom everything.

Until Doug.

The dark cloud turns black. The memories stop cycling through the land and fade away.

"I'm so sorry," Cora says.

Mom shakes her head. "I didn't bring you here for that, dear. I brought you here to remind you of the strong and independent woman you once were, full of moxie. You can be her again. She lives within you. Deep inside. It will be hard to dig her out, but she's in there."

The cloud recedes. The memories return and run rampant. Mom reaches out as Ben runs by, a Super Soaker 500 in his hands. The memory unfolds.

Cora sits under the shade tree with *Harry Potter* in her lap. It's her turn to read out loud. It's book one at the very end. Cora closes the book just as Jamie jumps out and blasts Ben with his larger Super Soaker. Water splashes onto the book and Cora shrieks.

In Remembra, Mom laughs. The memory ends with Cora joining the water fight.

Cora sighs. She used to be so carefree, relying only on herself instead of asking other people permission for what she needed or wanted to do. Doug specifically. Doug always shot down her creativity. Stifled it. Could she really be that person again? Could she pick up her pen and notebook and write? Could she travel the world?

"You must go now," Mom says. "The world is out there, full of possibilities."

"No, please. Let's stay a little longer." Cora watches another memory run by.

Mom takes her hand. "Remembra is a powerful place,

butterfly. We must remember this is the past. You cannot live here." She smiles, but her eyes are sad.

"Mom?"

"I'll be staying this time, butterfly. You go on. Live your life. Live your dreams. And always remember, I love you."

Suddenly Cora is in the park under the sapling again. Mom is gone. The *Harry Potter* book lies on the grass, the pages warped from Jamie's water gun. Cora picks it up and rushes down the path toward the park entrance calling to her mom, panic building in her chest.

An ambulance waits at the street, lights strobing red-blue-red-blue onto the trees. Cora glances around and finds the paramedics huddled over her Mom. She rushes to them, but they force her back. They start chest compressions and pump a resuscitation mask.

"What happened?" Cora can't get a full breath. She feels her face contort with sadness.

"We're not sure," the paramedic performing the breaths says. He squeezes the bulb. Condensation forms inside the mask. Does that mean she's breathing?

"George called us," the other paramedic says.

Cora looks toward the street. The truck that was parked there when she arrived is no longer idling. She scans the area for the man, finds him, and rushes to him.

He holds out a hand to her. "Your mother, I reckon she is, came out of the woods smiling about five minutes ago and collapsed there on the lawn."

Five minutes ago? Mom was with Cora in Remembra five minutes ago. Wasn't she? Cora blinks back tears. The sudden weight of despair makes her knees buckle.

Helpless, she watches the paramedics stop what they're doing. The one doing the compressions shakes his head. The other removes the mask and covers her mom's face. Lifting together, the two paramedics load her body onto a gurney and wheel her to the ambulance. Cora sprints after them.

"We did all we could." The paramedic has the sad eyes of a Bassett hound. "I'm sorry."

"What happened to her?" Cora whispers.

"Her heart," he says. With a wince he adds something that sounds like, "it was too full of love," but that can't be it. She doesn't ask for him to repeat himself.

CORA *One Month Later.*

Cora boards her flight to Italy with Mom's warped copy of *Harry Potter* in her carry-on. She finds her seat, sits, and fastens the seat belt across her lap. She lifts the book and opens it. A piece of paper flutters out.

My butterfly,
Remember who you were, but don't forget to live
for today.

LUMP'S DREAM

Lump lumbered out of the forest with a black-haired woman slung over his shoulder. She hung limp and unconscious. With his thick, scarred hands, he swung her to the ground and lay her on the grass, cradling her head as he lowered her. He looked at her face, her smooth skin. He trailed his wide fingers down her cheek. He felt his own face. His fingertips travelled over the ridges and grooves in his flesh. He ran his palm over his scalp, over the lumps and scabs. The scars.

He lifted the woman back onto his shoulder, the perfume in her hair, apple blossoms, touched his nostrils and he breathed in. His own stink mingled with hers, tarnishing it. He took her to a small stone house. He halted. His mother stood in the doorway.

"Bring her inside." His mother twirled away into the dark interior.

Lump ducked under the doorway and lowered the woman onto the table. Her dark hair splayed out behind her. Again, he cradled her head in his massive hand.

"Hm," Mother said. "I wish you'd bring me a blonde one." She turned her wicked eyes to him. "You have some grime on your chin, dear." She reached up and wiped at his face with a rough cloth. It scraped a scab. He grunted and pulled his face away from her.

Mother turned her attention back to the woman on the table. She pulled a knife from her belt and thrust the blade into the woman's chest. Blood poured from the wound. She filled a chalice with the woman's blood, chanted an incantation over it, and drank. She turned away from Lump, gasping.

He knew she would cry out and cover her face and when she moved her hands away she would be young again with the woman's black hair. Her skin would be smooth, not wrinkled. So, instead of watching like he usually did, Lump gazed at the woman and stroked her cheek with the back of his rough fingers. He touched her hair. Never once did his eyes stray from her smooth face.

Mother wouldn't send him out again for a few days, so Lump went into the woods. While he walked, he looked at a brochure for a music school called Juilliard. He stared at the pictures of the symphony and the violins for a long time before folding the wrinkled and creased pamphlet and tucking it away in his back pocket.

He reached his favorite clearing and pulled his violin out from under a bush. He played a song he made up. The music caressed his mangled, cauliflower ears and he closed his eyes. It transported him to a better place. A place where his skin felt smooth and unblemished under his fingertips.

"Lump!" Mother's voice, inside his head, said under

the music. "You'll never be beautiful, you'll never be accepted, you'll never, never, never."

He squeezed his eyes shut tighter and tried to block her voice from his mind, but it did no good. Her taunts plowed through the melody. He missed a note and stopped playing, looking at the violin so small in his hand.

"There you are," Mother's voice said behind him. "You play so beautifully."

He turned and looked at her. The knife in her hand worried him but he didn't move from the rock.

"I found this on the path." She held up the Juilliard brochure.

He grunted and felt his back pocket where the brochure should have been.

"You'll never go there. You will never leave this forest." Mother paused. Her voice softened. "You'll never leave me . . . will you?" Her voice quavered, and Lump hefted his form from the rock and approached her.

He reached a hand toward her face, her smooth skin. He touched her cheek and with his other hand he touched his face.

"Why?" The word came as a groan, thick in his throat.

"Lumpy," Mother said in a soothing voice. "I had to, to protect you." Her face hardened, and she slashed across his face with the knife, spraying blood onto her soft, smooth skin. The pain burned across his forehead, over his nose and down the other cheek. Lump grabbed his face and cried out. He backed away from Mother until his legs hit the stone and he fell onto his butt. He cried into his hands. Wept like a child.

When he stopped crying, Mother was gone, had likely been gone since right after she slashed him. He felt his face, his new wound. The blood caked in the gash. Another scar to disfigure him even more.

"Lump want," he said to the quiet forest. He swallowed hard. "Lump want new skin." His thick, swollen lips curled into an anguished frown.

He got up from the stone and picked up the Juilliard brochure Mother had dropped, then lumbered deeper into the forest until he came upon an old shack. He pushed the door open and went inside the dark space.

A table and two chairs took up the majority of the space inside. Off in a dark corner, a door stood ajar. The door led down to a basement much larger than the tiny shelter built on top of it. Lump clopped down the stairs and lit a lantern.

The room smelled like old, damp rags. Mold and mildew and mustiness. Lump went to a table in the middle where shackles hung from the edges of the marred wood. He touched one. It tinkled in the gloom and his thick lips spread into a smile.

He dreamed that night. He dreamed about drinking the magic blood and getting a new face, new skin. Smooth skin. He dreamed about being accepted into Juilliard with his new skin. He played the violin for them and they loved him. He dreamed of Mother's face, her fists hitting him, slashing at him with her knife, disfiguring him. He dreamed of the things she told him, the words that kept him deep in the forest with her. Protected by her. He woke up.

Mother came to him a week later. Her skin sagged. A gray streak shot through her dark hair.

"It's time, Lumpy." She caressed his cheek, grimacing as she touched him. "Bring me a blonde one this time."

Lump eyed the knife at her belt.

"Well, go then," she said, shooing him.

"Hhhh," Lump said. He held out his arms. "Hhhug."

Mother's face, stern and pinched, relaxed into a smile. She hugged him. Lump lowered his hand to her belt and slipped the knife from its sheath. He left before she could see he was hiding it along his arm, palming the handle.

When he came back with the blonde woman slung over his shoulder, he didn't take her to Mother. He went into the woods, through the clearing where he played his violin, and into the shack. He took the woman into the basement and lay her on the table. Ever so gently, he shackled her wrists and ankles. He didn't bother to gag her. No one would hear her way out here.

He touched her face, her smooth skin. He stroked her arms, loving the smoothness beneath his fingertips, then went to a whetting stone in the corner and sharpened the knife. As the blade scraped along the stone, he imagined his new skin. His new face. Smooth and beautiful. He felt the knife. Sharp.

The girl woke up. Her head moved from side to side. In the low light, Lump watched her, moving his eyes over her, looking for all the smooth skin he could use. Her eyes opened. Lump moved closer, his boots thumping on the stone floor. He leaned over her and her eyes grew wide. She didn't make a sound until Lump lifted the knife.

"Lump want new skin." He lifted one shackled arm and dragged the blade down the length of it, shaving off a slice of pale, smooth skin. The girl screamed. Lump hated the way it grated on his ears. He sliced away another filet of skin and set it aside. She kept screaming.

"New skin," he yelled over her cries. He didn't understand why she kept screaming. He wasn't going to kill her. He just wanted her skin. He moved to her other arm and kept skinning until her cries ceased.

"What are you doing?" Mother's voice screeched from the bottom of the stairs. She rushed into the room. "What are you doing?" She shouted again when he only looked at her.

"Lump . . ." he said. "Lump want . . ." He panted, and tears trickled from his eyes, coursing down the jagged scars. "Lump want new skin." He held out the piece he just sliced off so his mother could see.

She came closer, her hands outstretched. "Lumpy," she cooed. "What have you done here?"

"New skin," Lump said again. He laid the last piece on top of the pile. Before he could move to her legs and all the smooth skin they would give him, his mother's hands touched his, stilled them.

"She was mine," she said in a low voice. She squeezed his hand until he released the knife. Lump backed away from her, holding up his hands, knowing she would slash him with the knife again. Instead, she turned to the girl and stabbed her.

"Nooo." Lump moaned. He didn't want to kill her. "No, ma."

"You made me do this, Lumpy," she said. "You made me kill her. Just like you made me hurt you."

Lump held up his hands. Mother stalked toward him, the knife gripped in her fist. He backed away from her, knowing she would slash him again. He covered his face. The knife bit into his palms. He cried out. It bit into his wrists. She slapped his hands away and cut into his face again, reopening the wound from the week before.

Lump's tears blinded him. His mother kept slashing. The knife kept biting and slicing. He sharpened it so well. Blood gushed from his hands and wrists, from his face, blinding him and burning his eyes, mingling with his tears. He slid to the ground.

"Ma," he moaned. "No."

Mother crouched in front of him. "You did this to yourself," she said. Her teeth clenched. She pulled her arm back to slice at him again, but Lump lunged forward. He wrapped his hands around her neck and squeezed. The knife dripped to the ground as her fingers clawed at his around her throat. Her eyes popped wide. She struggled for breath. He squeezed and squeezed until he felt the bones in her neck break. She stopped struggling. He let go and she fell to the ground in a heap.

Lump picked up the knife. He hummed the tune he made up on his violin as he finished skinning the blonde woman. Then he skinned his mother.

Lump carried his violin and a burlap bag dripping with blood through the forest to the edge of town.

Juilliard would take him now that he had new skin.

ACKNOWLEDGMENTS

My deepest gratitude goes to the following people who helped make this book possible:

Angela Alsaleem, who wrote alongside me for several years. She probably has matching stories for about 80% of the tales in this book. If I didn't have Tim, I would have dedicated this to her.

My editor, Kristen Hiatt, for finding all the little fiddly things I can't seem to see. Let's get crab again soon! My cover designer, Steven Novak. Thanks for taking Bryan Sakti's artwork and turning it into the exact cover I had in mind, even though I didn't even give you hardly any guidance on what I was looking for. Bryan Sakti, who took my shitty doodle and turned it into the amazing figure on the cover. Your patience with me while we worked through draft after draft is admirable.

To my parents, who *never* told me, "You can't make a living as a writer." Your support and love and care has shaped me into the person I am today. Thank you for keeping my dream alive! My brother, James, who is a guaranteed source of weird conversations.

To my twin, Wissa (Melissa Sirevog), who has *always* been my #1 fan, even when I told lame stories in the womb about our amniotic fluid turning us into zombies. WTP!

Finally, to my devoted, amazing, wonderful husband, Tim. We met in 2006 when I started to seriously get back into writing. "The Big Toe" is *still* not about your toe, I promise. Thank you for reading all of these and still deciding to love me forever.

And Belle. Because, dogs.

ONE LAST THING...

Did you enjoy *LUMP: A Collection of Short Stories?*

One of the best ways to show how much you enjoyed it is to give a review on Goodreads or your favorite online retailer, even if it is only a few words. It'll help exceptional readers like you find great books!

THE BLOOD OF SEVEN:
CHAPTER 1

DAY 1: FRIDAY

Fake it till it feels right again.

Or run as far and as fast as possible to try to escape it. Detective Ann Logan, if she could even call herself a detective anymore, ran along the trail, gravel crunching beneath her feet. Lodgepole pines towered overhead, blocking out most of the stars still visible in the early morning sky. According to her GPS watch, she was on mile three, but the nightmare images from the Salida Stabber case threatened to break her mind further than they already had.

She pushed faster. Sometimes it took only one mile, sometimes five, sometimes a sixer of her favorite brew. Her therapist urged against the latter. So, Ann ran deep into the San Isabel National Forest in Colorado's Rocky Mountains.

The usual nightmare had awoken her at three in the morning and left her shaking under the sweat-filled sheets. It was the version in which Bruce, her old partner, came back from the dead to tell her his death was all her fault. Then, the Stabber's last victim—Elizabeth Bradshaw, seven years old—did the same. Even though Ann didn't believe in zombies or ghosts or anything like that, the dream wormed its way under her skin where it ate away at her sanity little by little.

They said two words over and over again. The same two words she chastised herself with.

Too late, too late, too late.

Their voices chanted in her ears in rhythm with her footsteps and the bouncing light from her headlamp. She hit mile four, and still they chanted. Images from the case flipped through her mind like a grotesque slideshow. She shook her head and squeezed her eyes closed. When she reopened them, she broke into an all-out sprint.

A tree root arched over the trail in the light's beam. Ann jumped too late. It snagged her foot and sent her sprawling onto her stomach. The air rushed out of her body. The voices stopped. She rolled onto her back and looked up at the stars peeking through the trees.

After a few gasping breaths, she got her wind back and climbed to her feet. She walked a little way to catch her breath before breaking into a run again.

The clearing where she usually turned around to get six miles out and back came into view. The crescent moon hung in the sky like the Stabber's sadistically perfect smile. Ann stripped her running jacket off and tied it around her waist, despite the fact that her breath puffed in front of her face with each exhale.

She walked in circles to keep her legs warm while her lungs returned to a normal breathing pattern and turned to head back down the trail when a tingling sensation spread over her skin. Ann rubbed her arms, but her flesh was free of goosebumps. The moonlight illuminated her skin. But no, that wasn't it. The veins just beneath the surface glowed blue-white. She rubbed at it again, but the illumination didn't go away. She lifted her shirt, then her pant leg. Her whole body glowed.

The tingling intensified. It burned. Like lava flowing through her nervous system.

She dropped to her knees, closed her eyes against the agony, and let out a low wail of pain. Static filled her ears.

Through the crackle, a voice compounded of many voices said, *"Protect her."*

Ann opened her eyes. Bright light flooded her vision, blinding her. A thin black figure appeared in the distance. It came closer until it resolved into the silhouette of a young girl around six or seven—long, curly hair stood out around her head. Her eyes glowed the same blue-white. Her hands moved, and she lifted something, a book, the interior gilded with the light. The book flew toward Ann. Scribbled words filled the pages. One of them flared, blinding Ann even further.

Sophia.

Ann's heart boiled inside her chest. She cried out again.

Then the book and the girl faded away, replaced with a flash of light that burned three familiar mountain peaks —the Royal Mountains outside her hometown—onto her retinas. When she regained her vision, the clearing came back into focus. No girl. No book. No Royal Mountain peaks. Just the clearing surrounded by towering pines.

Ann's breath came in short, painful gasps, as if she had just arrived in the clearing from the previous sprint. Her head swam. She must have pushed herself too hard out on the trail. That was all. Her brain was signaling a blood sugar crash or something. Her stomach growled as if to confirm.

She jogged back down the trail.

Or maybe it was stress. Stress did all kinds of things to people. Couldn't it cause hallucinations? A second failed psych evaluation *had* taken its toll on her psyche.

Inside her truck, Ann pulled on her jacket. The fabric rubbed over a sore spot on her chest. She touched it and winced. The skin was raised and felt raw. She flipped open the collar and peered down at it. Then she grabbed the rearview mirror and jerked it in her direction.

At first, she thought the two-inch-long, raw and red brand was an Egyptian Ankh, but on closer inspection, it sort of resembled an upright Jesus fish. Three bands encircled where the lines met to become the tail.

"What the fuck?" Her voice rode on gasping air. "No, no, no. What is this?" She poked it again and winced. Nothing had touched her out there. She hadn't even crashed into any overgrown bushes. She looked at it again in the mirror and then angled the reflective surface away from her. She gripped the steering wheel. Tears sprang to her eyes. She willed herself to keep it together until she got home and could assess the situation. Figure out the facts—what happened and what didn't.

The keys jangled in her hand, but she managed to get the right one in the ignition.

She wasn't ready. She knew that. No matter how ready she may have felt before this, no matter how ready she was to take another eval—she couldn't go back to work. Her mind went into preservation mode. Her Lieutenant would understand. He already thought she was back too soon. She called him from her truck once she pulled up to her apartment building. He told her to take two weeks. Longer if she needed.

Ann shuffled to her front door, eyes on the ground in front of her. Footsteps took off down the corridor. She looked up, but they were gone around the corner already.

A box about two feet square sat on her doorstep. UPS was on top of it today. She'd never received a package during the night. On closer inspection, however, there was no postage of any kind. Just her name scrawled on the top in black marker.

She jogged to the end of the corridor, but the person who must have dropped it off was long gone.

Ann squatted next to the package and examined the outside. She took it to the coffee table in the living room. Using her keys, she sliced open the tape and folded back the flaps.

The first thing she noticed was the smell.

**THE BLOOD OF SEVEN:
CHAPTER 2**

Teresa Hart sprayed furniture polish onto a rag and wiped dust from the crib. "Dusting day." She sang and hummed a lullaby.

After wiping down the nursery furniture, she rearranged and fluffed the stuffed animals at the foot of the crib. She folded the down edges of the pink and white blankets. She stood back and admired how inviting the tiny bed looked waiting for the baby to be tucked inside.

" 'Blessed are they who mourn, for they shall be comforted.' " She kissed the cross hanging from a chain around her neck and left the basement.

At the top of the stairs, she closed and locked the door with the key she wore on her wrist. In the bathroom, she made herself beautiful for her husband, Derrick. She met her clear blue eyes in the mirror and wondered when the lines had formed around them. When did her frown become so permanent? Someone once told her the lines on one's face were a road map to the life the person lived.

She stopped a scowl from emerging at the thought and smiled instead.

Hair perfectly coiffed, makeup expertly applied, she went into the kitchen to pack lunch for Maggie, their adopted six-year-old. By the time she finished the peanut butter and jelly sandwich it was already a quarter past seven, and Maggie hadn't come downstairs.

Teresa went to the landing. "Maggie, you're going to be late."

Back in the kitchen, she flipped on the coffee pot. When she turned around, Maggie stood behind her. Her long dark hair stuck out from her head in frizzy ringlets, a stark contrast to Teresa's smooth blonde lob. That mess would take twenty minutes to comb out.

"What took you so long?" Teresa asked.

"I didn't sleep very good," Maggie said. She yawned.

"You didn't sleep very *well*." Teresa corrected her. "Here's your lunch. Your backpack is in the living room."

Maggie went around the breakfast bar and pulled her backpack onto her shoulders. She started toward the hallway.

"Maggie," Teresa said. "Where's my hug?"

Maggie shuffled back to Teresa, gave her a half-second embrace around the waist, and turned back toward the front door.

Derrick's footfalls came from the stairs. Teresa watched from the kitchen. He met Maggie in the foyer. Her face lit up.

"Hi, Daddy," she said. She hugged him tight. She looked up at him and whispered, "She forgot breakfast again."

Teresa sighed. Rearranging her routine to make the child lunch every morning was hard enough, but breakfast, too?

Derrick said something about the muffin store in a low voice, and Maggie smiled and nodded. He pulled her hair back into a ponytail and fastened it with a pink scrunchie. When he glanced toward the kitchen, his mouth turned down at the corners.

"Wait on the porch. I'll be right out." He came into the kitchen while Maggie went outside.

"Good morning," Derrick said. He pulled a travel mug out of the cupboard and filled it with coffee. He turned to Teresa. "What's wrong?" His tone suggested, *What's wrong this time?*

Teresa busied her hands with the dishes in the drying rack. Derrick touched her wrist and stopped her. She didn't look at him.

"What's wrong, honey?" The softer tone, the nicer one. He was pretending to care.

"Maggie doesn't like me."

Derrick shook his head. "Not this again." He put his mug on the counter and crossed his arms. "Why do you think that?"

"She doesn't hug me like she hugs you." Teresa fiddled with her necklace. "She rarely makes eye contact." What else? Oh yes. The most important. "She never calls me Mommy."

"Don't be silly," Derrick said. "She's just getting used to us."

"She's been here for three months." Teresa dropped her arms. "How long until she settles in?"

Derrick shrugged. "I need to get to the clinic. I have an eight o'clock."

The usual excuse to not deal with things. To leave the situation. To leave her. Harmony was a fifteen-minute town. It took him five to walk Maggie to school, another ten from there to the clinic.

He brushed a kiss across her cheek and grabbed his briefcase from the living room.

"Derrick," she said, her voice cracking. "You know what today is, right?"

He shook his head. So easy for him to forget now that he had a replacement daughter.

"The baby . . . our baby's . . . anniversary. . . . of her . . . of her death." She held the tears in, but her voice hitched.

"Oh, Teresa." Derrick came back to her, hugged her. "I'm sorry. I forgot. I know how important it is to you."

But not to him.

He kissed her forehead and released her, turned to leave but stopped. "You know," he said, then paused.

Teresa knew what he was going to say. He was going to tell her to get over it. That's what it always came to. He didn't understand. He didn't know what it was like to grow a human in his body only to have it ripped away. But he reached for her again and awkwardly held her by the shoulders. His voice softened.

"It's been seven years. Maybe you should . . . I don't know . . . call your therapist. Start seeing him again."

He wants me medicated.

"Or you could come help out at the office. Perhaps some . . . normalcy . . . or a new routine would help."

"It was so easy for you to move on, wasn't it?" Teresa said in the voice she used when she wasn't sure if she really wanted Derrick to hear her. "So easy to be *normal* again. To forget our baby."

"It was *never* easy, Teresa." His nostrils flared. "I just . . ." He lifted his hands, then dropped them. "Never mind. I have to go. I don't have time for this."

She stood in the kitchen and listened to the front door open and close. At least he didn't slam it this time.

Teresa scurried to the front room and looked out the window. Derrick and Maggie strolled down the sidewalk and out of sight. His smile was for her now. Teresa sat on the love seat. Across from her, an upright piano stood against the wall. Pictures in silver frames sat in a cluster on top of lace doilies from Bruges, from another time, another life. Pictures of them, together. Happy. Smiling. Carefree. She and Derrick.

Tucked in the middle, partially obscured by the music stand, captured for the rest of time in black and white, was Teresa holding the baby. They had the same fair skin and pale hair. She was only seven weeks old.

A tear welled in Teresa's right eye but didn't fall. She went to the bathroom, snatched a tissue from the box on the counter, and dabbed, careful not to mess her makeup.

Mommy . . .

A distorted voice, like a child talking into a fan.

Teresa whirled and peered out into the hallway. Across from the bathroom, the basement door stood wide open. She checked her wrist for the key. Still there. No one else had a key. She knew she locked it. She always locked it. The only other way to unlock it was from the inside.

She slid to the door and peered down the darkened staircase.

A shadow drifted by at the bottom. Prickly chills washed over her scalp.

"Who's down there?" Her voice cracked. "Maggie?" she called, even though she knew she was home alone. Her mouth went dry.

Teresa took one step down the stairs and stopped. She didn't want to be the idiot bimbo in a horror movie. She backed out into the hallway, closed the door, and locked it, jiggling the handle to ensure it was secure.

The water heater, the furnace kicking on, wind in the ducts, rats . . . She'd call an exterminator.

Glass shattered in the front room. She spun toward the noise.

No, the kitchen. She found a tipped glass in the sink. Nothing broken. She rinsed it under the tap.

Mommy . . .

She shut off the faucet and listened, holding her breath. Her hand went to the cross at her neck.

The clock on the wall ticked off the seconds. Ten. Twenty.

Mommy . . .

From the front of the house. Teresa nearly shrieked. She took small, slow steps back down the hall. She stopped at the doorway and peeked into the front room.

The frame with her and the baby lay on the hardwood floor surrounded by pieces of glass. The other pictures remained untouched in a circle around a now empty space where the portrait had been.

There had to be an explanation. She just couldn't think. Not with a mess on the floor. She knelt and picked up the larger pieces but needed a broom. She took one step toward the hallway and tripped over something soft and yielding.

Teresa caught herself on the doorframe, turned, and gasped. The antique stuffed bear she'd had as a child stared up at her.

Big Bear.

She lifted him to eye level. What was he doing here? Derrick had put Big Bear in the garage. He'd wanted to throw the stuffed toy out, but she begged him not to. It had been hers when she was little. It hadn't been in the house since…

Since the baby died.

"Mah-mee," Big Bear said in the voice she'd heard.

Teresa dropped him. He landed face down. The pull string on his back slid inside his body. She let out a relieved laugh and tucked Big Bear on the love seat and arranged the pillows around him.

"Mommy."

The voice came from behind her. Not distorted. A child's voice. Crisp and clear. Not from the bear's old voice box.

Teresa turned around and froze.

A girl in a frilly white dress stood in the doorway. A black ribbon held her long pale hair away from her face. Dark eyes peered up from beneath a fringe of blunt-cut bangs.

"Mommy," the girl said in a sickly sweet voice. She cocked her head. "Why did you kill me?"

ABOUT THE AUTHOR

Claire L. Fishback lives in Morrison, Colorado with her loving husband, Tim, and their pit bull mix, Belle. Writing has been her passion since age six. When she isn't writing, she enjoys mountain biking, hiking, running, baking, and adding to her bone collection, though she would rather be stretched out on the couch with a good book (or poking dead things with sticks). She can be reached at info@clairelfishback.com. Please visit: clairelfishback.com for more books and updates!

Or, follow on your favorite social media platform:

facebook.com/clairelfishback

twitter.com/clairelfishback